He gently stroked  **that**
only a   and
his pal   , and
like her   ~~ give in to the
grief gna

"It w   ...y fault. I ordered the men forward."

"You were following orders." She relaxed against him a bit more. "It's no one's fault."

He nuzzled her hair, breathed in the lingering aroma of lilacs. For the rest of his days, he'd associate that heavenly smell with Alexa Winters. "I hate this damn war."

She raised her head from his shoulder, and though shadowy leaves dappled her face, making it impossible to clearly see her, he could feel her gaze on him.

Without a thought, he brushed his lips against her forehead, intending only to comfort her as he would his sisters. The teasing smell of those damn lilacs and a scent that was uniquely Alexa filled his nostrils. Tormented by the soft curves pressed against him, his manhood roared to fully erect. A dizzying sensation enveloped him, urging him to move closer, hold her tighter. He forced aside the thoughts even as he struggled against the demands of his body.

"Alexa," he whispered against her ear. "I came here tonight with honorable intentions."

She turned toward him, the movement bringing her face into close contact with his lips. "A-and now?"

He stroked her cheek with the back of his fingers. "God help me, right now all I can think about is kissing you."

Northern Temptress

by

Nicole McCaffrey

American Heroes Series

Northern Temptress

Cover Art by *Debbie Taylor*

The Wild Rose Press, Inc.
PO Box 708
Adams Basin, NY 14410-0708
Visit us at www.thewildrosepress.com

Publishing History
First American Rose Edition, 2014
Print ISBN 978-1-62830-047-5
Digital ISBN 978-1-62830-048-2

American Heroes Series
Published in the United States of America

Dedication

For Wyatt and Colton
May you never lose your love of history, your thirst to know more and the desire to dig deeper and find out "why?"

Now, put this down because this is as far as you're allowed to read until you're older.

Acknowledgments

Debbie Taylor
for making my dream cover a reality

~

Stacy "The Flyswatter" Holmes
for her support, encouragement and making me
dig deeper to pull more emotion from this story
than I could have on my own…
and for plenty of pest control.

~

The angels of Lindsay Place,
who take such wonderful care of my dad.
Thank you from the bottom of my heart
for patiently answering my medical questions
as I researched this book.

~

And in loving memory of my uncle, Gary Meade, Sr.,
who never tired of those long-distance debates over
North versus South, Lee versus Grant,
the Civil War in general—
and always had a good book to recommend.
You are missed so much.

One

Gettysburg, PA
June 30, 1863

The crunch of wagon wheels on gravel blended with the rapid clip of horse hooves and the shouts of an army on the move.

"Whoa, Girl." Caleb McKenna paused astride his mount to take in his surroundings. The lush green farm land promised unspoken riches. Not a wealth of coin or jewels; something far more valuable. The brick-red barns, wheat fields of gold that waved in the slight breeze, and rolling meadows spoke of fertile land. A place where the hungry and weary might find the luxury of food and rest.

Rest, however, would have to wait. The small town, so quiet when he had surveyed it earlier this morning, bustled with panic and chaos. He understood the fear of the townsfolk, had witnessed their terrified and angry stares in other towns. His dust-begrimed men and their filthy horses made for a strange sight. But in recent days there had been no time for a change of clothing or a shave, or time to properly wash the dust from their faces, beards or uniforms.

Simon Edwards, the young corporal who was never far from his side, rode up alongside him. "Major, do you think General Lee will give us orders to fight?"

Caleb glanced at the boy-faced corporal. "I do."

"*Here*?" Edwards emphasized. "Such a quiet little place. Kinda seems a shame."

"Indeed it does," Caleb said to himself as much as Simon. Word had already reached the Confederate army that General George Meade, now commander of the Union army, was marching northward from Virginia to meet them. A sizable battle was imminent.

"If we're successful here, it would mean a clear march to D.C."

"You really think we could take Washington, Major?" Edwards gave a low whistle. "That would mean negotiations to end the war, wouldn't it?"

The farther into Pennsylvania they rode, the more that very thought taunted him. "Precisely."

"Sure is a nice thought."

Caleb swallowed his affirmative response. Like most of his men, he was sick of this damned fight. Sick of men reeling and falling; of dodging splinters that flew from wheels or axles where bullets struck; of horses wild with terror from their wounds, shells shrieking overhead, bullets whistling everywhere and the incessant pounding of cannons that he heard even in his sleep. Tired of the whole damned thing. But as an officer, he couldn't vocalize that thought.

He rode ahead, taking time to reassure the citizens he encountered that none would be harmed or captured. Despite his assurances, he sensed their anxiety. Women stood on their porches, clutching small children to their bosom, watching with a mixture of fear and hatred in their eyes.

Their worried faces brought to mind loved ones left behind in Georgia. Like their sisters in the south, the women of Gettysburg were conspicuously on their own. Not an able adult male anywhere to be seen. The militia his brigade had chased through town earlier today had undoubtedly warned the men to avoid contact with the enemy.

The pounding of hooves came from ahead, and one of his men reined to a halt. "There's trouble up ahead, Major."

Caleb wheeled his horse around. "Yankees?"

"No, sir. Civilians. Well…one."

"I thought the men were all in hiding?"

"It's not a man, sir."

Kneeing the horse into a gallop, Caleb rode forward. A crowd had gathered on the lawn of a residence up ahead. He recognized the large brick house from his earlier reconnoiter of town as belonging to a local doctor.

Several foot soldiers had paused to rest in the shade of the wide, inviting porch. The yeasty aroma of freshly baked bread wafted to him, bringing a groan from his stomach as it reminded him how long it had been since breakfast.

"Take one more step, soldier, and I'll end your hunger pangs permanently." The cold female voice sent a shock through him. The Confederate army had assured the residents they would not be harmed. Perhaps the tantalizing smell of oven-warm bread had enticed the soldier to ask for a bite to eat. Dismounting, he pushed his way through the crowd toward the house.

Annoyance prickled as he made his way up the front steps to where a butternut-clad foot soldier braced himself against the open front door.

A dark-haired woman stood on the threshold, the

barrel of a small gun pressed to the intruder's forehead.

Caleb hesitated, not wanting to move too quickly and startle the woman into firing, especially once he noticed the death grip the soldier had on her free arm and the way she struggled to keep her footing as he pressed his weight against the door.

"No man who would take arms against his own country will set foot in this house," she said loud enough for the others to hear. "If I have to shoot one man, or a dozen."

Several snickers came from below.

"She's gonna have to re-load that little gun right quick." A soldier standing near Caleb cast him an amused glance, then paled and quickly saluted. "Major McKenna, sir."

With a wave, he scattered the men from the porch. "What in the devil is going on?"

A wail came from inside the house. For the first time, Caleb noticed a young girl, perhaps fifteen years of age, and an old woman standing inside. Both were wide eyed with fear. The old woman, bent with age, brandished a wooden spoon like a warrior prepared for battle. As though the sight of Caleb spurred her to action, she reached over the dark-haired woman's shoulder to thunk the soldier's head.

He let out a howl of pain, but didn't release the young woman. "You're gonna take y'self and that other pretty gal right on inside and cook us as fine a meal as we've ever seen."

"I'd be happy to," the dark-haired woman spat. "But I'm afraid I haven't enough hemlock for all of you."

Caleb had seen enough. "Private!"

The solider turned to look over his shoulder, then abruptly released his hold on the woman. She stumbled backward, nearly toppling the old woman and girl behind her. The little gun exploded with an angry blast, and her entire body lurched with the kick from the weapon. It flew from her hands, landing on the porch and skidding a distance. Amid a shower of whitewash and wood chips, Caleb stopped the gun with the toe of his boot.

The solider quickly saluted. "Major McKenna, sir."

Caleb bent to retrieve the weapon from the floor. "Explain yourself, Private."

The woman stepped out onto the porch, rubbing her arms as though her muscles ached. "Are *you* their commanding officer?"

He removed his hat and gave a sweeping bow. "Major Caleb McKenna, Army of Northern Virginia. Ma'am, on behalf of General Lee, I offer my sincere apology. You have my word as a gentleman these men will be properly punished for their behavior."

She jabbed a finger in the direction of the private. "He tried to force his way into my home."

"An empty belly will make a man reckless."

"Empty belly?" she scoffed. "He saw my cousin in the window; I doubt his *belly* clouded his judgment."

Caleb had never heard a woman speak so frankly in his life. For the first time since she'd come out onto the porch, he took a good look at her. She wore man's trousers and a work shirt tucked into them. Dark hair was pulled back in a simple braid, but half had come unbound to trail over one shoulder. Her face and clothes were smudged with flour and dough. Emerald green eyes flashed with enough fire to warn him she wasn't

5

through arguing.

"She tried to shoot me," accused the private.

Caleb turned to the soldier. "This woman is defending her home against the enemy."

"But she—"

"*Dismissed*, Private."

Gathering what little patience he had left, Caleb pulled in a deep breath and waited until the private left the porch. But he felt the full weight of the woman's angry stare on him.

"That's it? You send your men around to tell us we won't be harmed, but then one of them tries to force his way into my home and you do *nothing*?" She shook her head. "I should have shot him."

"Any solider who disturbs a private home and insults a woman answers to me, whether he's under my command or not," Caleb replied, attempting to keep his temper in check. "And while he's not one of my men, I assure you, he *will* be punished."

"Nonetheless, I feel the need to protect my family." She held out a palm. "My gun, please?"

He supposed it was pointless to tell her the tiny gun was useless except at very close range.

A rustling of the curtains at the window drew his attention...the young girl, saucer-eyed with fear, and the old woman, spoon at the ready. The girl was quite lovely, with ivory skin and long, honey brown ringlets. No doubt the sharp-tongued hellion before him had correctly guessed the soldier's intent.

Reminded of his sisters and mother left alone to defend themselves, he pressed the gun into her waiting hand. "Your husband should have left you a more suitable weapon."

"I have no husband."

He frowned. "Is this not the residence of Doctor Winters?"

"It is." She pocketed the gun. "My father, Doctor Edwin Winters is in Harrisburg helping with the wounded—I assume you know all about *that* battle." Her voice dripped with sarcasm. "I stayed here to tend to our patients locally."

"You are…"

"Doctor Alexandra Winters."

Caleb took a moment to digest the information. A female physician? He'd heard of such a thing, but never actually encountered one.

"Has the cat got your tongue, Major?"

He recognized the challenge in her tone. No doubt she met with quite a bit of opposition in her position, but he'd be damned if he'd let her draw him into an argument. "Quite the contrary, Miss—*Doctor*—Winters. I was thinking how absurd it is that a physician who has taken an oath to heal would sooner put a gun to a man's head than food in his belly."

"It was more than food he wanted, and we both know it."

"I intend to learn exactly what his intentions were." With that, he placed his hat on his head and turned to leave. But then another thought struck him. Pausing on the porch steps, he faced her once more. "Should the battle that looks to be taking shape actually materialize, there will be many injured men in need of care. Tell me, Doctor Winters, will you check the color of a soldier's uniform before treating his wounds?"

He was rewarded by a slight tightening of her jaw.

"I treat anyone who needs care. Regardless of the

color of their uniform." She folded her arms and met him with a challenging stare. "Or their skin."

Caleb held back a sigh of resignation. He had neither the time nor the desire to engage in a debate over slavery. "I see. Good day to you then."

She glanced behind her, where the two women stood watch in the window, then hurried toward the steps. "What exactly do you mean by a battle 'taking shape?'"

Well aware of the men lounging in her front yard and the number who had stopped to stare at the spectacle of a woman dressed in man's trousers demanding answers from him, Caleb tensed. "It may be only a day, or less time than that. But your General Meade is marching north to meet us as we speak. A battle is imminent, Doctor Winters. A sizable one at that."

Another flutter of the curtains pulled his attention to the old woman and girl. He had a sister about her age and another two years older. If any man laid a hand on them… His stomach twisted at the thought.

"Corporal Edwards!" he barked.

The young man appeared as if out of nowhere. "Sir?"

"See that a red flag is hung from this residence to indicate the presence of a doctor. And find two men to stand sentinel at the Winters' residence. I don't want anymore incidents at this home."

After scattering the remaining men from the lawn, he mounted his horse, wondering at the sudden pang of longing he felt for his family, the nagging worry for their safety and well-being.

"Major McKenna?"

That feminine voice with the Northern lilt was familiar now. He forced himself to draw a calming breath before turning toward the porch. "Yes, Doctor Winters?"

"I'd prefer not to have Rebel soldiers posted outside my home, thank you just the same."

"You don't have a choice," he said, not even trying to hide the frustration he felt. "The Confederate army is in command of this town, and those are my orders." He tipped his hat in her direction. "Besides, I have the odd feeling it's my men who will need protection. From you."

Without awaiting her reply, he kneed Girl into a gallop and was off.

****

The next morning, Alexa rose before the sun. Father had yet to come home, and with the Confederate officer's warning of a looming battle, sleep eluded her. It didn't help that her cousin, Felicity, was visiting and sharing her bed. Sleep was hard enough to come by in this heat without a warm body crowding the space beside her.

Now, with the kitchen windows and door open to catch the cooler morning air, Alexa busied herself baking bread, as she had yesterday. If the battle came, there would be wounded men to care for. And wounded men would need to eat. Baking kept both her mind and her hands busy in the meantime.

With one loaf ready to bake and another batch of dough set out to rise, she turned to open the oven when a resounding boom shook the entire house. She gripped the edge of the table for support as the ground beneath her feet trembled.

Cannons! *Oh dear God, it's happening.*

Footsteps raced across the upstairs hallway and down the stairs. Wide eyed and breathless, her young cousin appeared in the kitchen. "It's the Rebs," she whispered. "What shall we do?"

Alexa searched her mind for words to reassure her. Poor Felicity had come from war-torn Maryland to spend the summer in Pennsylvania, after her father had been killed at Antietam last September. There likely wasn't a thing she could say to calm the girl.

"This is the battle that Rebel officer warned you about, isn't it?" Felicity asked in a rush.

Another boom rattled the windows and the floor beneath their feet. "The fighting is probably miles off. We'll be fine."

Grammy Winters shuffled into the room. "To the cellar girls. Now!"

Felicity scampered for the door. Her grandmother moved slower, but was right behind her. At the kitchen door, the old woman turned. "Child, there's no time to waste."

"I'll be along." Alexa mentally calculated the things she would need to gather. Sheets to tear into bandages, a basin for fresh water, her medical bag...

"Alexandra," Grammy's worried voice broke into her thoughts. "I've already lost one son to this war, God alone knows where your father and my grandson are at this moment. I won't stand by and—"

"As soon as I get this bread from the oven, I'll be along."

"You're not too big for me to take a wooden spoon to your backside."

Alexa fought the beginnings of a smile. Her

grandmother had been threatening with that spoon for as long as she could remember, but until yesterday, she'd never actually used it on anyone. "You go and take care of Felicity. She must be scared out of her wits."

"And you're not?" Grammy shuffled off as quickly as she could.

"Not at all." Worried, yes, but how big could the battle be? Another boom shook the house, and Alexa watched at the window as her grandmother and cousin tugged the doors to the fruit cellar open and disappeared inside. The minute the doors closed, she headed for the front porch. She had to know what was happening out there.

She searched for the guards the Confederate major had posted at her home yesterday, but they weren't in sight. Alexa nearly sagged with relief. They were nice young men, but as no one had bothered them again, their presence was unnecessary. Grammy had insisted on taking food to them at suppertime, and they had seemed grateful enough, wolfing down the simple meal of stew and biscuits as if they hadn't eaten in weeks. But just the same, Alexa was glad they were gone. She didn't need a battle on her doorstep. And even though most of the town had evacuated at the first signs of the Rebel army, she didn't want those who remained to see Rebs guarding her home.

Enough scandal was already attached to her name without giving the town gossips more fodder for their stories.

As she stood there, a troop of Union soldiers rode past. One of the men broke from the group and wheeled his horse around.

"Alexa!"

She recognized the voice and raced down the porch steps to greet her brother's oldest friend. He jumped from his horse and enclosed her in a warm hug, lifting her off her feet and twirling her around.

"I'd heard you were home again. I was hoping to see you while I was here, but under better circumstances," he said, setting her back on her feet.

Quentin Lord had been close friends with her brother since their days at West Point. Alexa always thought him quite handsome, but a tad too aware of his own good looks. Still, he had visited the Winters' home so many times over the years he was practically kin. "Are you well, Quentin?"

"Fine. A few scratches here and there, that's all." He glanced up to see his unit moving on without him. "I really must ask that you take shelter. You'd be much safer inside."

"I'm going to the cellar soon, I promise. Is it over? Have you beaten back the Rebs?"

"Naw, but the infantry's here now, we're just riding in. We'll lick those Johnnies in no time." He glanced over his shoulder to where the long line of soldiers continued to move on. "You be sure to get inside, now. Your brother would never forgive me if I let anything happen to you."

She placed a hand on his arm. "It's been a year since we've heard from Nate. I don't suppose you've—"

"I'm sorry, Alexa. I haven't seen him."

Her heart fell. "I thought perhaps—"

He gave her hand a gentle squeeze. "I get letters from home that are months old."

"You're right, of course. I'm worrying needlessly."

"While I'm here, I'll do my best to come by for a visit."

"We'd like that. Take care of yourself, Quentin."

He smiled at her, his dark eyes twinkling. She recognized the look, had seen him use it on nearly every female he encountered. She'd have to remember to keep Felicity away from him. "How about a kiss for a solider riding into battle?"

She leaned in toward his cheek. "You haven't changed a—"

He turned his head and the rest of her words were muffled against his lips. She jerked back, startled. Quentin really *hadn't* changed.

With a wink, he swung onto his horse.

Alexa stared after him, frowning. She had no intentions of becoming another of Quentin's ladies in waiting. One man had already ruined her life and reputation. She wouldn't give another the chance.

Aware her bread would soon be done, she hurried into the house to gather supplies. If nothing else, caring for the wounded would remind the judgmental town folk and old pea hens that, like it or not, she was a doctor, just like her father.

Maybe then they'd stop gossiping about her scandalous divorce.

****

After taking the last loaves of bread from the oven, Alexa reluctantly retreated to the fruit cellar. She'd never cared for the musty, damp room, even if the cooler temperature provided relief from the heat of the day.

A lantern helped to cast away much of the

shadows, and Grammy sat beside it, knitting socks for the soldiers. Felicity sat on a cot along one wall, a candle beside her as she, too, knit, though her young fingers didn't move with the same skill and speed as Grammy's.

"Does someone sleep down here, Alexa?" the girl asked during a lull in the booming. "This cot is freshly made up, and I found these candles and some matches in the cupboard over there."

"I'm sure I don't know what you're talking about," Alexa murmured, taking a seat beside her cousin. She took up a ball of wool and turned it in her hand, considering the idea of knitting, but she hated fiddly activities such as knitting or baking pies and pastries.

"That's what Grammy said. But aren't cellars for storing food?"

"There are jars of preserves and vegetables behind you, child," Grammy spoke up.

Felicity gestured toward a small table beside the cot. "But there's a lantern—"

Any further words were cut off as a resounding artillery assault began in earnest.

Soon the crack of gunfire was added to the boom of cannons. Felicity huddled closer to Alexa, and she tried to comfort her. Staying brave for her cousin's sake was better than giving into her own fears, but it sounded as though the end of the world had come.

As the hours passed, the house shook with the explosion of cannon fire. More than once it sounded as though a shell had torn through the upstairs, and the house shook so violently Alexa feared it would collapse. Quentin had been right to insist she take shelter.

"There can't be anything left of either army after all of this," Felicity wailed, her hands covering her ears. "Why don't they just get it over with?"

"They are," Alexa soothed, pulling her close. "I'm sure they're trying their best."

For what seemed an eternity, they listened to the ongoing assault. Was Nate out there somewhere, or did he lie dead on a battlefield somewhere far away? Or rotting in some prison camp? Why hadn't she heard from her brother in more than a year?

Her body lurched as another blast rocked the house to its foundation, and she forced her mind away from the dark subject of her brother's whereabouts. Were the two young men sent to guard her home out there fighting? Probably with the Confederate officer she'd met yesterday.

Now, why did *he* cross her mind? More than once today, Major McKenna's face had returned to haunt her. It was a handsome face, she grudgingly admitted, saved from being too pretty only by the deep cleft in his chin. He cut a dashing figure in his uniform, the width of his shoulders emphasized by the fitted gray coat, hair the color of maple sugar just brushing the collar. A smile tugged at the corners of her mouth as she recalled the expression in his dusky blue eyes when she'd announced *she* was the doctor.

And Quentin. What had gotten into him to steal a kiss that way? Nate would be furious if he thought his friend had tried to take liberties with her.

Felicity raised her head from Alexa's shoulder. Slowly, almost expectantly, she removed her hands from her ears.

"Is it over?"

Alexa strained to listen, but only silence remained. She met Grammy's gaze across the room. They held still for several long seconds, scarcely daring to breathe.

Hurried footsteps ran past outside, and then the doors were pulled open, spilling bright sunlight into the cellar.

Squinting against the light, Alexa rose to her feet. A group of soldiers filed down the stairs, their tattered butternut and gray clothing proclaiming them Confederates.

Felicity screamed. Grammy dropped her knitting.

"What do you want?" Alexa was grateful her voice didn't crack or waver, despite the trembling in her knees.

Two soldiers moved past Alexa to look under the cot. Another grabbed as many jars of preserves and vegetables as he could carry.

Her cousin shrieked and jumped to her feet.

Grammy rose. "You boys get out of there!"

"We're lookin' for yanks," answered one soldier with a thick Southern accent.

"Any yanks hidin' down here?"

Alexa raised her chin to meet his gaze directly. "We're *all* Yankees in this house."

The young men chuckled, and one tipped his hat toward her. "It's *soldiers* we're lookin' for ma'am, not women."

"Is the war over?" Felicity asked in a small voice. "Did you win?"

"The Confederate army has control of the town right now, little lady. You're welcome to come out, you won't be harmed."

Three more soldiers trooped down the stairs.

One of the men broke away to meet them. "Was there anyone in the house?"

"Jam, molasses and lots of bread." One Reb gestured with the loaves Alexa had left cooling in the kitchen, then took a big bite. "But no Yankees."

Felicity's jaw dropped. "That bread's not for—"

Alexa squeezed the girl's arm to shush her, then turned to glare at the soldiers. "Obviously, there are no Federal soldiers here or you would all be dead by now. I think it would best if you went on your way."

The two men exchanged amused smiles. "We'd be glad to leave ma'am, but which one of you is that lady doctor I heard about?"

"She's not here," Grammy spoke up quickly.

"It's all right. They said we wouldn't be harmed." Alexa disentangled herself from her cousin and stepped forward. "Which one of you is hurt?"

"It's not us, ma'am," answered one soldier from the stairs. "It's them outside. Some are bad hurt."

Alexa followed the men up the stairs. The full light of the sun knifed into her eyes when she stepped out of the cellar, and she had to blink from the pain of it.

But the light wasn't as painful as what met her eyes once they adjusted. Her yard, and the street before it, were littered with blankets, clothing, cartridge boxes, knapsacks. And bodies. Men, horses, mules—all of them horribly still.

She'd have remained frozen to one spot, but one of the soldiers who had escorted her from the cellar tugged at her elbow. "Over here, ma'am."

He led her to the front of the house where dozens of men lay wounded and bleeding on the porch. Several dozen more streamed toward town. The badly wounded leaned on the not-so-badly wounded, some were carried on stretchers or the backs of their comrades.

Hundreds of them.

She had hoped for the chance to put her skills to good use. But never in her worst imaginings had she anticipated anything like this.

Two

Alone in his tent, Caleb bent over a portable writing desk, the dim yellow light from a nearby lantern casting shadows on a blank sheet of paper. Well, it wasn't entirely blank. He'd gotten as far as "My dearest mother and sisters." He removed his spectacles, rubbing eyes that ached with the need for sleep.

He was running out of ways to disguise the truth in his letters home. But his family anxiously awaited word from him.

His father had died in January of sixty-one, just one day after their home state of Georgia had seceded from the union, a move his father opposed. His older brother had been killed at First Manassas.

Caleb was all they had left.

It was easy enough to write and tell them he was alive and well, but they expected more. Despite dwindling food rations, frostbite during the winter months and lean circumstances overall, he made sure to tell them he was fine, everything was going well and that the war would end soon, and he would be home to look after things.

News of today's battle would reach them, and he hated that they would worry until they heard from him.

But words could not adequately describe today's events. He'd seen his share of battles these past two years, but none like this. Though Union forces were initially outnumbered, reinforcements came from seemingly nowhere. His men had fought bravely, as they always did, believing that death was better than defeat.

And death had been plentiful today. Men he'd grown up with, rode with, drank with…gone.

A short time ago, he'd learned that a Union general had been killed almost at the onset of the fighting. Caleb recalled John Reynolds from his days as commandant of the cadets at West Point. He had been a cadet under Reynolds and had respected—even admired—the man.

He sighed and shifted position, reaching around to massage a stiffness in one shoulder. The damn war needed to end. He no longer gave a damn who won, he just wanted it over. He hoped to God the battle in this little Pennsylvania town would decide that.

The South had been victorious today. But tomorrow would bring more fighting. And if additional reinforcements came from the North, Confederate forces would be badly outnumbered. Being outnumbered wasn't unusual, they frequently were, but his men were sick, hungry and tired. He didn't know how much more they could withstand.

Caleb rose from the chair. Words of reassurance for his family were lacking when he was this restless. He'd come in a short time ago, intending to rest; tomorrow was only hours away. General Longstreet conferred with General Lee even now, and he'd have his orders soon enough. But rest, as always, was a luxury he could ill afford.

He took his coat from the back of the chair and shrugged into it, wincing as the movement reminded him of the piece of shrapnel he'd taken to the shoulder earlier today. He made a mental note to have one of the field surgeons look at it when things settled down.

Buttoning the coat, he stepped outside and started toward the field hospital set up in a nearby barn. At least there he could be of use.

He'd gone no more than half-a-dozen steps when Edwards ran up to him, panting as though he'd run a long distance.

Caleb frowned. "Didn't I send you to keep an eye on the Winters' residence?"

"Yes sir," he pulled in a deep breath. "I followed her all the way here."

"Who?"

"Doctor Winters, sir."

Caleb looked over the boy's head, scanning the area for any sign of the sharp-tongued hellion he'd encountered yesterday. "She's *here?*"

Edwards gulped visibly. "No, sir, I uh, lost her at the field hospital."

He frowned. "What in the devil is she doing there?" An image of dark green eyes flashing with anger came to mind. Surely the same Doctor Winters who had offered to poison the men on her lawn yesterday wouldn't volunteer to doctor wounded Southerners? There were more than enough wounded from either side to keep her busy without her seeking more.

"Does she know you followed her?"

"I don't think so, sir. She stopped at the Presbyterian Church first, they've a hospital set up there. But she didn't stay long."

"And the men patrolling the town didn't stop her?"

"No, sir. She stayed pretty well hidden, darting between houses and through yards. She kept to the shadows the whole time."

"Kept to the shadows, did she?" The town was under siege. Confederate pickets were stationed to keep the citizens from milling about. Yet she had managed to avoid them. Almost as if she knew how.

Was it possible she was more than a doctor and a loyalist? Was the lovely Doctor Winters a spy, as well?

****

"Water..."

Surrounded by the moans and cries of the wounded in a field just west of town, Alexa knelt beside yet another Confederate soldier. "Nate?"

"Water," the man croaked in a raspy voice.

She tipped a canteen of water to the man's lips. The soldier didn't have the strength to drink, but seemed grateful for the liquid that drizzled over his lips and chin. She forced a smile when his pain-filled gaze landed on her. No, he wasn't Nate. He was much too fair.

The soldier shuddered in pain.

She touched his arm. "Where does it hurt?" There was no visible injury, but blood soaked the ground beneath him

He mumbled something.

"I'm sorry, I don't..."

He reached a hand toward her face. "*An...gel.*"

"No, no," she protested. "I'm not...I'm looking for..." His hand went limp. "Sir?"

No response. She felt for a pulse at his neck, then somberly pulled the gray cap down over his face.

As she moved toward the next man, liquid oozed

through the worn leather soles of her work boots. She glanced down and gave a little shudder. The ground here was so soaked with blood that puddles of it had formed. She knelt down beside another soldier and pulled his cap back from his face. Her heart gave a small leap. He had dark hair. "Nate?"

No response. She heaved a heavy sigh. He was too small to be her brother anyway. She moved on to the next. He, too, was dead.

On and on it went until she found another dark-haired soldier. A full beard covered his face, making it impossible to distinguish his features. And he was breathing! She knelt beside him. "Nate?"

"Ma?" The soldier grabbed her hand. "Is that you?"

Alexa's heart fell. The voice had a heavy southern accent.

"I knew you'd come."

The moon slipped from behind a cloud, spilling silver white light across them. Crimson stained the man from waist to throat. How on earth was he still alive?

"Ma? You still there?"

Alexa closed her eyes. If it comforted him to believe she was his mother, then so be it. "I'm here."

"Would...would you sing to me? That song you sang when we was little babies?"

"Not just now," she crooned, stroking his brow. "You rest first." She pulled a clean cloth from her bag, soaked it with water and moistened his lips.

"Water," croaked another man somewhere nearby. "*Water...*"

"I tried to do ya proud," the soldier continued, his voice fading. "We won, you know. The South won."

"Shhh... You need to rest." When he grew quiet,

she slipped her hand from his to fumble in her bag for her stethoscope.

He tried to rise. "Don't leave!"

"I won't," she whispered, hoping her quiet tone would soothe him. "I was only looking for something."

"Don—don't leave me."

"I won't. I promise." Resigned, she stroked his hand and murmured soothing words, assuring him she would stay. At his insistence, she began to sing a song Grammy had often sang to her and Nate. Whether or not it was what the soldier longed to hear, it seemed to comfort him. A short time later, still clinging to her hand, he slipped from this world to the next. She brushed dirty hair back from a face that was more boy than man and closed his eyelids.

Tears welling in her eyes, she rose to her feet and pulled the hood of her cloak closer about her face. Sweet Mother Mary, but the enemy took on a different face this way. Though Rebels, these men were suffering. They were all so helpless, so frightened. And so young. They called out for mothers, wives, sweethearts. And water. A heavy weight settled over her; she was no closer to finding her brother. And the canteen was empty.

She'd have to fetch more water and return, but the need to know if Nate was here, if he was hurt was more than she could bear. Even while tending the wounded at home, her mind had continually strayed to her brother's whereabouts until she could stand it no more. When the last bloody limb had been stitched, the last broken bone set, she had slipped out to look for him, fully expecting to return before more wounded arrived.

She'd never expected to find anything like this.

Strong fingers closed around her upper arm. She whirled, a scream ready.

Before she could utter a sound, a hand clamped over her mouth.

"What the hell are you doing?"

The voice was familiar. Cultured Southern tones. She closed her eyes long enough to let her senses take over. And inhaled the scent of bay rum. The smell brought to mind a perfectly chiseled face and eyes the dusky blue of twilight. *Major McKenna.*

She sank her teeth into the fleshy part of the palm covering her mouth, rewarded when he gave a hiss of pain.

"Don't scream. And for Christ's sweet sake, stop biting me."

When she failed to follow orders, he tightened his hold. She brought her foot down hard on his instep.

He groaned. "For the love of—will you listen to me? You need to get out of here. If you scream, you'll bring dozens of men running."

She gave an exaggerated nod, wordlessly telling him that was her intent.

"*Men,*" he added with emphasis, "who haven't seen a woman in a long, *long* time."

She swallowed hard. So, being held prisoner by *him* was the lesser evil?

"I'm going to take my hand away now." His hold loosened ever so slightly. "You won't scream?"

She released a small huff of defeat and shook her head. One insufferable soldier was preferable to dozens.

The minute he released her, she turned to face him. "Is the Confederate army so heartless it can't provide water for the wounded? I demand to see the officer in charge!"

"Keep your voice down or I'll have you bound and gagged."

She folded her arms. "You wouldn't dare."

"*I* am the division commander, and therefore the officer in charge." He raised his voice an octave, as though talking to one of his men. "I'll ask you again, Doctor Winters. What is your business here?"

"I should think it's obvious."

A harsh choking sound came from nearby. Alexa whirled and cautiously stepped around several horribly still men before finding the one in distress. She dropped to her knees, tore open her bag and fumbled for the knife she needed. "He can't breathe," she explained, sensing the major's watchful gaze. She pressed the blade to the soldier's throat and prepared to make an incision.

McKenna seized her wrist in a vice-like grip. "Guns, threats of poison and now *knives*? Has the Federal army commissioned you?"

She wrenched back violently, but he held tight. Her fingers began to go numb, and she lost hold of the knife. "Damn you, let go of me. His airway is blocked."

"Come with me." Placing a hand beneath her shoulder, he pulled her to her feet.

"No—let me help him." She fumbled on the ground for the knife, but his arm snaked around her waist, half-lifting, half-dragging her.

"*Water*..." croaked a distant voice. "Please, water..."

"Private Edwards!" the major barked, again in a tone that suggested his patience had worn thin. "Round up every available man you can. I want canteens filled with water and brought here immediately."

He moved forward, but she held back. The gurgling had stopped. An eerie silence descended until another pitiful wail for water pierced the stillness.

Alexa looked over her shoulder to where the soldier lay motionless. "I could have helped him."

"And prolong his agony? Death is the only friend these men have right now." He forcibly guided her away from the wounded, pulling when she hung back, pushing when she paused to offer aid. Finally, when they were several yards from the men, he stopped and released her arm.

"May I remind you this town is under siege? No one, and that includes you, is permitted to travel outside town lines. I will ask once again, Doctor Winters, what is your business here?"

"I was looking for a soldier."

"Wouldn't an able-bodied one be more to your liking?"

So much for Southern gentlemen. "I'm trying to find my brother."

"You do realize these men are *Confederate* soldiers."

She closed her eyes for a moment, well aware of his meaning. Yesterday she had threatened to kill a Confederate soldier—many of them, actually. "I'm sure you will find this amusing, Major, but my brother fights for the South." She raised her chin, mentally bracing herself for whatever remark he would make.

Instead, the moonlight reflected understanding, perhaps even weariness in his face. That perfectly chiseled, handsome face.

"I'm sorry," he said, his tone far gentler than she'd

have hoped. "I can only imagine how that must have torn your family apart. Do you know what division he's with?"

"He wouldn't tell me. I don't think he wanted my father to know."

"May I ask his name?"

"Nathaniel Winters. I've always assumed he was with a Virginia regiment."

"Most of these men, myself included, are from Georgia."

She turned to take a lingering look at the dying men. "Please let me help them. Perhaps one of them will know my brother."

When he said nothing, she laid a beseeching hand on his arm. "Please."

He glanced down into her face, and his expression softened. "Doctor Winters, few men could deny such a heartfelt request, but try to understand." He lifted the hand she'd placed on his arm, tucked it into the crook of his elbow and stepped forward, as though they were out for an afternoon stroll. "There *is* no help for these men. Most will be dead before daybreak. Those who aren't will soon wish they were."

"I'll do what I can." Tugging her hand away, she turned back toward the wounded.

Warm heavy hands clamped her shoulders and spun her around to face him.

"I can't leave you here. If the wrong officer happened to find you, you'd be arrested for a spy." His gaze raked pointedly over her shirt and trousers. "Or worse."

Worse?

She considered his words for a moment. Was he

suggesting she looked like a—"How dare you!"

"Dammit, listen to me." His tone was hushed, but the meaning was clear. "This is no place for a civilian, certainly not a woman. Union sharpshooters are camped in the woods nearby. At first light, they'll begin firing at anything that moves."

She glanced toward the dark copse of trees in the distance, but saw nothing save the inky blackness of night. "That's a chance I'll have to take, isn't it?" Yanking away from him, she strode back toward the wounded. Blast him, even if she didn't find Nate, or anyone who knew him, she'd help these poor suffering souls.

She gave a yelp as her feet were swept from the ground.

"You can risk your neck in someone else's battlefield." Major McKenna grunted as he shifted her weight in his arms. "Not mine."

"Put me down!" She flailed, and though she heard another grunt and a muttered curse, she failed to free herself. "I want to find my *brother*."

"He's not here." He stopped walking and shot her a warning look. "It's too dangerous for you here, and if you keep screaming and thrashing about, I'll drop you on your stubborn little head." He shifted her to redistribute her weight as he crossed the field in angry strides.

"But—"

"Shush!"

"Where are—"

"*Miss* Winters!"

Though she didn't appreciate being hushed, she recognized the lack of patience in his voice. She'd simply let the arrogant lout wear himself out carrying her around, then return to the wounded.

She shot him an angry glare. "That's *Doctor* Winters to you."

Three

Either the doctor was heavier than she looked, or exhaustion had taken a toll on Caleb's strength. The sight of his tent up ahead was welcome relief. More than once she had opened her mouth to speak; each time he'd silenced her with a warning look.

Corporal Edwards stepped up to pull back the entrance flap, curious gaze moving from the sulking Alexa Winters to him.

"Don't ask," he warned, brushing past him.

Inside the tent, he dumped her onto his cot. She scrambled to her feet and faced him, green eyes flashing with defiance.

"Sit," he said, reading her thoughts. "I don't intend to ravish you."

She made no move to follow orders. "Why did you bring me here?"

"Because you were attracting far too much attention where you were."

He strode across the tent, eager to put some space between them. Being in such close proximity to her was…unsettling. He hadn't noticed the brilliant green of her eyes the other morning, or the stark contrast of her dark hair and porcelain skin. Or how those damn trousers hugged the curve of her hips and the length of her legs… "Why *do* you dress that way?" Every ounce of frustration he felt was reflected in his voice, but he was too damned tired to care.

"Have you ever tried moving around in a tight corset and long, heavy skirts, Major McKenna?" she asked, at last plopping unceremoniously onto the cot. "They get in the way. Especially when tending the sick or injured."

He glanced in her direction, but had to force his gaze away from the fullness of her breasts, emphasized by the shirt tucked into the waist of her trousers. "Is there nothing more modest you could wear?"

She glanced down, as if considering her attire. "When I was three, my dress caught fire on an iron grate. I wasn't badly injured, but after that, my Father began to dress me in my brother's old clothes. As I got older, I could climb trees and scale fences as well as any boy in town, so a dress never made sense." She shrugged. "I've always dressed this way. It's comfortable."

Not for the men she came into contact with it wasn't. The entire way across the field to his tent, he'd been acutely aware of the curve of her buttocks against his lower body, the softness of her breasts against his chest. Not to mention the pain in his shoulder. Carrying her hadn't been easy given his recent injury, but her stubborn refusal to listen to reason had ignited his temper.

Still needing distance, he paced toward the writing desk he'd left unattended earlier. "When did you last hear from your brother?"

"It's been more than a year."

"You do realize it's next to impossible to get letters from south to north?"

"I do. I just thought…well, hoped that he was here.

And that he'd try to see me."

He thought of his own sisters, and worried about their well being constantly. Nothing and no one could stop him from seeing them if he were close to home. "I'm sure if he's here, he'll make every effort."

She shook her head. "It's not likely. He and my father argued bitterly over his decision." She rose and placed her hands on her hips. "If you won't let me tend the men here, there are dozens at home I need to look after."

He sighed. "I haven't yet figured out how to get you there."

"I walked here from the Presbyterian Church. I think I can manage to get home."

"Do you have any idea how lucky you are you weren't captured, or shot or accosted by men like those I removed from your porch yesterday?"

"I'm sure it's not as dangerous as you believe. Besides," she patted her pocket. "I have my gun should I need it."

Her confidence did little to reassure him. "I'll escort you home, Doctor Winters, if only for my own peace of mind."

"It's not necessary. But thank you."

"Before we go, I have one request. A favor, actually." He unbuttoned his coat and slid out of it. "I don't wish to offend your sensibilities, but since you're so intent on treating the injured—"

"My God, you're bleeding!"

He glanced at the brownish red stain on his shirt. "It wasn't this bad before."

"Before you insisted on carrying me half a mile?" she demanded. "Sit down so I can get a look at it."

Her authoritative tone made it clear she was in charge, and if the pain throbbing in his shoulder hadn't been so fierce, he might have found it amusing to be ordered about by a woman. Instead, he draped the coat carefully over the chair near his writing desk, then strolled toward the cot. Her huff of irritation reached his ears as he sat.

"You'll bleed to death before you're seated, at this rate."

Caleb watched with interest as she took up her bag and pulled out a sliver of soap. Moving to the stand that held his washing water and basin, she plunged her hands in, then proceeded to lather thoroughly.

"What are you doing?"

"I should think it's obvious. I'm washing my hands."

He'd never seen any of the field surgeons do such a thing. "Why?"

She removed her hands from the water and shook them to dispel the excess, then reached in her bag for a cloth to dry them. "Apart from the fact it's simply good manners?"

"Yes," he said, wincing as his shoulder throbbed.

She took the lamp from across the room and carried it closer, then knelt so the wound was at eye level. "It has been my personal observation that women who deliver babies with a midwife or another woman present have far fewer occurrences of child bed fever than when they deliver with a doctor present." She touched the jagged edges around the wound, frowning. "Do you know why that is?"

"I'm sure I don't, Doctor Winters."

She held up a hand and wiggled her fingers.

"Women are much more likely to wash their hands before touching a patient. It makes sense when you think about it; dirt from the hands is introduced to the body."

"I've never heard one of the doctors here speak such nonsense." A twinge of pain shot through him as she probed the edges of the wound.

"Mmm," she admitted. "Nor will you. They'd laugh me out of the profession if I made such a claim. It's certainly not as though I have any proof; people do still die, after all, of infection or disease. It's merely a theory."

The doctor sat back on her heels. "Major, I'll need you to remove your shirt." She glanced behind him. "Unless there's an exit wound, I'll need to remove whatever's in there."

"There isn't one."

It seemed strange to remove his shirt in the presence of a lady without her turning bashfully away, but Doctor Winters seemed more intent on rummaging through her bags and washing her hands and instruments again.

"Lie back," she said when she'd returned to his side. "This is going to be painful, Major, but I don't have any means of putting you out or easing the pain."

He'd expected as much.

"Just lie still, and I'll move as quickly as I can."

He lay back and focused on the ceiling while her gentle fingers probed the wound. Pain roared through him, but he refused to give voice to the sensations ricocheting through his brain. One sensation repeatedly pushed through the red haze of pain clouding his mind. Something soft against his arm each time she leaned forward.

He chanced a glance in her direction. Sure enough, each time the doctor leaned in closer to examine the wound, her breast brushed his upper arm.

"I'm nearly done," she whispered. "Just a few more minutes, I think I have it…"

Her voice soothed, as did the sight of dark lashes against creamy cheeks. But the feel of her soft breast against his arm was better medicine than anything she might have offered.

"So, your father being a physician undoubtedly influenced you?" he asked, trying to steer his mind to a more innocent topic. "Is that why you chose to become a doctor?"

"Yes and no." She pulled a pair of long tweezers from her bag. "My grandmother was probably a bigger influence. She's delivered most of the babies in this town, and has always kept a garden of herbs and plants grown specifically for medicinal purposes. I spent much of my childhood at her side, assisting her."

He ground his teeth as she probed the wound with the metal instrument. His mind screamed every obscenity he'd ever heard, but he forced himself to remain quiet, lie still even as his brain ordered his body to flinch away from the pain.

Her voice reached him as if from a dream, and he realized he must have passed out. "I have it here, Major." She held up the tweezers for him to see, a bloody piece of metal clamped within.

"Shrapnel," he murmured.

"Yes." She set it aside, then reached for something else in her bag. "I need only to stitch up the wound. I have whiskey to help dull the pain, if you'd like."

He shook his head. He needed to see Doctor Winters safely home; he wouldn't dull his senses with strong spirits.

"Stubborn, but typically male."

The shadow of a smile tugged at the corners of his mouth a second before the needle entered his flesh. He tensed, willing the pain away. When that failed, he focused once again on the lovely sight before him. With Doctor Winters so intent on her task, he could study her physical attributes unnoticed.

"I imagine you've encountered a great deal of opposition as a female physician?" he asked, feeling the need for conversation to distract from the pain.

"Most people prefer to be seen by a man, but then that's what they're used to. It's hard to see a woman in any role other than wife or mother."

"How does your father feel about your chosen profession?"

"Father is somewhat of a free thinker. He believes strongly in educating women. He never treated me differently than Nate, not as weaker, nor more feeble. He encouraged me. As did my brother."

Her voice, steady and strong yet so feminine, washed over him, taking the worst of the sting out of each tug and stab of the needle. One of the things he'd missed most while at war was the gentler company of a female, the sound of a feminine voice, or the sweet, soft smell of their skin.

The whores who followed the army camps did little to make up for the lack of feminine companionship. Nor much else, in his opinion. Nearly all were diseased, and he forbade his men to visit them. Never a hypocrite, he steered clear of such pursuits himself. Normally, he kept his urges well under control, but the close proximity of Doctor Winters was almost as much torture as her needle.

"Done, just let me tie this off." He glanced down to study her neat handiwork while she again rummaged through her bag. "I know I have a knife in here—"

"Major McKenna, sir." Corporal Edward's voice from outside the tent flap held an air of urgency.

The young corporal most likely carried orders for him to report to General Longstreet. "Are we nearly finished?"

She nodded. "I need only to cut the thread, but I seem to have lost my kni—oh, I dropped it earlier, didn't I?"

"I have a knife," he said. "I'll just—"

"I can bite it off."

Before he could react, she laid a hand to his chest to still him and leaned in to take the thread between her teeth. The sweet smell of lilac water wafted to his nose, assaulting his senses in a way shrapnel and shell never could. For the brief moment it took her to nip through the threads, her breasts were completely pressed against his bare chest, eliciting a moan from his throat that had nothing to do with pain.

She abruptly straightened. "I'm sorry, did that hurt?"

Hurt didn't begin to describe it. "Not at all." He offered no further explanation for his involuntary response, and instead rose, hastily buttoned his shirt and strode to the tent flap to allow the corporal entrance.

The corporal saluted, though his gaze moved from Caleb to the raven-haired doctor once again washing her hands and instruments.

"You hurt, Major?"

"A bit of shrapnel, nothing serious."

"General Longstreet wants to see you right away."

"Very well."

The young man's gaze strayed to follow Alexa Winters' movements. Caleb heaved a silent sigh. "I'll need you to stay here and guard her," he said in a low voice. "Under no circumstances do you allow her to leave. And no one, save myself, is allowed inside. Understood?"

He nodded.

"Did I hear you correctly?"

Suppressing a groan, Caleb turned. Those bewitching green eyes were alight with fire again.

"Did you tell that young man to guard me—like a prisoner?"

He motioned for the soldier to leave. "I did."

Hands on her hips, she faced him defiantly. "You can't hold me here against my will."

"I can. And for the time being, I am."

"I have patients—"

"Then that makes one of us, Doctor Winters," he said, wincing at how loud his voice had grown. He stepped closer, the pain in his shoulder throbbing, tempting him to give his temper free rein. "You are far too much of a distraction to be wandering about at will. And without someone here to guard the tent, you'd likely prove a temptation."

Her arms remained folded, and she raised a dark brow. "Am I supposed to swoon now? I appreciate your concern, Major, but I'm hardly some simpering belle. I'm older than half the men out there, hardly a 'temptation,' as you so kindly put it."

She never failed to astound him. Did she truly not realize the danger she'd already placed herself in this evening? No wonder he'd never cared for independent-minded females; they were exasperating.

He strode angrily toward the tent flap. "Need I remind you these men haven't seen a woman in months? You could be decades older, wrinkled as an old prune and missing half your teeth, and you'd still prove a distraction *and* a temptation."

He paused to meet her gaze just before exiting, smugly satisfied to find her slack jawed. "I trust that explanation is more to your liking."

Four

As the minutes stretched into hours, Alexa paced restlessly around the little tent. Once again, she strode to the entrance and peered around the flap where Corporal Edwards stood dutifully on guard.

"I can't stay here all night." She did her best to sound pleasant and reasonable though she felt anything but. "I have wounded men to care for."

The young soldier said nothing.

"Some of them are Confederate," she offered hopefully.

Still nothing.

Annoyed with his silence, she threw back the flap and stepped into the heavy, damp night air.

He stepped in front of her, blocking her path. "I can't let you do that, Doctor Winters."

"I can find my own way home." She pushed past him.

"Orders are orders, ma'am. Just doing my job."

He blocked her way once more. The men around them had gone silent, and several pairs of eyes were on her. Soldiers who had been sitting by the fire, sharing stories, or playing cards stared up at her with interest. A bit too much interest. She backed up a step. Damn McKenna, this was his doing. The men were only curious, but thanks to him, she felt as though she stood there as naked as the day she was born. Their friendly, curious gazes appeared *too* friendly. Too curious. Too…everything.

The broad grin of one soldier reminded her of the Reb who had tried to force his way into her home. Despite the reassuring weight of the gun in her pocket, she felt suddenly vulnerable.

She glared at Edwards, who watched her with a knowing smirk.

"Still want to find your own way home?"

It was on the tip of her tongue to demand he escort her himself, but she doubted he'd be much protection; he was little more than a boy. She had no choice but to wait for the major.

Without another word, Alexa turned and stepped back into the tent, dropping the canvas flap into place behind her. Damn the man, even when he wasn't here, he made things difficult.

With a loud sigh, she pulled out the folding chair near a portable writing desk and sat. A pen and a pair of spectacles lay discarded atop a piece of paper. A letter home, she guessed, but the major hadn't gotten past the salutation.

The longer she waited, the more weary she felt. The sight of the neatly made up cot on the other side of the tent beckoned to her. How she longed to rest her head on the small pillow, just for a few moments. She wouldn't sleep…only rest. Rising from the chair she walked to the cot and sat, testing the comfort of the small bed. It wouldn't be wise for her to be lying there when he returned, he might think…

Oh the hell with what he might think, she was exhausted. She pulled her feet up and lay down to rest her head on the pillow. Just for a moment.

****

Though the night sky was still inky black when Caleb returned to his tent, dawn's pearly glow would soon lighten the sky.

He clapped Corporal Edwards on the shoulder. "Get some rest, soldier, we've another long day ahead."

Blinking wearily, the young man nodded.

"Any trouble with my guest?"

"She wanted to go home, demanded I release her." The corporal yawned. "But that was a while ago. She's been quiet as a church mouse ever since."

Caleb could only wonder what had kept her so quiet as he stepped cautiously into the tent. A moan reached him, and he made out a small form on the cot. On the table beside it, a candle burned low, casting that side of the room in shadows.

"No...please lie still." Doctor Winters stirred fitfully. "I'm sorry...so sorry."

A wave of compassion washed over him. The first glimpses of war were difficult for even the most hardened soldier. For a young woman like her, they had to be brutal.

He placed a gentle hand on her shoulder, careful not to startle her. "Doctor Winters."

"I can't," she sobbed. "No more water."

He knelt beside the cot. "It's nearly daybreak, Doctor Winters." He gently shook her again.

"Nate!" The sound tore from her throat in a panicked scream.

Caleb couldn't allow her to remain in the dream a moment longer. He sat on the cot beside her and gathered her into his arms. "Alexa, wake up."

A choked sob followed and her fingers curled into

his jacket. "I thought you were…that I'd never…"

"Shhh," he soothed. The faint scent of lilacs teased his nostrils. The softness of her pressed against his chest, and it felt so damn good to hold a woman again, even one he suspected despised him. He gently stroked her hair, enjoying the feel of her velvety tresses beneath his palm. "You were dreaming."

She sniffled and pulled away enough to sit up, then lurched away from him. "McKenna?"

"You were calling for your brother." He rose reluctantly from the cot, well aware of the impropriety of sharing it with her.

"I don't remember."

"I should have warned you what the first sights of war can do. My men wake up screaming on a regular basis."

"Do you?" she asked, shifting to sit straighter. "Wake up screaming, I mean."

"I don't know. I sleep alone." In truth, he woke up in a sweat, his heart pounding and orders on his lips more often that he cared to admit. He took her hand to help her up. "I'm glad you took the opportunity to rest. I have a feeling it will be another long day."

"Please don't say there will be more fighting." She sounded every bit as weary as he felt.

"With the two armies this close together, they have to try to end things."

"You mean end the war?"

"It's possible, yes."

She stifled a yawn. "Oh that would be heaven. Life could go back to normal."

"Whatever normal will be, Doctor Winters, but yes, it would be a relief. Are you ready to go home?"

"Yes, please." She rubbed her eyes, reminding him more of a sleepy child than the spitfire he'd left behind a few hours ago.

Outside the tent, the sky toward the east showed faint streaks of light. Heavy, damp air closed in, the night having done little to dispel the heat of the previous day. Caleb inhaled the smells of campfires and food, his stomach grumbling in response. His men turned curious faces toward them. Seeing him exit his tent with a woman was unheard of, but there was no doubt what most would think had taken place. A few flashed knowing grins his direction.

"Lead the way, Doctor Winters."

She moved forward, her own gaze just as curious at the men they passed. "Don't they ever sleep?"

"It's hard to sleep when you're facing death."

As they passed groups of men, tents and equipment he realized the darkness had masked much of the carnage last night. But the dawning light made it painfully visible. He placed a hand to her elbow, steering her around a dead horse.

"By mid-day the stench from these dead animals will be unbearable," he said. "Try to stay indoors as much as possible."

She nodded. They were about to step around another horse when he heard a soft, pitiful whinny.

"Oh God." She dropped down beside the injured animal.

He sucked in an irritated breath. Must the woman attempt to heal everything? The animal tried to rise, but it was evident more than one leg was broken. White foam oozed from the corners of its mouth, and the eyes were weary with pain.

She stroked the animal's side. "Poor baby."

With a sigh, he removed his coat, drawing her gaze. Without explaining his actions, he pulled his pistol and wrapped the coat around it. She spoke soothing words to the animal even as the muffled shot sounded.

He shook out his coat, brushing gunpowder from it. "I hope your Federal troops didn't hear that shot and decide today's fighting has begun."

Eyes wide, she rose and glanced quickly about, as though expecting to see blue-clad soldiers rushing toward them.

"Shall we?" At his words, she rose to her feet and fell into step beside him.

The further they traveled, down the slight incline of Taneytown Road, past the tree-lined cemetery, the more he marveled at the foolishness of her venturing out alone in the dark of night. Confederate sentinels were everywhere, and while he was allowed to pass with more knowing chuckles and grins, he couldn't help but wonder how she'd gotten as far as she had without encountering trouble.

Male voices and the crunch of wheels on gravel carried on the early morning air. He took hold of her arm to pull her behind a tree, praying she'd keep quiet for once. Soldiers came into view, leading a horse and wagon laden with what could only be stolen goods. Anger gnawed at him, such behavior not only went against the General's orders, it reinforced the notion of the Southern army as looters and Rebels. He tried to make out their faces in the moonlight, but didn't recognize them.

She gasped. He placed a hand over her mouth, not

as roughly as he had earlier but enough to warn her to silence. "Shhh..."

He watched as the soldiers moved past, half afraid she'd start shouting at the sight of the goods piled atop the wagon. He didn't normally choose to avoid conflict, but he was well outnumbered and had her safety to be concerned with. Once the soldiers were out of earshot, he removed his hand.

"They're looting our homes," she hissed. "Why didn't you stop them?"

He sighed, wondering if shaking her would rattle common sense into her head. "Right now, my responsibility is you, and time is running short." He took her hand once again, giving it a squeeze for urgency. "Let's get you home."

"You're just going to let them go?"

He'd find out who they were one way or another, but not right now. "I am."

"No Federal officer would allow that," she muttered.

He slowed his pace. "Would you prefer to remain my prisoner? The Confederate army could certainly use more doctors."

Her mouth dropped open, then snapped closed.

He purposely kept his pace brisk and businesslike as he led her in silence toward the town. She had to double her footsteps to catch up, but time was of the essence, and he needed to see her safely delivered home and return to his duties.

A few houses from her own, she stumbled to a halt
"What is it now?"

"This is far enough."

"If memory doesn't fail me, your house is further

ahead." He started forward, tugging her hand in the hope she'd follow.

The doctor pulled back, feet not budging. "I don't want the soldiers recuperating in my home to see you. Nor you them."

Exasperation warred with exhaustion. "You think I'd harm a wounded man?"

"No… Arrest them perhaps."

"If we are victorious again tomorrow," he sighed, "Yes, we'll take what prisoners we can. It's war, Doctor Winters. Federal troops would do the same."

She nodded. "I know."

"Wounded soldiers—of either side—are of no interest to me at present." He started forward again, certain she'd follow. "Seeing you home safely is."

"There's something else."

He sighed louder, no longer concerned if she knew patience was a luxury he lacked the time to indulge. "Surely you're not concerned about my intentions."

"You know my brother is fighting for the south."

"Yes." He clasped his hands behind his back.

"Half this town thinks I'm a Southern sympathizer—they blame me for the rift between my father and brother."

"Why would they blame you?"

"Because I encouraged Nate to follow his heart rather than do what Father expected of him."

"I see."

"For that reason—and a few others—the very last thing I need is to be seen with a Southern officer at an indecent hour."

He rocked back on his heels, struggling to keep his hands clasped behind him and not use them to drag her toward her destination. "And your neighbors are all awake at this hour, peering out their windows?"

"No, most of them fled town before your army arrived."

"Then you have no one to hide from."

He strode forward, not bothering to look back to see if she followed.

"No one indeed. Merely every sharp-tongued pea hen in town."

He had taken only a few steps when the predawn twilight revealed a Union soldier dangling lifelessly from a nearby sycamore tree. Caleb abruptly pivoted to stand in front of her.

She collided into him, the close proximity bringing the heady smell of lilacs and a uniquely soft, feminine scent to tease his nostrils. "What on—"

Settling his hands on her shoulders, he held her in place. "Before you take another step—"

Her gaze settled somewhere over his shoulder. "Oh my—"

She lurched forward, but he held her back. "He's dead. There's nothing more you can do for him."

"You don't know that."

Caleb turned to follow her gaze. Even in the faint light, he could make out the lifeless stare, the gaping hole in the middle of the soldier's forehead.

She wrenched from his grasp, but he grabbed her about the waist and held firm. Her soft body pressed against the length of his, and a faint breeze lifted a strand of raven hair to tickle his chin.

"It's over for him. Let him go."

"That's someone's son. Someone's *brother*."

The raw emotion in her voice tugged at his heart.

He'd seen enough death and dying to become almost numb to it. Caleb pulled her around to face him, taking her chin between his thumb and forefinger to prevent her from looking away. "Treat the ones you can. Let the rest go."

"I can't do that. I took an oath."

Was she this exasperating all the time or only when in his presence? "Does your oath include raising the dead, Doctor Winters?"

"No, but—"

He gently squeezed her chin. "Then what is it you'd like to do for him?"

"I could…"

She tried to turn away again, but he held tight.

"…write a letter to his family."

"I'll have his personal effects delivered to you."

"Thank you." Her cool tone implied the effort was far too little.

He stared into her face. "Do you have any idea how much you try my patience?"

She nodded. "Somewhat."

"I don't know whether to throttle you or—"

"You're not accustomed to women who can think for themselves."

Her matter-of-fact tone sent a pang of annoyance through him, and he abruptly released her. "That's precisely what I mean. Someday I hope you have the chance to see how mistaken you are about Southern women. They may be kind and gentle, but they're certainly not weak." He clasped his hands behind his back again to quell the temptation to wring her lovely neck.

"Are you married, Major McKenna?"

"Affianced," he said with a stab of guilt. He rarely gave Melody a thought, though she dutifully sent letters.

"When are you planning to marry?"

"We were to be wed in April of sixty one, but the war came. First my brother died, then hers. There never seemed a proper time." He winced at the emotionless way he said it, without a tinge of regret.

"It's been more than two years, and she hasn't pressed you for a wedding date?"

He shrugged, noting the grand brick structure of the Winters' residence just ahead. "Melody is…" Exactly what Alexa Winters would sarcastically call a belle—and not in a good way. "She's loyal, devoted. She knows we'll be wed when the time is right."

"Major, for all the passion in your voice, you might as well be talking about your favorite hunting dog."

"Passion has its time and place." He stopped walking since the house was within view. "This is as far as I'll go, lest I sully your reputation."

He captured her left hand in his, stroking his thumb over her empty ring finger. A wave of arousal moved through him. Had it been so long since he'd been near a woman that any female—even one who so obviously loathed him—provoked long-repressed needs? "And what about you, Alexa Winters? Too busy trying to be a man to allow one into your life?"

Brows drawn together, she frowned at the clasped hands between them. "I don't want to *be* a man. I just don't want to answer to one."

He couldn't help but smile at her determined tone. "I'd like to meet the man who finally tames you."

"Not tames me, Major, accepts me for who I am.

Most men aren't secure enough in themselves for that, so I'll gladly remain single."

"Under different circumstances, you would be a challenge I'd relish." He brushed his lips gently over her fingertips. "Stay safe, Doctor Winters. If I learn anything about your brother, I'll send word."

She glanced up at him, and for a moment, his breath caught. Her lips were as plump and inviting as sweet raspberries and the temptation to taste them nearly overwhelmed him.

"Th—thank you, Major McKenna. For everything. Please have someone look at that wound in the next day or so to make sure there's no sign of infection."

"I will. Thank you again for suturing it."

"You're welcome."

Caleb took a step backward, needing more distance between his thoughts and her delectable mouth. What was it about this sharp tongued, opinionated woman who vexed and frustrated him, yet at the same time, tempted him to forget his promise to Melody?

She hurried away, and the waning moon painted shades of midnight blue in her hair. He caught a glimpse of pale ivory skin a second before she blended into the shadows near the porch steps and disappeared. Surely the nagging physical attraction he felt was one sided. She hadn't seemed nearly as fascinated by him.

He turned to head back to camp. Now that she was out of his care, he could forget his fixation with the lovely Doctor Winters.

Perhaps, though, she was right about him leaving his fiancée to wait. When this battle was over, he'd write to Melody and tell her to make arrangements for a wedding when he came home on Christmas leave.

Five

After seeing to the soldiers recuperating on the porch, Alexa stepped inside. Wounded men lay everywhere, and she stepped carefully around those who were sleeping.

In the parlor, she came across one of the patients who had worried her the most, a sharpshooter from a Pennsylvania regiment. She had bound his broken ribs and removed a bullet from his shoulder yesterday and was pleased to see him resting peacefully. The ball had shattered a bone in his shoulder; she doubted he'd ever have full use of the arm again. But at least he'd have his arm. A field surgeon would have removed it.

Pausing beside the sleeping soldier, she placed a hand to his forehead, relieved to find it cool. His chest gently rose, then fell in a normal, reassuring rhythm.

"Hi, Doc."

She smiled warmly. "How do you feel, Captain Carter?"

He shrugged. "Good as can be expected, I guess. Shoulder hurts a bit."

"I could give you some of Grammy Winters' herbal concoction," she offered. "It will help you sleep." He had been awake the entire time she'd removed fragments from his shoulder and hadn't complained even once. If he was admitting to even "a bit" of pain, it must really hurt.

He shook his head. "No disrespect to your Grammy, but that there potion would grow hair on a dead flea. I reckon I can tolerate the pain."

She laughed. These poor, wounded boys had come seeking medical care and had no idea what they were in for. Unlike her father, Alexa believed in her grandmother's use of herbs and liquor for medicinal purposes. She'd seen Grammy's cures work too many times to dismiss them as easily as Father did.

"I want to thank you. You saved my life yesterday, Doctor Alexa."

A warm flush came over her at the nickname the soldiers had given her. "I don't think you were quite at death's door, but you're welcome just the same. You get some rest."

He smiled and closed his eyes. Of all the wounded soldiers she'd cared for yesterday, Captain Will Carter, with gentle brown eyes that reminded her of an old hound dog, was the least demanding.

She moved about quietly, preparing to check the other soldiers.

"He's gone," Will said as she approached the next patient. "Died just before dawn. Strangest thing—he looked up and said 'we sure could have used you down here' and then…he just passed."

She turned to look over her shoulder at Will, and he shrugged.

"Kinda makes you wonder who he was talkin' to, doesn't it?"

Sorrow pierced her heart. In spite of the young man's serious wounds, she'd hoped he would survive. *Treat the ones you can, and let the rest go.* The major's words, undoubtedly jaded by the suffering he'd witnessed during the war, came to mind, and she forced her shoulders back. When Major McKenna's guards returned later—if they did—she'd have them lay the poor man to rest. Felicity could write a letter to his loved ones.

A short distance away, another soldier's head rested on a book, since they'd run out of pillows and lacked any better substitute.

"There's my girl," rasped a hoarse Quentin Lord.

"I'm hardly a girl." She found a pitcher of water and poured some into a cup for him to drink. "And most certainly not yours. Haven't you collected enough hearts in the towns you've marched through?"

"Ahh but I haven't collected yours."

She resisted the urge to roll her eyes. Though his harmless flirting didn't cause the warm flush to her cheeks it once had, she'd expect nothing less from him. "Nate would have your head and we both know it. Now, how is that leg feeling?" She checked the cast she'd placed on his broken leg yesterday. "It looks good. You'll be up and about in no—"

A sudden, fierce cannonading began in the distance. The house shook and the windows rattled with each successive boom. Rapid footsteps from upstairs told her Felicity had been awakened by the racket. Unlike yesterday, they wouldn't spend today hiding in the cellar, there were too many wounded to care for.

"You be careful today, Alexa." Quentin met her gaze and for once he seemed sincere. "These boys need you."

****

Hours later, the wounded began to stream into town. Alexa stepped out onto the porch. While Grammy stayed inside, cooking broth and baking bread, Felicity took a position at the well, ladle in hand, to offer a cool drink to any who stopped. Both Union and Confederate soldiers filed past, some wounded, others hollow-eyed and dreadfully thirsty.

Many of them suffered from heat exhaustion or sunstroke, and while Alexa treated them, they brought news of the day's battle, where it had taken place and how it had gone.

Perhaps what amazed her most was how they intermingled, uncaring about the color of one another's uniforms now that the day's fighting was over.

In the welcome shade of the porch in the front yard, she'd just finished bandaging a foot soldier who had lost a thumb in the day's fighting when a gray clad soldier ran up to her. "You're the lady doctor, ain't ya?"

"Yes, I'm Doctor Winters."

He motioned over his shoulder with a thumb. "I got a man here says he has to see you."

She followed the direction he'd pointed. A Confederate soldier, barely old enough to shave from the looks of him, stared at her with worried eyes. Despite an injured arm, he bent low over another man, his blood-soaked hand pressed to a wound high in his friend's thigh.

The other soldier lay on a makeshift litter supported by two more gray-clad Confederates. "It don't hurt much at all, ma'am," he said, drawing her gaze. "Just wont' stop bleedin'. Major McKenna said maybe you could—"

"Corporal Edwards?" she gasped, recognizing the young man who had guarded her in McKenna's tent last night. "Set him down. Gently," she ordered the soldiers carrying the blanket. When Edwards' friend tried to move his hand away, she stilled it. "Not yet."

She bent to take a closer look, her heart thudding heavily at the sight. The position of the wound, and the dark red blood that stained his friend's hand, confirmed her worst fear.

"I-is he gonna make it?" one of the soldiers asked.

Alexa stared into the hopeful gaze that held only a hint of fear. "Damndest thing," Edwards said. "One minute I was fine, the next I took a hit. Happened so fast."

"Corporal, what is your first name?"

"Simon, ma'am. Simon Edwards"

"I'm Alexa."

"I…I know. The major said I'd probably bleed to death waitin' for a field doc," he added with a nervous laugh. "Said you'd be glad to sew me up."

"I would." She tried to swallow past the lump in her throat. "Only…I can't. This kind of wound can't be sewed fast enough."

He swallowed, his Adam's apple rising and falling convulsively. "Ma'am?"

She reached up to brush a lock of sandy blond hair from his forehead. "Simon, you've sustained a wound to a major artery."

Felicity, hovering nearby, gave a slight cry. Alexa shot her a look meant to silence her.

Dark red blood gushed from the wounded man, and she pressed her hand over his friend's to form a tighter seal over the wound.

"It don't hurt none," Edwards said.

"It wouldn't," Alexa reassured him. "Arteries carry blood away from the heart. The femoral artery—where you were injured—is the largest one in your body. I couldn't suture it quickly enough...before..."

"Golly," he said, looking down at his blood-drenched lower half. "That was some hit."

"Those damn yanks," said one of the soldiers nearby. "Those God*damned*—"

"Hush," Alexa scolded, afraid they'd start another battle right here on her front lawn.

Simon stared up at her, eyes reflecting understanding. "Smitty here can't hold his hand on my leg forever."

"No," his face blurred and danced as tears filled her vision, but she forced them away.

"How long?" he asked.

Alexa glanced at the blood soaking hers and Smitty's hands. "Soon. But there's enough time to write a letter. To your mother or wife, perhaps?"

"My son?" he asked. "Me and my wife just had a baby boy a few months back. I ain't even got to see him yet. I'd sure like..." His Adam's apple bobbed again. "I'd like to address it to him."

Fighting back tears, Alexa motioned for Felicity to come closer. "This is my cousin Felicity. She's written a great many letters home for soldiers. She's quite good at it."

"I...have the best penmanship in my school," Felicity offered hopefully. She sent Alexa a beseeching glance, as if begging her to do something more.

With a shake of her head Alexa rose, instructing Smitty to press both hands on the wound. She cared for another soldier patiently waiting nearby, trying not to be affected by Simon's heartfelt letter home lest she lose control of her emotions. She tied off a bandage and rose to tend another man when Felicity beckoned her back to Simon Edwards' side.

"I'm ready now," he said. "Miss Alexa, that thing you did when you brushed my hair back? My mama used to do that. Would you…would you mind?"

Unable to speak over the ball of emotion lodged in her throat, Alexa gently stroked his hair.

Simon nodded. "Okay Smitty, I'm ready now."

"No, Simon, I'll take you back to the field doc. I don't mind. I can keep my hand there a day or more. We'll find someone—"

"If Doctor Alexa says it can't be fixed, then it can't," Simon insisted. "The major trusts her. And so do I."

Hot tears slipped down Alexa's cheeks as Smitty removed his hand. Felicity began to softly chant the Twenty-third psalm. Soldiers around them removed their caps. After a moment, Smitty joined in, his voice cracking with emotion.

Alexa continued feathering her fingers through the blond hair, her gaze intent on both Simon and the blood that steadily soaked the ground.

When an elderly person died after a long life, it was natural; when a baby or mother died during childbirth it was sad, yet not uncommon. A young man bleeding to death hundreds of miles from the newborn son he'd never seen—would never know—was beyond comprehension.

All she had ever wanted was to heal and comfort. She'd never felt so helpless, so completely useless, as she had these last two days.

"He's gone," she whispered at last, fingers still absently combing Simon's hair. She turned her attention back to his face, willing herself to memorize it. For some reason, she wanted to remember him, remember the true face of war.

Smitty and the other soldiers picked up the blanket holding Simon's body and began to move away.

"You should let Alexa look at your arm," Felicity said.

Smitty stopped, casting them both a bitter glance. "I'll take my chances with a real doctor."

"Don't you speak that way about Doctor Alexa, son," warned a soldier recuperating on the porch.

"Fixed me up good," said another.

Alexa stepped away, hurrying toward the back of the house before the tears she'd been holding back could burst forth. A trampled hedge and ravaged garden were the only obvious signs of destruction from the past two days. At least here there were no bodies, no cartridge boxes strewn about. No blood soaking the grass beneath her feet.

She leaned against the house, hugging her arms about her waist. Her chest ached with the unfairness of so much suffering and death. A horrible need to scream built inside of her. She drew in a shuddering breath and waited for the sobs to begin.

All that came was a pitiful squeak.

Tears that threatened moments ago were gone. Nothing remained but a dull ache in her throat.

"Alexa," called Felicity from the front yard. "More soldiers are coming."

Pushing herself away from the house, she moved slowly across the yard.

Maybe when this nightmare was over, she would find time to cry.

****

Caleb sat in his tent, brandy glass in hand. He rarely allowed himself the luxuries his men had to do without, be it food or fine spirits. His sisters had sent the bottle quite some time ago, but no occasion had warranted opening it. Until tonight. He shared it with the men who were close enough to feel the day's losses as keenly as he.

Simon Edwards' loss weighed heavily on his heart. He'd lost men before and usually didn't let it bother him, but dammit, Edwards left behind a young wife and infant. Now it was up to Caleb to tell a newly widowed woman that her husband had died a hero. To find the words that would reassure a child in years to come that his father had died for a noble cause.

"To the Cause," he raised the glass in silent toast before gulping the contents. He set the empty glass aside and made an effort to gather his thoughts; he had more than one letter to write this evening, by far the one to Simon's wife would be the most difficult.

His gaze came to rest on the bundle he'd left on his desk this morning, the personal effects of the dead soldier he'd encountered with Doctor Winters. With all that had happened, he'd yet to fulfill his promise to have them delivered to her.

An image of raven hair and raspberry lips stole into his mind. How was she holding up? Guilt stabbed at him for ordering Smitty to take the wounded Edwards to her. At the time, he'd thought the boy's injuries minor, since he wasn't in pain. And he'd truly believed Alexa would be able to help, it was the sort of thing she'd relish.

Knowing her stubborn refusal to admit defeat and

the tender heart she'd displayed with the wounded horse and the dead soldier, Simon's loss would surely weigh heavy. He owed her an explanation for that, and an apology.

And since Edwards was no longer here to deliver the dead soldier's personal effects, or the news Caleb had learned about Nathaniel Winters' whereabouts, he would rather do so himself than trust the task to another.

He shrugged into his coat, wincing as the wound Alexa had sutured last night pulled painfully. Stepping outside his tent, he knew a moment of grief at the sight of his division. Less than half the men he'd arrived with were still alive.

"Join us, Major?" asked a lieutenant, gesturing to the deck of cards in his hand.

"Thanks just the same, O'Toole. Perhaps another time."

Another soldier chuckled. "Just how far is it to that doctor gal's house?"

Hoots of laughter and knowing chuckles followed.

Caleb brushed the dust from his coat sleeves before glancing at them. "Doctor Winters has a brother who fights for the South. That was her only interest here last night."

O'Toole gave a knowing chuckle. "What's your interest, McKenna?"

"Aw come on, fellas, his heart belongs to Miss Melody," another Georgian said.

Caleb handed the bottle of brandy to O'Toole. "I trust you'll all be able to march and fight come morning."

For most of the day, he'd managed to keep

thoughts of Alexa Winters at bay, the spirit in her vibrant green eyes, the cascade of hair that felt like velvet beneath his palms. Ignoring personal feelings in battle was second nature. But ignoring his physical attraction when she was nearby was quite another thing.

He forced himself to think of his fiancée, whose face hadn't crossed his mind in days. Sweet, gentle Melody with hair the color of...of...

What the hell color *was* her hair? He could no longer bring her image to mind. Yet the face of Alexa Winters was clearly embedded.

Damn the woman, if she hadn't been holding a man at gunpoint on her porch, hadn't turned up in the field hospital, she wouldn't be haunting his thoughts so now.

It had been too long since he'd seen his betrothed, far longer since he'd held her close. And too long since any woman had stirred his blood the way Alexa did. Now that he thought about it, he wasn't sure any woman ever had.

It didn't take long before he found himself near the Winters' home, pondering the Union soldiers inside. He didn't need to start another battle by boldly announcing himself. Nor did he want to upset Alexa, given her concerns about being viewed as a Southern sympathizer.

As he stood considering his options, the front door opened. A young girl came out, pausing to wipe a hand across her brow before she bent to retrieve a bucket. He recognized her as the cousin Alexa had been protecting the other day. Her small shoulders sagged wearily before she straightened and headed down the steps.

Caleb stepped back into the shadows as she came

off the porch. He was uncertain if he should speak to her, but the need to see Alexa propelled him forward again before common sense could mount an argument.

The girl started and gave a small cry, the bucket tumbling from her hands. "You nearly scared me to—oh!" She put a hand to her open mouth, regarding him with wide, frightened eyes.

"Here now," Caleb soothed, bending to retrieve the bucket. "I mean you no harm, young lady."

She studied him curiously for several moments. "Do I know you?"

"We've not formally met." He bowed and introduced himself before heading for the well with the empty bucket. "I was looking for Doctor Winters."

She fell into step beside him. "Where are you hurt?"

"I assure you I'm quite well." Her innocent curiosity in the midst of such destruction reminded him of his youngest sister, bringing a fond smile. At the well, he attached the bucket to the winch and lowered it, aware of the girl's questioning frown. "I have news of her brother."

The girl's hand fluttered to her heart. "No. Oh no. He's not—"

"The news isn't all bad. If you don't mind, I was hoping to speak with her personally."

"Of course." She waved a hand toward the house. "Won't you please come in—oh, dear." Eyes wide, she stared up at him as though she'd made an unforgivable etiquette breach. Caleb grinned at her predicament. His presence would only make the wounded Federal soldiers uncomfortable. "I'll be glad to wait here."

"I'll tell Alexa straight away. She's stitching a

soldier, but shouldn't be long."

He raised the bucket and removed it from the windlass. "Miss Winters? I think it would be best if you didn't say who is calling. It might upset your other...guests."

"I won't say you're a Reb." She stopped abruptly. "I didn't mean—"

"I've been called much worse." When they reached the porch, he handed her the full bucket, then stepped back into the shadows beside the house.

He had to wait only a short time before the door whined on its hinges. Alexa stepped onto the porch, flexing and unflexing the fingers of her right hand as though the muscles were cramped. She strolled to the opposite end of the porch. "Is someone there?"

She was only a few feet away, but the urge to touch her was overwhelming. What was it about her that drew him so?

Reminding himself she hadn't come out to be accosted, Caleb stepped into the faint moonlight. "Good evening, Doctor Winters."

"Major." Her shoulders visibly relaxed at the sight of him. "I'm glad to see you're all right."

"Is that so." He purposely didn't phrase it as a question.

"When Corporal Edwards...I didn't know if you'd been..." She lowered her gaze.

"I was nearby when it happened." He cleared his throat to rid the emotion from his voice. "But no, I wasn't hurt."

"I see."

She stepped to the porch railing, and he could see dark splotches of blood staining her shirt and trousers.

This day had surely been as long for her as it had him.

"You know then, that he…"

"Yes." A pang of grief stabbed him. "But I didn't come to talk about Simon. Not yet anyway. I have the personal effects from the soldier we found this morning. And I have word of your brother."

She hesitantly accepted the bundle he handed her, then squared her shoulders and met his gaze. "Nate is dead, isn't he?"

"Missing. Since July of last year."

"I would have heard from him by now if he's still alive."

"Not necessarily."

"Thank you, Major." She smoothed a hand over the bundle of personal effects. "I appreciate you taking the time to ask after my brother with all you had to deal with today."

Caleb stepped closer to the porch. He should leave now, return to his men. He'd given her what little information he had. But the time spent with her wasn't nearly enough to satisfy his yearning for her company. "Do you have a few moments to visit with me?"

She glanced briefly toward the house. "I have patients waiting. But yes, I'd like that."

He met her at the steps, reaching out in an automatic gesture to assist her, tucking her hand in the crook of his arm. "How are you this evening?"

"Me?" Her voice rose an octave, as if he'd taken her by surprise. "I'm fit as a fiddle."

His gaze traveled once more over her blood-stained clothing. "I doubt that very much. I wanted to apologize for sending Corporal Edwards your way this afternoon. Had I known the gravity of his wound, I would have never put you through that."

She remained silent for several moments. "I appreciate your faith in me as a doctor, just the same."

"I know it must be difficult, but try to remember that Corporal Edwards, and all the men lost here today gave their lives for a cause they believed in." It was a phrase he'd uttered too often since the war had begun.

She stopped abruptly and removed her hand from his arm. "Do you truly believe that?"

Not anymore, but it was the only comfort he had to offer. "Alexa—"

"Did you come here to placate me with stories of honor and valor? I've seen nothing today but blood and death and young men ripped to pieces. Tell me, Major, where is the honor in that?" Her voice broke. "Secede if you want, but dammit, stop killing each other."

She reeled away, hurrying down a slight incline in the yard toward the back of the house, and disappeared beneath the low-hanging canopy of an enormous weeping willow.

Caleb followed, stooping beneath the dangling leaves, but there was no sign of her. A few stray leaves and a rustling sound came from over head. A glance upward revealed her sitting on a sturdy branch a few feet off the ground. So that was where she'd gone.

"Would it help to know I share your feelings?" After two and a half years of war and the loss of countless friends and relatives, he was ready for it to end, too.

"I'm sorry. I shouldn't have lost my temper. It's not your fault. But for every wounded soldier I've seen today, I've thought, 'did Nate do this to you,' and I felt almost guilty. And then I thought of you and wondered..."

"If I did it," he finished for her.

"Caleb, how can you shoot those poor boys?"

His youngest sister had once asked him much the same thing. He still lacked an easy answer to the question. "I'm a soldier, Alexa. It's my duty."

"To kill innocent men?"

"Before they kill me or invade my country. Yes."

"It sounds so heartless."

He leaned a shoulder against the branch, looking up at her in the shadowy light. "It's no different than you not fainting or feeling ill at the sight of blood. Your training has prepared you for what to expect, and experience has made you less sensitive to it."

"But I'm trying to save lives and you're…"

"You're seeing a side of war that few civilians ever will. But you have to trust that we know what we're doing."

She turned toward him. "You really believe all those men knew what they were getting into? What of all that 'the war will be over by Christmas' talk?"

True, when the war had begun, the south had thought it would whip the north in a short time. Their earliest battles only reinforced that belief, with the Southern army winning easy victories. He sighed. But now, more than two years in, it seemed the war would never end.

"No, they didn't. But even so, I assure you there isn't a man going into battle who wants to die—but we're prepared to do so if that's what's required."

She didn't speak, and he strained to see her in the dark, wondered what was going through her mind. By what little moonlight filtered through the branches, he saw her swipe at her cheeks and heard a small sniffle. She probably wouldn't like to be caught crying. He averted his gaze, instead studying the bark of the branch she sat upon, scarred in places from years of climbing feet, and worn smooth in others from hours of someone seated there.

He patted the sturdy wood. "I take it this was a special spot when you were a girl."

"I don't know what possessed me to climb up here." Another sniffle. "I'm surprised I still can."

Her legs swung to one side, and without thought for propriety, Caleb put his hands to her waist to lift her down. Through the thin fabric of her blouse, the warmth of her flesh met his palms. He set her before him, leaf-speckled moonlight casting a glow on her tear-streaked face.

He stroked a thumb over the moisture on her cheeks. "Alexa," he sighed. "Don't cry."

Her hot tears spilled over his thumb.

"He was so calm, so much braver than I'd have been."

Edwards had been like a brother to him, he'd felt every damn bit as helpless when his friend had been hit. "I shouldn't have put you through it."

"There was nothing I could do for him." Her voice was raw with pain and exhaustion.

He pulled her into his arms, needing to comfort her and needing comfort himself.

She held herself rigid for several moments before settling her head on his shoulder. "I'm sorry. I don't usually give in to such feminine displays."

"I won't tell a soul."

He gently stroked her back, keenly aware that only

a thin cotton barrier stood between her flesh and his palms. A tangle of emotion tore through him, and like her, he fought against the need to give in to the grief gnawing at him.

"It was my fault. I ordered the men forward."

"You were following orders." She relaxed against him a bit more. "It's no one's fault."

He nuzzled her hair, breathed in the lingering aroma of lilacs. For the rest of his days, he'd associate that heavenly smell with Alexa Winters. "I hate this damn war."

She raised her head from his shoulder, and though shadowy leaves dappled her face, making it impossible to clearly see her, he could feel her gaze on him.

Without a thought, he brushed his lips against her forehead, intending only to comfort her as he would his sisters. The teasing smell of those damn lilacs and a scent that was uniquely Alexa filled his nostrils. Tormented by the soft curves pressed against him, his manhood roared to fully erect. A dizzying sensation enveloped him, urging him to move closer, hold her tighter. He forced aside the thoughts even as he struggled against the demands of his body.

"Alexa," he whispered against her ear. "I came here tonight with honorable intentions."

She turned toward him, the movement bringing her face into close contact with his lips. "A-and now?"

He stroked her cheek with the back of his fingers. "God help me, right now all I can think about is kissing you."

"Caleb…"

The strangled whisper tore his resolve to shreds. Trembling with the need to touch her, he lowered his head, closing the distance between them until their lips were only a breath apart. He gave her time to retreat, to pull away or slap him.

With a moan, she slid her hands behind his neck, and he pulled her closer, groaning when her lips parted beneath his. One taste…he'd only allow himself one taste…

Barely able to control the passion rushing through him like a raging river, he took her lips hungrily, pouring the need he felt, the grief, the guilt at being tempted by the forbidden—and failing to resist—into the kiss.

He slid his hands to her back, molding her close until her breasts melded against his chest. A shudder moved through her as his tongue entered her mouth. She tasted of coffee, heavenly, sweet and warm, and when her tongue shyly met his, it took all of his strength not to ease her to the ground and make love to her right there.

His mind swam with recriminations; he was betrothed to someone else, he had no business kissing Alexa. But dammit, he'd wanted to kiss her practically from the moment they'd met. And now that he had tasted the sweet, forbidden fruit of her lips, he didn't want to stop.

Her hands glided up his chest, and he couldn't contain an involuntary flinch when she brushed the wound she'd treated yesterday.

In an instant she pulled back. "Did you have that checked?"

"Not yet." He nuzzled her neck, eager to bring her focus back to kissing. The lingering scent of lilac water clung to her, and he inhaled deeply, drinking in the heady aroma. He opened his mouth to taste her skin and felt the shiver that moved through her. A tug in his lower region sent a tremor of raw need through him. When was the last time he'd felt this alive?

She moaned. "I should look at—"

"It can wait." He continued his unhurried journey up her neck, lingering at the hollow behind her earlobe. It, too, smelled like lilacs, and he couldn't resist sampling her delicate lobe.

Another moan. He found her mouth again, this time lazily acquainting himself with the feel and taste of her. The war—hell, the world—could wait, just this once.

"Alexa? Are you here?"

The voice belonged to the cousin he'd met a short time ago, and the doctor tensed in his arms. He abruptly stepped back.

"Hide," she whispered. "Please, I can't be found like this."

He barely had time to register the request before she scrambled up the tree again.

The cousin's voice came closer, still calling.

"Hurry!" Another urgent whisper.

Caleb could understand her not wanting to be caught in a moonlight embrace—especially with a Confederate officer—but even so, her reaction seemed unusual.

With no other means of disappearing and the cousin coming closer, he followed her up into the tree. The limb creaked beneath his added weight, and Alexa climbed with feline-like confidence to a higher perch. Uncertain this branch would sustain his weight, he stayed still, scarcely daring to breathe.

"Why are we hiding?" he whispered.

"Because I can't let those gossipy pea hens catch me with a man."

"You're a doctor."

"Yes, but to them I'm something much worse. Shh…"

He glanced down as the cousin came into sight. Through the dangling leaves, two plump, dark-clad figures he presumed were the aforementioned "pea hens" emerged to follow close behind Felicity. With them was a Confederate soldier who most likely had escorted them from town. But he couldn't see the soldier well enough to recognize him.

"She came out here a short while ago," the girl said. "Wait here, I'll see if Grammy has seen her."

The cousin hurried off, leaving the soldier and the pea hens standing in the yard. Caleb hoped once more that the limb was sturdier than it looked—and the leaves thick enough to hide him.

"Clara, are you sure we should wait? God only knows where that woman is or what she's up to."

Condemnation all but dripped from their voices and he slid a glance at Alexa. Why would they speak so harshly of a woman who devoted herself to caring for the sick?

"St. Francis Xavier is overrun with wounded, I need to know if she can take any more men." Venom dripped from every syllable. "Much as it pains me to ask *her* for anything."

"It's a disgrace the way she has that young girl helping her. Why, a girl that age taking care of full grown men...who knows what her delicate eyes might see."

A low growl came from the limb directly above him. "Miserable old bat."

"Well, if you ask me," came the first voice, "Ned should never have allowed her to wear her brother's clothes and behave like a boy. And now running about in trousers at her age. Why, it's positively scandalous."

An amused grin twitched at Caleb's lips. Scandalous perhaps, but he certainly appreciated the way she filled out the seat of those trousers.

"I heard she was in town last week wearing britches."

"She certainly was. No wonder that husband of hers divorced her."

Divorced? Caleb arched a brow in the doctor's direction, but she refused to meet his gaze. That explained a great deal about Alexa's reaction to being discovered with him. And it certainly explained how she knew how to kiss like that. Heat flared through him at the memory of how eagerly she'd responded.

A movement below drew his attention.

"I can't find her." Felicity came into view. "But Grammy said you ladies are welcome to come inside and wait."

They followed the girl, and the voices drifted away as the group moved around toward the front of the house, the foot soldier dutifully following.

Moments after they rounded the house, Alexa stepped onto the lower branch. Instead of climbing down to accommodate her, Caleb stayed put, forcing their bodies into close contact.

He heard her breath catch and caught her elbow to steady her.

"What are you doing?" she asked. "I'm not sure

this limb can hold us both."

He wanted to question her, demand answers to questions that had yet to form in his mind. But he had no right to ask her anything. In another day or less, he'd never see her again.

Reluctantly, he released her.

She jumped down, landing with a gentle thud on the ground. "I want to check that wound. Come with me."

Caleb climbed down, taking more care in reaching the ground than she had, pausing to brush off his uniform as she marched across the yard, confident that he'd follow.

Reaching a set of doors built into the ground near the house, she tugged them open, then turned to look over her shoulder. "Hurry up."

Curious—and well aware of the throb of his wound—he crossed the yard and peered into the dark entrance.

Alexa moved inside and hurried down the steps. A candle flared to life. She lit several more until the room was bathed in soft light.

"Over here," she said, indicating a table in the center of the room.

Caleb pulled the doors closed and moved cautiously down the cement steps. On the opposite end of the room sat a cot, blankets neatly folded at the foot, and ready to be used. He strode across the room, taking in the meager supplies, including a wash basin and bowl. Not the usual things one kept in a fruit cellar.

He came to stand beside Alexa as she bent to retrieve a basket filled with strips of cloth, glass bottles and scissors.

"Exactly how many escaped slaves have you treated and hidden here, Doctor Winters?"

Her hands stilled over the basket. "I don't know what you—"

"You have medical supplies and provisions down here, not to mention a bed. And this table certainly looks sturdy enough to hold an injured man."

"I'm guilty of no crime except storing furniture and medical supplies in my fruit cellar." She met his gaze with a challenging look he knew all too well. "The Confederate army is in charge of the town—if you don't like the contents of my cellar, I suggest you arrest me."

"Dammit, Alexa. It's not that I like slavery, but every escaped slave you helped was someone's property."

A half-smile played over her lips. "Not anymore."

"You're the most mule-headed, frustrating woman—"

"So I've been told. Remove your jacket and shirt, please."

He unbuttoned his coat and yanked it off, tossing it carelessly on the table before walking, slowly, deliberately toward her, stopping when their bodies were mere inches apart. "Do you even realize how much danger you placed yourself—your family—in?"

Her eyes darkened, and she swallowed visibly. "Y-your shirt."

Unfastening the buttons with jerky movements, he was aware of her steady gaze on him.

When the shirt hung open, she glanced up. "Would you..." Her voice sounded strained. "Mind sitting on the table so I can take a look at your chest—your wound?"

He did as she asked, sitting so that his chest was at her eye level, then shrugged out of his shirt

If he'd hoped to see any reaction to the sight of his bare chest, there was none. He closed his eyes as an unbidden memory of her hand sliding over his chest minutes ago returned to taunt him. She held the candle up to better see his sutures.

"I don't like how red it is. Does it hurt?"

"No." Throbbed like a damn toothache was more like it.

She turned to reach into the basket and pulled out a bottle, uncorking it with her teeth.

The fumes alone nearly knocked him over, but before he could speak she splashed the liquid onto a cloth and pressed it to his wound. The stinging pain of hell's eternal flames rushed over him. "For Christ's— what *is* that?"

"Corn liquor," she said. "I'm not sure why, but it seems to help infection."

"You've used this before?"

"Yes, many times."

"On your former husband, perhaps?" The moment the words left his lips, he regretted them. It wasn't his business, nor his concern if she'd been married.

A slight tightening of her jaw, barely visible in the dim light, was her only noticeable reaction. "I told you I had no husband. I didn't realize I was obligated to explain I had one previously." She doused the cloth again and pressed it to his chest, not nearly as gentle this time. Droplets of liquor dribbled down his skin and soaked into the waist of his trousers.

"It's not my business. I shouldn't have asked," he

said by way of apology. "Those women—the gossipy ones—they're why you couldn't risk being seen with me."

"They've made my life a living hell since I moved back to town last year. They disliked me when I was a young girl for wanting to become a doctor rather than being content to be a midwife. Now that I'm divorced, I've given them more to gossip about."

She dabbed the wound again, and this time, he held her hand firmly to his chest. "I can see that."

"I won't give them the satisfaction of riling me. I simply ignore them."

But he could hear the hurt in her voice and wondered if she was as unaffected as she claimed.

He moved her hand from his chest until the cloth fell, then placed it back on his bare skin, away from the wound. Her fingers curled into the hair sprinkled across his chest. He shifted, pulling her between his open legs.

Her wary gaze flew to his face. "Caleb…there are soldiers upstairs who need me."

He lifted her chin on his finger, gazing intently into her passion-darkened eyes. "There's a solider right here who needs you."

Without giving her time to react, he brought his lips to hers. She stepped in closer, arms twining around his neck, the softness of her pressing against him. His hands slid to her hips, tempted to explore the warm curve of her buttocks, slide upward to fill his palms with the weight of her breasts. But propriety forced him to keep them where they were.

He wondered if she missed her marriage bed, longed for a man's touch—his touch—the way he yearned for hers. Knowing she wasn't an innocent sent the blood pounding through his veins. No worries about offending or frightening delicate sensibilities. She was a woman in every sense of the word.

Alexa took a step back. "This is wrong." She distanced herself from him by moving to the other side of the room. "Y-you're engaged to be married."

Realization washed over him like a sudden rain shower. God above, how could he have done it again?

Caleb slid off the table, grabbing his shirt in a fist. "I behave completely out of character every time I'm near you."

"It's hardly my fault."

He glanced at her as he shrugged into the shirt and began to button it. "I wouldn't be so sure. You dress in a manner that—"

"That what?" Hands on her hips, she met his gaze with a challenging look.

"That makes it easy for a man to forget himself."

"I explained to you why I dress like this. If you don't like it, you don't have to look at me."

He crossed the room in angry strides. "I like it too damn much, that's the problem."

Her jaw dropped. "You think I dress this way to be provocative?"

"Quite the contrary. I think you dress that way because it pleases you. But you might not have nearly as much trouble with your so-called pea hens if you gave a thought to how others perceive your manner of dress."

She folded her arms over her chest. "By *others* I assume you mean men?"

"I do."

"I should slap your arrogant face."

"Surely I'm not the first man to tell you that. I doubt your husband allowed you to go about dressed this way."

"My husband had no say in how I dressed."

"And thus we've come full circle. Right back to headstrong and defiant, which undoubtedly is why you're divo—"

Full force, her hand met his cheek, the crack echoing in the stillness of the small room.

She stared at him, wide eyed, horrified.

He put a hand to his stinging face, rubbing the place where her imprint undoubtedly remained. "I deserved that." He strode across the room to take his jacket from the examination table, aware of her watchful gaze as he slipped it on. "As I said, I seem to lose my head when I'm around you."

She crossed her arms over herself and turned her back to him.

"I apologize, Alexa. Exhaustion and grief have made me insufferable this evening." Not to mention a nagging sexual frustration, but he wasn't about to share that. He waited for her to turn around or speak, but recognized the purely female response of stone cold silence. "As you said, there are soldiers who need you upstairs. And I, undoubtedly, will have my orders for tomorrow very soon." He strode toward the steps.

"To leave or to fight?"

He stopped and turned to face her, though she had yet to turn around. He heaved a silent sigh of resignation. "To fight, of course."

Her shoulders sagged for a moment before she turned, arms still crossed. "More boys blown to pieces. More suffering and dying."

"Sacrificing for a cause they believe in." The words hung between them, a reminder of their differences and the war that had thrown them together in the first place.

He slowly moved up the steps toward the doors.

"Major?"

He half-wished she was calling him back to her side; more than anything he wanted to kiss her again, propriety and consequences be damned.

"Alexa?" He purposely chose to use her given name even though she'd switched to formalities again.

"For what it's worth...*I* divorced *him*."

"I never thought otherwise." He pushed open the doors, careful to check for anyone who might witness his exit, then strode out into the inky black night.

Six

Breathe.

As the cellar doors closed behind him, Alexa struggled to get her breathing under control. Her insides quivered, her hands and knees trembled. But was it from his words, which had cut closer to the bone than she'd have liked—or his kisses?

Her stomach hollowed out at the very memory of kissing him. She'd never felt that way in a man's arms before—she'd wanted to forget herself, forget her duty to her patients, forget everything but the nearness of him and the thrill it sent through her.

In the small confines of the fruit cellar, he'd seemed taller somehow, even more handsome in the gray uniform that fit him precisely.

She pressed fingertips to her lips where they still tingled from his passionate assault and her willing surrender. She could still smell the bay rum that lingered on his skin, still taste him...

Little wonder women made such ninnies of themselves over men. She'd never understood it, until now.

Alexa pulled in a deep breath and forced herself to release it slowly. She had no time to act like an addlebrained fool. There were men to be cared for, not to mention more mouths than she would be able to feed. The major had provided a pleasant diversion from an unpleasant situation, but their time together had ended and there was work to be done.

She gathered up her basket of medical supplies. It wouldn't go far toward helping if tomorrow's fighting came to pass, but every little bit was needed right now.

Extinguishing the candles, she headed up the cement steps and out the doors. The humid night air and the lingering stench of death greeted her, an unpleasant reminder of what her world had become. She'd barely stepped onto the porch when the door opened and Felicity darted out.

"Oh, Alexa, thank heaven you're home. I was beginning to think that Southern officer kidnapped you!"

"I'm fine," she paused to check on a wounded man she'd cared for earlier in the day. He slept deeply, probably as much from exhaustion as blood loss.

Another reached for her, and she took a moment to speak with him.

"God bless you, Doctor Alexa," yet another murmured.

Tears stung her eyes. This was her calling, not behaving like a loose woman in the arms of a man who was betrothed to another.

"Well?" Felicity stamped an impatient foot. "What did he want? Where is Nate?"

Straightening from the soldier she'd been comforting, Alexa placed her hands to her back. The dull ache from bending over so frequently returned, along with a bone-weariness that made her wonder when she'd last slept.

By now, Granny had come to stand at the door, face drawn with exhaustion and worry.

"Nate is missing. He has been for over a year. Which means he's either a prisoner, or…" Unwilling to complete the thought, she let the words die on her lips.

Inside the kitchen, she stepped over another wounded man who slept on the kitchen floor and made her way to the stove for a cup of coffee.

"I don't know what we're going to feed them tomorrow," she said, sinking gratefully into a chair.

"Why not eggs?" Felicity chirped.

Alexa rubbed her hands over her face, wishing she dared take a moment to put her head down. "The Rebs took all the chickens, Felicity."

"Not all."

Intrigued by her cousin's smug tone, Alexa glanced up at her. "What do you mean?"

Her smile turned into a bubble of laughter. "Earlier today, I caught some Reb soldiers taking our last two chickens. I asked them how we'd ever be able to feed all the poor wounded Southern boys in our care if they took our last chickens."

"Child, you're lucky you weren't harmed," Grammy scolded.

"Not at all. In fact, they said they'd gladly bring us more food—for the poor wounded Southern boys."

Too exhausted to be relieved by this news—or concerned that any food delivered was undoubtedly stolen—Alexa stretched an arm along the table and rested her head on it.

Granny placed a bowl before her, and despite the tantalizing aroma of broth causing an interested rumble from her stomach, she didn't have the energy to raise her head. A shawl was draped over her shoulders, but she was too sleepy to protest that she didn't need it in this heat. Instead, she gave herself up to the waiting arms of slumber.

****

The first gun sent the signal for a hundred more to open. In his military career, Caleb had never seen such artillery fire. The air was filled with the hiss and scream of missiles bursting overhead, the ground littered with the bodies of dead horses and soldiers.

Following the barrage, thousands of Confederate troops began advancing. They marched abreast in a long, straight line, uphill toward the waiting Union army, their stride that of men who believed themselves invincible. General Lee seemed to believe they were, but Caleb knew how exhausted, weak and worn his men were. A lump rose in his throat at their bravery. Shells struck about them, the sun beat without mercy, yet still they moved forward.

And then the Union artillery opened fire again, blasting a gap in the Confederate line. Under orders not to fire, the Confederate ranks closed the gap and continued to advance. Federal infantry sent volley after volley of gunfire in their direction, but the men continued to march forward.

At last the Union line was penetrated and the hand-to-hand fighting ensued. Caleb urged Girl forward, galloping into the midst of the fighting. Around him, men swore and cursed as they struggled in deadly combat.

"Fall back!" came the echoed cry from behind him. "Fall back!"

And still the caissons exploded.

He wheeled around to lead his men away from certain death, defeat leaving a bitter taste in his mouth.

Spying one of his men on the ground, wounded, he leapt from his horse and rushed toward him. "O'Toole!"

"I'm fine, Major. It's just me leg..." the other man shouted above the din. "I got me another one."

Caleb spied two of his men nearby. "Get O'Toole to the field doc—"

A sudden, sharp pain blasted through his hip, the momentum spinning him around, and the ground rushed up to meet him with a thud. For a moment, he lay there stunned, scarcely able to believe he'd been hit. He felt no pain, and for a brief moment, wondered if he'd suffered the same fate as Edwards. Refusing to die in the dirt or give up so easily, he jabbed his sword into the ground, pulling himself upright to assure his men he was all right.

He had no idea how long he actually stood there before the world exploded in a kaleidoscope of color, spiraling about him, until he rushed headlong into blackness.

****

The cannons began late in the afternoon, their racket rumbling across the sky like an endless clap of thunder.

Determined to stay with her patients, Alexa tried to convince Felicity and Grammy to retreat to the cellar, but Grammy wouldn't hear of it and her cousin refused to go alone. Instead, they stuffed cotton in their ears and went about caring for and feeding wounded.

The soldiers offered steady reassurances. Those who were able to gathered on the porch, staring longingly toward the column of white smoke curling toward the sky.

Quentin leaned heavily on Alexa as she and Felicity helped him out to the porch.

"Sounds like it's south of here," one southern man commented after a particularly loud series of booms.

"The two ridges just south of town, on that open plain, I'll wager," Will Carter added with a nod in that direction. "I think we're whupping you boys pretty good."

Alexa followed his line of vision but saw nothing to indicate victory. "How on earth can you tell?"

Will turned to her, brown eyes soft and warm. "For every cannon that's fired, one answers back," he explained patiently. "The Rebs can't afford to waste ammunition like that. Sooner or later, they'll run out."

"You really think so?" Felicity asked with a sniffle.

Alexa placed an arm about the frightened girl's shoulders. There were several affirmative nods.

"Those Rebs got nothing left to give," spoke up a Minnesota man. "Poor miserable sons of—"

A nearby southern man cleared his throat.

Alexa scarcely heard his murmured apology. She stared toward the rising smoke, emotion choking her so that she could hardly breathe. With each explosion men were being torn to pieces. Was it wrong to pray for Nate's safety when he fought for the enemy?

And what of Major McKenna? The thought of him sent a wave of hot, unsettled feelings through her. His kisses had left her trembling and breathless. No man had ever made her feel that way. Even after the bitter words they'd parted over, the memory of his mouth on her skin sent a shiver through her despite the warmth of the day.

She sent up a silent prayer for his safety.

A large, warm hand settled on her shoulder. "There, there, Doctor Alexa," Will said, patting her a bit awkwardly. "Don't fret so. It could be the end of the war we're hearing today."

Hadn't she just wished for that last night?

For long moments, no noise came, the silence almost deafening. Sporadic pops of gun fire sounded, followed by the occasional blast of a cannon, and then…silence.

Alexa exchanged weary glances with Grammy and Felicity, wondering when the wounded would begin to arrive.

The soldiers talked among themselves, speculating as to what had happened.

A young boy Alexa recognized from town came running down the road, fists pumping the air in triumph.

"We licked 'em," he shouted, not slowing a bit as he ran past the house. "The Rebs are pulling back! They're retreating!"

A cheer went up from the soldiers on the porch. They shook hands and clapped one another on the back. Then they broke into an impromptu, slightly off-key version of "Hang Jeff Davis from a Sour Apple Tree."

Relief flooded her, but Alexa couldn't share their exuberance. Not when so many men already lay dead and wounded on the fields around town. How many had been added to their number today?

Hands folded under her chin, Felicity gave a contented sigh. "We can truly celebrate tomorrow."

"Tomorrow?" Alexa frowned. "What on earth would we have to celebrate?"

Will Carter broke away from the celebrating to

approach her, a smile lighting his hound dog eyes. "Doctor Alexa, surely you haven't forgotten tomorrow is Independence Day?"

****

The soldiers were still in a celebratory mood later that evening as news of the day's events continued to pour in. The South had been defeated. The Confederate army was retreating. Most felt it would be the end of Lee's army, and soon, the war.

Dusk was fast approaching when Alexa stepped outside to draw another bucket of water. Exhaustion had been her companion for so long, she couldn't remember the last time she'd felt like herself. She paused for a moment to lean against the house and collect her thoughts.

Retreat meant the end of the fighting, the end of the steady stream of wounded men pouring into town. Relief nearly brought her to her knees. Though it would be a lifetime before their little town was back to normal—if ever—at least the fighting was over.

Would the war really end now, as so many believed? And if it did, would she ever see Nate again? And for the thousandth time that afternoon, she wondered if McKenna was all right, if he'd been in the thick of today's fighting. Had defeat left a bitter taste in his mouth or was he glad to have it over with for now?

She didn't expect to see him again, but for the rest of her life, she'd remember the way the world had tilted beneath her feet when he'd kissed her, the delightful shivers that had coursed through her when his tongue stroked the hollow behind her ear.

A movement near the road caught her attention—two gray clad soldiers carrying a wounded man on a litter. She stifled a groan and, forcing herself upright, stepped forward, praying for the energy to care for every last man who needed it.

One of the men was familiar, short and stout with a bristly red beard. Smitty? Was that his name? The one who'd held his hand over Simon Edwards' wound yesterday.

Yesterday? How in Heaven's name was it possible that had been only a day ago?

Smitty's face all but crumpled as she rushed toward him. "Doc, you gotta help him." He set the litter gently down.

"I'll do the best I can," she said, leaning in to see how badly wounded the man was.

"Field surgeon says there's nothing can be done. I thought maybe you..." His voice, raw with emotion, broke, and he turned away.

How on Earth had they made it here with Federal troops in control of the town? They must care a great deal about their comrade.

She knelt down. The wounded man lay on his side, his trousers torn and bloodied, a wound packed with blood-stained rags over one hip. He moaned in pain.

"It's all right," she said soothingly as she removed some of the bloody rags. "I'm just going to examine you."

He mumbled something incoherent. Reminded of her vow to look each of them in the eyes, memorize their face, she took a moment to stroke the hair back from his face. Hair the color of maple sugar that felt like silk beneath her fingers… *Oh, God, no...*

Startled, she turned a shocked gaze to Smitty. "This is the major."

"Colonel, Ma'am," said the other man. "General gave him the promotion right there on the battlefield."

Alexa glanced back at Caleb then into the worried faces of the men who had risked capture and imprisonment to bring him here. She pulled in a steadying breath. "I'll do what I can, but I'll need both of you to hold him down. Come with me."

Seven

Sunshine, golden and bright bathed the land in warmth, the crisp blue sky promising a beautiful spring day.

"Has there ever been a lovelier day for a picnic?"

Caleb chuckled at the delight in his younger sister's face. It seemed ages since he'd seen her, yet for some reason, he couldn't recall why. But it was all he could do to keep from staring at his family. Mother, serene and lovely, with just a hint of a smile revealing her own excitement at the prospect of a picnic. Aurora, two years older than Savannah, but nearly her twin with their long golden hair and blue eyes.

And his baby sister, sweet Savannah, who had always held a tender place in his heart.

He glanced toward the buggy that carried his mother and sisters, but saw no sign of his father. Turning in the saddle, he looked behind him. Normally, his brother and father rode alongside the buggy on a favorite mount as he did.

There was no sign of them. Something nagged at the edges of his brain, there was a reason why his father and brother weren't here, but he couldn't remember.

Savannah beamed a smile at him. "Will Melody be there, Caleb?"

He couldn't help another chuckle. "Of course. She'll be meeting us with her family."

"Which means Ty will be there," Aurora said with a pointed look at her sister, and Savannah blushed, her cheeks turning a becoming pink.

"Caleb?"

Oh how he'd missed Mother's soft, honeyed voice.

"Have you set a date for the wedding yet?"

Dread tangled through him. He loved Melody, he truly did. But he wasn't ready to marry her. There was something he needed to do first. Something important. He just couldn't remember what it was. "Not yet." Trying not to notice the concern in Mother's gaze as she studied him, he forced a relaxed smile. "Soon. I promise."

Aurora adjusted her parasol as they rounded a bend in the road. "Well, this war surely can't last much longer, and then you can marry her."

War? The word echoed in his brain. War stood in the way of marrying Melody. War was why his father and brother weren't here.

I'm supposed to be at war…

Pulling his mount to a halt, he faced his family, only to see them fade before his eyes until they were nothing but misty shadows. In their place lay the bodies of his friends and fellow soldiers, bloodied and horribly disfigured.

The sharp crack of gunfire and thundering boom of cannons flooded his brain. And then the pain. Burning, searing pain. A scream tore from his throat, and he fought to sit up.

"Be still," a female voice soothed. "You'll drain what little strength you have."

He frowned. He knew that voice. And for reasons he couldn't fathom, knew it was important to do what she said. A familiar, musty smell filled his nostrils. He'd been here before but…when? Darkness surrounded him; a lamp glowed on the other side of the room, but didn't cast enough light for him to focus.

"Drink this."

That voice again. It nagged at the fuzzy edges of his brain.

Something cool and metallic was held to his lips and a gentle hand supported his shoulders as he leaned up on an elbow. Lilacs teased his senses, pushing aside the pain for a few seconds. *Beautiful…* Headstrong, stubborn…

For a fleeting moment, he grasped her name, but it fled his mind as quickly as it came.

Crisp, cool water moistened his tongue. Nothing had ever tasted so wonderful, and he greedily gulped the contents. "More."

"Not now."

She moved away, and he heard a splash of liquid and the soft thunk of something being set down. The smell of lilacs returned. "Take this." A cup was again pressed to his lips.

A bitter aroma met his nose, and he recoiled. "What is it?"

"Laudanum. It will ease the pain and help you rest."

"Am I ill?"

"You've been wounded."

His right hip throbbed a painful reminder of that fact. "Where are my men?"

"There will be time for questions later, Ma— Colonel. Right now, rest is all you need to worry about."

Colonel? Was it possible she didn't know him? Yet, somehow he knew her.

He drank the bitter liquid, grimacing as it burned his throat. The taste brought more fuzzy memories to mind. A cool hand on his brow, wet cloths bathing his face. And voices. Not hers—another woman—telling him to lie still, talking to him, forcing this same bitter liquid down his throat.

His head dropped back onto the mattress; he no longer had the strength to hold it up.

"Give in to the need to sleep. I'll be here when you wake again."

Her words comforted him as the effects of the medicine carried him away—he was relieved she'd be there, he trusted her ability to care for him. She was capable. *Why do I know that?*

"Just rest, McKenna."

For a moment, he clearly pictured her face, but the image faded as the haze around his brain grew, swirling around, carrying him down, down, down. Even as he fought against the tide pulling him under, one thought taunted him.

Who the hell is she?

****

Less than a day after the battle ended, trains began to run again and supplies, scarce with the stores closed up and deserted, were more easily come by, which made caring for and feeding so many considerably easier.

The Sanitary Commission had rolled into town with food and supplies for the wounded, setting up hospitals and relieving the burden from some of the residents. A group of nuns set up camp and took some of the wounded; homes and churches all around town overflowed with men in need of care.

Alexa had spent the better part of the night working in the field hospital at the Lutheran Church, but still had her own patients to care for at home. Placing a hanky doused in peppermint oil over her nose and mouth to mask the odors of death and decay, she headed back.

She forced herself not to look at the gruesome sights she passed, men and horses that had yet to be buried. Grammy refused to let Felicity leave the house, lest the young girl be overwhelmed by the sights that met her eyes just a few steps from their front door.

Caleb came to mind, as always. Alexa wouldn't be able to check on him right away and prayed he didn't regain consciousness and try to move. She had asked Grammy and Felicity to look in on him, but they couldn't stay in the fruit cellar with him indefinitely. Laudanum and his injuries had kept him unconscious for the better part of a week. She didn't know what she'd do if he didn't wake soon.

As she drew closer to her house, she noticed a group of Confederate soldiers standing in a line outside. Recognizing many as her patients, she quickened her steps.

Quentin Lord, leaning heavily on his crutch, held a gun while a blue clad officer escorted another wounded Confederate soldier down the porch steps.

She hurried over to them, tempted to wrench the gun from his hand. "What are you doing?"

"Alexa," Quentin greeted as if it were an ordinary day. "We're just rounding up some of the Johnnies that are well enough to be relocated."

One of the men, barely out of boyhood, appeared

ready to collapse. She stepped over to him and took hold of his hand. "Most of these men are *not* well enough to be on their feet. Where are they being taken?"

"Fort McHenry."

"Fort Mc—the *prison camp*?"

Quentin hobbled toward her. "What did you think we were going to do with them? Let them go?"

"Just days ago you lie side by side with these men recuperating and swapping stories. No one was worried about uniform color then."

He frowned. "It's war, Alexa. They'd do the same to us, you know."

The officer shoved the last man into line, then strode over to them, anger evident on his face. She noted the two gold leaves on his jacket collar. So, he was a major, which meant she couldn't ask Will or any of the other men in her care to intervene—they were outranked.

"Is there a problem here, miss?"

"These men are under my care. I demand you release them until they are well enough to be moved."

The major darted a glance at Quentin, apparently unaccustomed to being ordered about by a woman. "Is she that lady doctor?"

He nodded. "She is."

The man adjusted his hat. "Ma'am, you do realize the penalty for harboring a Confederate solider is prison?"

"I'm not *harboring* anyone; I'm caring for the sick and the wounded. These men are not well enough—"

"The Federal army appreciates your concern, but these here men are prisoners of war. Now, step aside or

I'll be forced to arrest you."

She opened her mouth to protest, but a movement on the porch caught her attention. Will stood there, his shoulders slumped, one hand in his pocket. Leaving her patients for just a moment, she stepped over to the porch railing. "Will, can't you do something?"

"I tried to reason with your friend over there." He nodded toward Quentin. "But this will get him a nice promotion, so he ain't interested in actin' like a respectable human being."

She studied Quentin over her shoulder. He didn't seem the least bit affected by what he was doing. How was it possible she'd known him for so many years, yet never really known his character? "I can't let them do this, those boys will never survive prison camp."

Will touched her arm, bringing her attention back to him. "Think of the men here who still need you, Doctor Alexa. All of 'em. What will become of them if you get arrested?"

Faces of men she'd spent days caring for came to mind. One in particular. Her shoulders sagged. He was right. "Thank you, Will, for being the voice of reason for me tonight."

Against her better judgment, she approached the officer in charge. "At least let me put fresh dressings on their wounds before you drag them off to God knows where."

The officer exchanged amused glances with Quentin. "You do that, ma'am, but be quick about it."

Alexa marched toward the house to retrieve the necessary supplies, a lump of anger and emotion stuck in her throat.

Grammy and Felicity met her at the door.

"You won't let them take those men, will you, Alexa?" Felicity asked.

"I'm afraid we don't have a choice." She met Grammy's gaze. "I should have known when Quentin announced he was ready to return to his duties he'd do something like this.

"Well, we couldn't keep them indefinitely," Grammy said. "Nothing good would come of it."

Well aware of whom Grammy really meant, Alexa nodded. "Help me dress their wounds, Felicity, it's the least we can do for them now."

****

The pain of a thousand razors slashed at Caleb's hip and abdomen. He thrashed, desperate to escape the sensation and reached for his sidearms. His hand brushed only thin air.

"Don't move so much," came a soothing female voice. "You'll pull your stitches."

He stilled immediately. It was her again, the sweet-voiced angel who smelled of lilacs and summer rain.

Something warm and leathery pressed against his forehead.

"He's feverish." The voice was older, graveled with age. "There's infection somewhere."

"Colonel McKenna, if you can hear me, please lie still. I need to remove your bandages."

The voice brought a heavenly vision to mind. Hair the color of midnight, skin like fresh cream and lips as sweet and juicy as ripe berries.

"There's no sign of infection here."

Her voice washed over him like the flutter of an angel's wings. Soft…sweet. So tempting.

"Then it's somewhere else." The gravelly tone

again, fraught with disapproval.

"No, there's nowhere—oh no. I wonder…"

Gentle fingers worked the buttons on his shirt, brushing his chest. Oh, how he craved her touch.

He could see her before him, smiling, laughing. She held raspberries in her outstretched palm, offering them to him. His mouth watered at the sight of the plump red fruit, so sweet…so juicy. So tempting. She took a small bite from one, the juice staining her lips a berry red, then laughed and danced away.

A toss of her hair and a seductive glance over her shoulder beckoned him to follow. To hell with the consequences. He wanted to taste the juicy, decadent fruit mingled with the sweetness of her lips. Wanted to taste all she had to offer.

"Dammit, McKenna. You promised you'd have someone check this."

"You'll have to lance and drain it."

"Pass me that candle so I can heat a knife over the flame."

Her fingers rested on his chest, their touch gentle, soothing. His temptress was close enough to reach, to touch. He grabbed hold of her arm and pulled her toward him. Eyes like green jewels sparkled with sensual promise. He bent his head toward hers, unwilling to be denied the taste of her any longer…

Searing pain shot through his shoulder, tearing a roar of agony from his throat. He tried to sit up, to move away from the torture, but his limbs felt heavy, weighted down by some unseen force.

"It's all right now. Just rest."

His temptress fled, but the heady aroma of lilacs lingered to tease his nostrils.

****

One of the doors to the cellar opened, flooding the small room with damp night air and the putrid smells filtering in from the battlefield. A dim light shone at the top of the stairs, and for a split second, Alexa's heart hammered in her chest. Had her hiding place been discovered?

But the slow, careful shuffle of feet on the stairs was familiar. Shoulders sagging with relief, she rose from the chair near the cot and hurried to help Grammy with the basket she carried.

Alexa set it on the table and unpacked a cup of broth, a slice of bread and a cup of hot tea, a spoon, napkins and linens for washing.

"How did you manage to get away with all these things?" Now that some of the women from town had seen how overrun the Winters' residences was with injured, many showed up to help throughout the day.

Grammy lowered herself into a chair near the table. "Just said I was taking food to the field hospital. Didn't say which field hospital." She nodded in Caleb's direction. "Any change?"

"He's resting more peacefully, I think."

"Sleep's the best thing for him now. If he doesn't come down with pneumonia or bed sores, he might just make it."

Alexa had been shifting and turning him as best she could for the past few days, propping rolled up blankets behind him to keep him from lying in one position too long, but because of his groin injury she could only move him so far. But Grammy was right, along with bed sores, pneumonia was a constant worry.

"As soon as he comes to, I'll get him up and

moving about."

Grammy nodded her approval. "Seen pneumonia settle in lots of times, but not so much in them that's up and active."

Alexa placed a grateful hand on her grandmother's shoulder. "You sit here and rest a while so it looks like you walked a long way to that field hospital."

Well aware of Grammy's sharp gaze on her, she approached Caleb with the cup of broth. She set the cup on the table beside the cot and bent to try and wake him. "McKenna? Can you wake up enough to eat something?"

He stirred and moaned.

Her heart constricted at the sound, worried that he was starting with another infection or worse. "Are you in pain?"

Another moan. Perching beside him on the cot, as close as she could get without hurting him, she clasped his hand in hers, her heart lurching when he squeezed tight.

"If you can hear me, tell me where it hurts."

He mumbled something incoherent. She clutched the hand that held hers while he shifted and moaned. It was so much easier to be nice to him when he was like this. Awake, he posed far too much of a challenge to her senses. This way, she could easily pretend he was just another patient.

With a bit of help from Grammy, she was able to prop him up enough to get a few sips of willow bark tea down him. Within minutes, though, he'd collapsed back onto the cot.

Grammy's iron gray gaze met Alexa's. "Let 'im sleep. His body knows what it needs."

With a nod, she tucked the thin blanket around him.

"You go on ahead and check your other patients; I'll keep watch over this one. Won't do me a bit of harm to be off my feet for a while."

She wanted to protest, wanted to be here if he woke. But she suspected Grammy already knew how deep her feelings ran for Caleb. Appearing reluctant to go would only inspire her grandmother to spend even more time in the fruit cellar. And as much as Alexa longed to be present if Caleb woke, she did have other soldiers who needed her time and attention just as much.

With a nod, she headed for door. She'd slip back down here after Grammy had gone to bed for the night.

****

Late summer sunshine streamed through the tree tops making it the ideal day for one last picnic. Caleb sat beneath the shade of an old oak tree, Melody beside him. Across the yard, his mother and Mrs. Chandler had their heads together, no doubt discussing wedding arrangements.

Melody picked up a golden leaf that had fluttered to the ground and twirled it between her fingers. "Mother thinks a spring wedding would be ideal. Perhaps in April, before it gets too hot?"

He forced worrisome political thoughts aside, determined not to spoil her happy mood. Georgia had secession fever, and if the anti-slavery Lincoln was elected president in November, they could be living in a very different country come spring. "Whatever pleases you, Melody. You know I have no objection."

Her golden-brown eyes sparkled with happiness.

Male laughter carried to them. His older brother, Matthew's distinctive laugh rose above the others. Caleb grinned, his father and Melody's were probably sharing the latest political joke. She turned at the sound of their laughter. For a split second, something sad clouded her expression, and she glanced down at her hands in her lap. This wasn't the first time he'd seen such a look from her, and he wondered what caused his future bride such sadness.

They had been friends since childhood, and she'd always confided her dreams and secrets to him. Upcoming nuptials shouldn't keep her from doing so now.

He took hold of her hand and gave it a gentle squeeze. "Is something troubling you, Mel?"

She smiled at his use of her nickname. "No, not at all." She gently pulled her hand from his, checking over her shoulder to see if her mother or brothers had witnessed the contact.

"How are you feeling today, McKenna?"

He puzzled at her odd question and use of his surname, but couldn't find the words to reply.

"I thought I'd read to you for a bit, if that's all right."

Again, though words formed in his mind, they didn't pass his lips.

"I'd love to read you the work of Miss Harriet Beecher Stowe, but I'm sure you've read it many times already."

Harriet Beecher Stowe? What had gotten into Melody? She'd never been sarcastic.

"Charles Dickens is more to my liking anyway. In fact, before you and your army rode through town, I was re-reading Oliver Twist. I don't mind starting at the beginning for you."

As Melody read, he wondered what had become of her soft, Georgia accent, and why it held a slightly nasal, northern cadence.

He glanced at her, and for a moment his breath caught. Dark hair spilled over her shoulders, and instead of her pastel morning dress, she wore a work worn shirt and trousers. A glimmer of recognition flashed through his mind. A willow tree. Kisses—sweet and soothing, then hot, passion filled and forbidden. Grief. Blood, so much blood.

Simon Edwards' face flashed through his mind and a pang of loss shot through him with such intensity it took his breath away. He hadn't just lost Simon; he'd lost her, too. They'd quarreled, and he'd left her here— here, in this musty little room. The very thought of her stirred the pain anew. He had to find her, had to see her one more time. He tried to move, but pain ripped through his hip and chest.

"Alexa…"

"McKenna? Are you awake?"

Her soft voice soothed the pain, and somehow made it more tolerable.

"Damn you, if you don't wake soon, I'm going to throttle you."

She hesitated, then continued to read, and her voice lulled him, soothing him toward sleep.

Eight

Alexa awoke with a start. Light showed around the edges of the door.

Across the room, Caleb stirred, moaning. She uncurled from the blankets she'd spread on the floor, grimacing as stiff muscles protested. Kneeling beside his cot, she pressed a hand to his forehead, relieved to find it cool.

It had been three days since she'd lanced the infected chest wound, and two weeks since she'd removed the fragments that had gone through his right hip and out his groin. She couldn't believe he'd survived, was still hesitant to think he would continue to improve. But he was fever-free today, and for every day he remained so she was grateful.

She stepped away to pour a cup of water from the pitcher she kept nearby. When she returned, his eyes were open, taking in his surroundings.

"I'll light a candle in just a moment," she assured him, and placed the cup to his lips. "Take a sip of this."

He pushed it back toward her. "No." His voice was raspy, but his tone determined.

"It's water."

She placed a hand behind his back to help him sit up enough to drink. He grimaced, but drank when she placed the cup back to his lips. "Slow," she cautioned.

He finished the contents, and as she set the cup

aside, she felt his gaze on her, studying her movements.

"Are you hungry?"

He nodded. The news sent a small surge of hope through her. Hunger was a good sign.

"I'll fetch you some broth in a few minutes."

"How long have I been here?"

She dreaded answering as she suspected what his reaction would be. Instead, Alexa bent to straighten the blankets she'd slept on so he wouldn't read the deception in her face. "A few days."

He rested back with a sigh, staring up at the ceiling. "My division?"

"General Lee has moved his army south." Finishing with her own blankets, she began to straighten his.

"How did I come to be in your care?"

"Your men—Smitty and Johnson, I believe— brought you here after the field surgeon declared your wound mortal."

"So you…"

Images of him lying still and lifeless filled her mind. There had been so much blood. She'd never performed such delicate surgery, never even knew she had it in her to do so. A hot ball of emotion wedged in her throat. "Yes."

"You…saved my life?"

Forcing aside haunting images of him thrashing as his men held him down, his screams as she probed his wound, she lit a candle and carried it to his bedside. "If you continue to improve, then I suppose I did."

"Why?"

She set the lamp on the table near his bed. "What sort of question is that?"

"We didn't part on pleasant terms, and you made your feelings about the Confederacy clear enough."

"I assured you I wouldn't worry about the color of anyone's uniform, Ma—*Colonel* McKenna."

"Why do you keep calling me that?"

So, he had heard her all those long nights at his side, comforting him through fever and pain.

"You were given a battlefield promotion. For your bravery."

Another loud sigh. "They only do that if you're dead."

"You nearly were."

His eyes darkened with emotion, and he lay there for several moments in silence. "This chatter will surely tax your strength—Ma—Colonel. I'll go and fetch you something to eat. Do you need…" Her cheeks burned. This had been so much easier when he was unconscious. "Do you need to…relieve..."

"No."

She breathed a silent sigh of relief and headed for the stairs.

"Alexa?"

No one said her name quite like he did, with that cultured Georgian drawl. Tears blurred her vision. She thought she'd never hear her name spoken so again.

Unable to turn around and let him see raw emotion on her face, she paused. "Yes?"

"Thank you."

No sound could squeak past the thickening of her throat, so she merely made her way up the cement steps as gracefully as she could and pushed open the doors.

Cardinals and sparrows chirped a greeting to the morning as she stepped outside, blinking against the brilliant sunlight of a summer morning. Tears blurred her vision, and she forced her feet forward, the smell of coffee pulling her toward the house.

In the kitchen, she helped herself gratefully to a cup from the pot Grammy had brewed earlier and sank wearily into a chair at the table. The trembling in her hands had nothing to do with exhaustion and everything to do with the man in her fruit cellar.

Treating him while he was unconscious hadn't been difficult. But awake, his presence filled the entire room.

Not once had she allowed herself to dwell on any lingering personal feelings while treating him. But just now, when he'd spoken her name, she'd been flooded with the memories of his kiss, his touch. The heat of his mouth opening over hers, his tongue delving inside, finding and coaxing hers into a mating dance.

Under no circumstances could she allow herself to lose her head again. He was her patient, nothing more. Giving in to passion could only lead to scandal and heartache, and she'd had enough of both to last a lifetime.

Keeping him alive and safe from capture long enough to send him home or see him on his way south could be the only thing she concerned herself with.

Male laughter floated through the closed kitchen door, along with a familiar deep voice from the parlor.

"That's a fine looking wound there, son. You'll be back chasing those Rebs in no time."

Alexa rose so quickly her chair tipped over and hit the floor with a loud clatter.

"Broken ribs, eh? Did you get the Johnny who did it, son? That's a boy. You'll be in pain for a while yet.

Don't let it be the boss of you and you'll be fine."

She pushed the door open a crack to peek out. There in the parlor, surrounded by wounded men, was her father. When had he returned?

He moved from one man to the next, pausing to tell the occasional joke or share an anecdote about his experiences in Harrisburg. Each story was met with laughter.

She couldn't help but smile at the sight of him, short, stout, his thinning gray hair looking even whiter than it had just days ago, spectacles perched on the end of his nose.

He moved effortlessly among the men. He had to be exhausted, though it didn't show. He seemed completely at ease, and she suspected every man in the room felt the same way. Tears filled her eyes for a moment. This was the doctor she had always wanted to be.

"Now, someone did a fine job stitching up this arm," he said with a wink as she came through the door. "I think I recognize that needle work."

Alexa crossed the room and bent to kiss his cheek. "You had us worried half to death."

He waved a hand in dismissal. "Who would shoot an old man like me? Certainly not those Rebs," he added in a jovial voice. "They couldn't hit the broad side of a barn if it was right in front of them."

Laughter and guffaws followed.

Catching her eye, he gestured about the room. "Tell me, where are the sick and wounded?"

Around them, soldiers enjoyed games of checkers, chess, or dominoes. Many talked openly of war news or read the paper aloud to those who were too ill to read it themselves. Most were laughing.

"A wise man once told me there is nothing so depressing as inactivity of the mind," she began. "And I quite agree."

He chuckled, but his eyes misted with pride. "Now, who would say such a thing as that?"

"Are you hungry?" she asked when the laughter had quieted.

"Famished. But it can wait 'til I've visited with the rest of these young men."

"We've had excellent care, sir," spoke up the ever loyal Will Carter. "Doctor Alexa has been a real blessing to us."

Her chest swelled at his flattery as she turned back toward the kitchen intent on fixing breakfast for her father.

Having Father home was a relief, but it would make hiding the Rebel officer in their fruit cellar that much more difficult.

Nine

Caleb pulled the blanket back and peeled away the dressings that covered his wound. Alexa came to change them each day and baptize him with corn liquor, but he was impatient to see signs of healing.

The skin surrounding the sutures was red and sore, but to his great relief, there was nothing to indicate infection. He pushed himself to a sitting position, as he had each day for the past three. The effort was painful on his injuries, but he didn't grow as lightheaded from the exertion as the day before.

A scraping sound came from the doors to his prison, and then they were tugged open. He pulled the blankets back over himself.

The fragrant aroma of coffee preceded Alexa into the gloomy little room.

"I thought you might like something stronger than tea today," she said, setting the tray on the table in the middle of the room.

His stomach grumbled in response.

"You're hungry, that's a good sign." She pulled a chair away from the table and dragged it over toward the bed. "Let's see if we can get you on your feet for a few seconds. Once you're able to move around a bit, you'll get your blood circulating and heal those wounds even faster."

He noted the determined set to her chin, as if no

force on earth, save her own, had a say in how quickly he healed, "Eager to see me on my way, Doctor Winters?"

"Eager to see you healed, if that's what you mean. First things first, I want to check your wound. Lie on your side."

As he had each morning, he rolled to face the wall, offering her his right hip. Her touch was purely clinical as she examined him, but he was nonetheless embarrassed to be naked from the waist down. He supposed it was pointless since she'd undoubtedly seen all of him during and after his surgery.

"Everything looks good," she said after she'd re-wrapped the wound. "Now, let's see about getting you on your feet."

"Am I allowed to wear trousers?"

Her gaze flew to his face as though the thought hadn't occurred to her before. "I cut your trousers and undergarments off the night you were wounded. I haven't given you anything to wear because I couldn't remove and replace clothing to dress your wound while you were unconscious."

"And now?"

"I could try to find something to fit you, of course. Meanwhile, let's wrap the blanket about your waist to preserve your modesty."

"It wasn't *my* modesty I was concerned with, Alexa."

Her lips pulled into a grim line. "After what I've seen these past two weeks, nothing will ever shock me again." She stepped up to the cot. "Sit up, and when you can, swing your legs to the floor."

He struggled to sit up and turn without tugging at

his sutures. The movement, however, left him lightheaded.

"Just take a couple of deep breaths. When you're ready to stand, I'll help you." She busied herself removing the blankets and pillow from the cot, tugging them from beneath him.

Finished, she tossed the linens in the corner and came to stand before him. "Are you ready?"

Probably not, but he'd never admit it out loud. "You aren't strong enough to support my weight by yourself."

"And you're not strong enough to stand without assistance. Between the chair and me, we'll get you upright, even if it's just for a moment or two."

He recognized the stubborn tone—arguing was pointless. "How many patients are left in your care?"

"About two dozen. Some were well enough to return to their unit, but not many."

"I'd like to know what's happening with the war." Between the inactivity and not knowing what was happening, he was nearly out of his mind.

"I can send Felicity down later with some newspapers for you to read."

He nodded. "What's become of the Confederate soldiers you were caring for?" She took a sudden interest in plumping his pillow and a knot of unease formed in his stomach. "Alexa?"

Rising, she faced him, her eyes reflecting anguish. "Those who were well enough... Federal troops have taken them to a holding place where they'll be transferred to prison camps."

Heaviness settled on his heart. "So, you kept them alive just so they could be taken to a prison camp where they'll likely die?"

She thumped the pillow with more force than necessary, then stood before him with her arm extended, telling him it was time. "I wasn't given a choice. Federal troops rounded them up."

"Well, at least now I know what I have to look forward to."

He shifted his weight to his feet and tried to rise. The room spun, and the floor pitched and swayed beneath him. Her shoulder caught him beneath the armpit and she tugged the chair closer with her foot.

"I said I'd help you."

"I don't want help." The words came out harsher than he intended.

"Stubborn fool. Hold onto the back of the chair for balance."

He had to bend to reach it and nearly toppled over. A tremor moved through her body and she began to sag under his weight. He wasn't sure how she got him there, but with a thud, he landed in the chair.

Nausea roiled in his stomach, and his head spun as though he'd consumed too much brandy. His chest heaved with exertion as he pulled in great gulps of air.

She rubbed her shoulder, and tipped her head to one side.

"Are you all right?"

"Fine," she sounded every bit as out of breath as he. "As long as you're in the chair, we may as well get you washed and shaved."

He'd be glad to be rid of the beard that had sprouted on his face during his recovery. But the idea of her bathing him was something he'd find more appealing if he were well.

"Do you want to try some coffee now?" She held out the cup toward him.

He took a sip of the now-warm liquid, savoring the rich brew on his tongue before swallowing. It had been months since he'd had real coffee—chicory was a poor substitute, but coffee beans were hard to come by unless his men came across some Union soldiers willing to trade coffee beans for tobacco.

"Would you like some bread? I brought you some to go with the broth this morning, but I wasn't sure your stomach was ready."

The news lightened his mood considerably, as did the sight of the thick slice liberally spread with butter and jam. While he sipped the coffee and ate, Alexa placed fresh linens on his cot.

He took note of the way she bent to smooth and tuck them around the mattress, but was too weak to truly appreciate the sight of her backside in trousers, as he had on other occasions. She straightened and he quickly looked away.

"Are you dizzy?" she asked.

He shook his head.

The sight of her, linens bundled in her arms, heading for the steps, stirred a nagging sense of isolation. "I'll put some water on to heat and be back."

He'd just finished the last of the broth when she returned with a soap cup, brush and razor. She slipped an apron on and reached behind her to tie it.

"Oh, I nearly forgot." From her pocket she pulled a tooth brush and a tin of tooth powder. "The sisters of something-or-other have been handing out clothing and hygiene items for the wounded men. I brought you these."

He nodded his thanks and set them in his lap.

"Lean your head back."

"Should I trust you with a straight razor near my throat?"

She laughed and brushed the shave soap over his face. "I guess you'll find out." Moving behind him, she placed gentle hands to the sides of his head. "Just relax your head back against me."

He did so, wishing he were well enough to enjoy having his head cradled between her breasts.

She began to shave him with gentle but confident strokes of the razor. "No one knows you're down here, save Grammy, Felicity and me."

"And why is that?"

"My father is back in town, and you know how he feels about Confederate soldiers."

He resisted the need to turn and glance at her, watching instead as she wiped the razor on a cloth. "Feelings I believe you share?"

Another smooth stroke of the blade. "I'll admit that seeing Rebel soldiers loafing on my lawn, smoking, laughing and demanding food made me angry. In fact, I'd go so far as to say I have no fondness whatsoever for any Reb who is able to walk and talk."

"But?" he asked, sensing she had more to say.

"But wounded men are another matter entirely. I can't seem to feel anything but compassion for them."

"Fortunate for me, considering the circumstances."

She finished one cheek and moved to the other. "Yes. But the men remaining in my care now are Federal soldiers. And I don't intend to let them know you're here."

"Why not?"

She moved around to study his upper lip and chin before taking the blade to him again. "You need more time to recuperate. I don't want to see you sent to a prison camp, you'd surely catch pneumonia and die."

Her tone was distant and clinical, much like any other doctor concerned for their patient. He ignored the jab of disappointment that speared him and instead focused on the more pressing issue at hand. "So, your plan is to keep me hidden in your fruit cellar indefinitely?"

"Until you're well enough to travel."

He absorbed that news in silence. Where exactly did she expect him to travel? She couldn't have thought this plan through; he'd need weeks of recovery. He let his gaze rest on her face as she moved in closer to shave him again. Dark purple smudges were evident beneath her eyes, and she had lost enough weight to hollow her cheeks.

"You look exhausted, Alexa."

"I'm all right."

"You wouldn't admit if you weren't." Her breath fanned his face. The sight of her raspberry lips up close reminded him of the kisses they'd shared beneath the willow tree. "How much sleep have you had?"

She shrugged, but didn't take her gaze from her task. "Enough I suppose."

"You were sleeping on the cellar floor beside me this morning. I doubt that was the first time."

"I needed to stay nearby in case you woke in the night."

He wondered if that was the only reason.

She finished scraping the last of the shave soap from his face and reached for a nearby cloth. He caught

118

her hand and took the flannel from her, wiping it over his face himself. "I want to apologize again for the way I left things between us."

Though the light in the room was dim, he saw her eyes darken with emotion. "There's no need."

"I disagree."

"You apologized that night. It's forgotten." She averted her gaze and wiped her hands on the apron. "I'll be back in just a bit with the water."

****

Juggling the water basin, soap, cloths to bathe Caleb and a nightshirt for him to wear wasn't nearly as difficult as getting back to the fruit cellar undetected.

Alexa had just slipped out the door and into the backyard when Will Carter rounded the corner from the house. She muttered a silent curse. His shoulder and ribs were in no condition for him to return to soldiering, but there wasn't a thing in the world wrong with his legs, making him one of her more mobile patients, and he helped out wherever he could.

"Something I can carry for you, Miss Alexa?" he asked, hurrying toward her.

"Uh…no, Will, thank you."

"Were you taking those things indoors?"

She glanced from the cellar doors back to Will, grasping for a way to explain herself.

"I guess you ladies don't have much privacy with all us men in the house," he chuckled. "I didn't realize we'd left you with no place to..." His ears reddened. "Well, to wash up."

"Yes, it's true," she said, forcing a bright laugh.

"I'd be glad to stand guard out here, ma'am, and make sure no one disturbs you."

119

Stand guard? While she bathed a man whose very presence set her knees to trembling and her mind to all sorts of improper thoughts? Once again, she scrambled for an explanation that wouldn't sound ridiculous. "Oh, that's so thoughtful of you. But I'm not sure how long I'll be."

"Well, the least I can do is open the door for you when you got your hands full."

She stepped back and allowed him to pull the doors open with his good arm. "I'll just tell the others to stay clear of the cellar for a bit."

"No!" The word escaped her like an explosion of gunfire.

Will's brows rose.

"I…I'd hate for anyone to get ideas. About what I'm doing. Just…please don't say anything. If anyone is looking for me, just tell them I stepped out for a bit." She gave him what she hoped was a genuine smile. "I'd be mortified if anyone heard I was taking care of something as silly as bathing when there's work to be done."

His eyes darkened and the tips of his ears reddened again. "Your secret is safe with me, Doctor Alexa."

"Thank you, Will." She stepped inside and down the first couple of steps, peering into the darkness below, praying the sunlight didn't illuminate the room far enough for Caleb to be spotted.

"Should I close them behind you?"

"I'd appreciate that."

She held her breath until the doors closed with a gentle thump and darkness surrounded her again. Remaining still, she waited for her eyes to adjust to the dim light before she dared move for fear of spilling the water and having to start over again.

Setting the bowl and cloth on the table, she hurried over to the chair where she'd left Caleb, praying he hadn't passed out and fallen off. "Are you still awake?"

"Awake enough to know you have an admirer."

"Who?" She tugged at his shirt. "Can you raise your arms for me?"

"The soldier who wanted to stand guard while you bathed."

She slipped his shirt up and off and tossed it on the table. "Oh, Will is just—" Why admit the truth, better to let him think she had feelings for Will instead of him. "We've grown quite fond of one another."

"I can tell."

Ignoring the implication in his voice, she checked the water temperature with her finger before dipping a cloth in the basin. "Do you feel up to washing or would you like some help?"

He took the cloth she offered and pressed it to his face. He held it there for a moment before wiping the remaining shaving soap from his cheeks and upper lip.

"Here." Alexa stepped closer. "Let me do the rest." She dabbed at a spot near his ear where the soap remained.

Rubbing a sliver of Grammy's kettle soap in the cloth, she washed the back of his neck, then moved around the front.

"You're risking a lot keeping me here, Alexa." He met her gaze over the cloth. "If I know the army, I'd have to guess imprisonment, possibly even hanging."

"You once accused me of harboring runaway slaves." She dragged the cloth along his back and shoulders, steeling herself not to notice how wide his shoulders were, or the way his muscled back tapered to a narrow waist. She forced her fingers and hands not to caress, but to treat him with the same efficiency she did any other patient. "Whether I did is of no importance, but does that sound like someone who cares a fig about consequences?"

Taking a deep breath, she dipped the cloth again and soaped his chest. She moved carefully around the wound she'd lanced, aware it was still tender. Soft golden hair swirled in circles beneath the cloth, and she remembered the feel of it beneath her hands when he kissed her.

"It sounds like the same stubborn, headstrong, Alexa Winters."

She paused and glanced down at him. A twinkle of amusement danced in his eyes.

"You can't accept women who think for themselves, can you Ma—Colonel?"

He took hold of her wrist, pressing her palm to his chest. "If it comes down to it, and it means saving yourself, hand me over to the Federal soldiers. I can take whatever they have in store for me."

Refusing to meet his gaze, she tugged her hand away and lifted his arm. "We'll discuss that when you're well enough for such bravado."

She'd admired the strong biceps and corded forearms more than once while treating him. Such strong, masculine arms. Now, she forced her attention elsewhere while she soaped his arm and the masculine patch of hair beneath.

"I think as long as I'm in your care, we should dispense with formalities. I've come to miss the sound of my own name after two years of being addressed only as Major McKenna. Caleb will do just fine."

Caleb. She remembered whispering his name under the willow tree when, for a brief moment of insanity, she'd forgotten about war and blood and death and allowed him to comfort her. "I'll try to remember."

"I appreciate that."

Alexa made quick work of washing his stomach, then knelt to wash his calves and feet. She took care in soaping his feet and toes, noting his appreciative grunt when she slipped her soap covered fingers over the arches. Most of her patients appreciated a good foot rub, so she took her time, kneading each foot thoroughly, pleased at the moans and groans it elicited.

"I take back every bad thing I ever said about you," he said when she finished. "You're a saint."

"Don't canonize me just yet." She rose and was faced with what to do with the blanket that covered him from waist to thighs. Soaking the cloth once again, and pulling in a bolstering breath, she reached for the edge of the blanket. This was no different than the other men she'd washed. He just happened to be conscious.

He seized her wrist. "Alexa, for the love of God."

She chanced a peek at his face, well aware of the heat blistering her cheeks. "I was only going to—" She swallowed. "Would you prefer to do it?"

"I would." The sound came out half-growl, half-sigh.

She handed him the cloth, unsure if she was relieved or irritated. "Suit yourself. If you get dizzy and fall, be sure to cover yourself to preserve my modesty before asking for help."

Moving back to the table where she'd left a pitcher of water for washing his hair, she made a production of arranging the bandages and folding washing flannels. She heard the chair creak, the splash of the cloth in the water and held her breath, worried he'd collapse any moment.

"It's not *your* modesty I'm concerned with." He sounded a bit out of breath, as though the exertion had tired him. "I may be injured, but I'm certainly not made of stone."

Her cheeks flamed even hotter. "What…what are you suggesting?"

The chair creaked again, and a groan sounded from behind her. "I'm suggesting that while you may be trying your damndest to pretend I'm just another bed pan to be emptied, I know for a fact there's more between us than that."

She lurched around before she could stop herself, but he'd already arranged the blanket over his lap. "Just because we shared a few kisses doesn't mean I'm besotted with affection for you."

"No. But there is an attraction, and a powerful one at that."

"I haven't time for attraction to you or any other man." She took up the pitcher and stalked toward him. "I've a house full of soldiers to care for, you're just another patient. If it pains your pride to hear that—"

He grabbed her about the waist, hauling her onto his lap. Water sloshed from the pitcher, soaking her shirt and his chest. His hand slipped to the nape of her neck, tangling in her hair, holding her firmly in place.

She hadn't expected him be so strong after what he'd endured. The stubborn fool would be lucky if he hadn't torn his stitches, let alone spent what little strength he had. Judging from the way his chest heaved, he'd come close.

"When I'm well enough to enjoy it, Alexa Winters, I damn well intend to kiss you again. Thoroughly."

Heat suffused her insides. She still relived his kisses at odd, unexpected moments throughout the day. But she wouldn't allow those feelings to cloud her judgment as a doctor. She squirmed to try and right herself.

"God's nighshirt, Alexa, don't—"

"Your stitches. Did you—"

A tell-tale bulge beneath her buttocks reminded her of his earlier warning that he wasn't made of stone, and she ceased struggling. Her gaze flew to his face. His eyes met hers in a look that clearly said she'd been warned.

Swallowing past a sudden thickening in her throat, she carefully sat upright. "I need to move—before we, uh…damage your…" Lord above, why couldn't she think straight?

Somehow, with his assistance, her feet met the floor. Hands quivering like leaves in a windstorm, she took up the pitcher, hoping enough water remained to wash his hair. Silence hung heavy and awkward between them as she moved behind him and placed the basin at the back of his neck. "Tip your head back." Her voice sounded breathless, shaky. She tried to pull in a deep breath to calm herself. And failed.

He did as she asked, and she poured enough water from the pitcher to wet his hair, the excess water draining into the basin.

Lathering her hands with the soap, she placed them to his scalp and began to massage.

"I suppose you want me to apologize."

She watched the silken strands twining about her fingers, marveling at the different shades of brown and gold the sun had painted them. "That would be the appropriate thing to do."

"Apologizing implies regret. I have none."

"I see." She stopped scrubbing and glanced down at his face.

His eyes were closed, but he opened them as if sensing her gaze. "Dammit, Alexa. You can't deny what's between us."

"Your fiancée would certainly disagree."

He sighed. "We need to talk about that."

Without warning him, she dumped the remaining water from the pitcher over his head. She knew only a twinge of regret when his gasp told her the water had grown cold.

She reached for the flannel she'd left on the end of the cot and used it to vigorously rub his hair until it was almost dry. She'd neglected to bring a comb so she smoothed the soft locks with her fingers, irritated to find that he was just as handsome with his hair mussed.

When finished, she took up the clean night shirt she'd brought with her and yanked it over his head. While he gingerly threaded his arms through the sleeves, she packed up her belongings.

"It doesn't speak well of you, McKenna, that you're betrothed to one woman and vowing to kiss another."

He winced and attempted to stand. "I suppose not."

She hurried to his side and braced him with a shoulder as he moved the few feet from the chair back to the cot. "One might even say it makes you a bit of a rat."

He groaned as he sank onto the cot and lay back. "I can certainly see why one would think that."

His eyelids were already drifting closed, so she tucked the blankets around him. He'd undoubtedly sleep for hours now, worn out as he was.

"Sweet dreams, McKenna."

****

The sound of the doors opening stirred Caleb from dreams of home. A brief gust of damp, fresh air wafted to him before the doors closed with a soft thunk.

Instead of Alexa's hurried footsteps or the slow careful shuffle of her grandmother, the steps were light and delicate. He wasn't surprised when Alexa's young cousin came into view. She moved slowly, as though afraid of spilling the contents of the cup she carried.

He shifted and sat up straighter. A grumble from his belly demanded real food, but it appeared beef tea was on the menu for dinner again.

A pang of disappointment pierced him at not seeing Alexa, but he supposed she wanted to keep her distance after their encounter this afternoon.

"Felicity, isn't it?" he asked.

"Yes." She set the cup on a table near his cot and pulled a linen wrapped bundle from her apron pocket. "I brought you this to go with the broth." She unwrapped it to reveal a thick chunk of bread.

"I appreciate that."

"I didn't butter it, I was afraid the grease would soak the napkin."

He dipped the bread in the broth and bit into it, grateful to have something besides liquid to eat.

A book and some newspapers were tucked beneath her arm, and she placed them on the bed. "I've been reading to the soldiers upstairs," she said. "I thought you might enjoy having something to read."

He glanced with interest at what she'd left for him. A collection of newspapers and Charles Dickens' *David Copperfield*. "One of my favorites."

"I could read to you if you'd like. Or…" She glanced away.

"Was there something else?"

"Yes, actually. Alexa suggested…well, she said I should help you write a letter. To your fiancée."

He nearly choked on the bread. He did owe letters home, but wasn't sure how far south letters could actually travel from here. A sip of the broth helped wash down the chunk of bread stuck in his throat. "Let's plan on that for another time. Right now, I'd enjoy some company. I'd be delighted to have you read to me."

She dragged the chair over to the bed and sat, taking care to tuck her skirts about her in a most lady like manner, bringing to mind his younger sister, Savannah, though Felicity's hair was a light brown whereas Savannah's was blonde. But the fresh face, wide-eyed expression and innocence reminded him fondly of home.

She glanced at him, then quickly looked away again.

"I assure you, I don't bite."

"I just…"

"What?"

"I've never met anyone from the south before. We had soldiers here, but they were hurt and didn't talk much."

"I'm from Georgia. Just outside of Savannah."

"Do you own slaves?"

He suspected the words came out before she could stop them, but the question didn't take him entirely by surprise.

"Do I personally own them? No. But my father did." To his father, slavery had made financial sense. To Caleb, the institution was outdated, but then, he'd grown up playing with the slave children and had never understood why his friends were also his servants.

She glanced down at the hands clasped in her lap. "I'm sorry, I shouldn't have asked."

"It's perfectly normal to be curious."

"Did he ever…"

He'd heard many of these questions before. "No, we didn't beat them. And no, I don't fool myself into believing they were happy living a life of forced servitude. I planned to free them after the war, but your President Lincoln took care of that earlier this year."

"Did they all go?"

"I haven't had a letter from home recently, but to the best of my knowledge, yes. All but those who were too old or sick to travel."

She tipped her head, and if he'd been looking for a hint of resemblance to her cousin, he found it. But while such a look from Alexa promised biting sarcasm, Felicity seemed sincerely curious.

"So, why are you fighting then if it's not for the right to own slaves?"

He finished the last of the broth and set the cup aside. "That, young lady, is a very long and very complicated story. Mister Dickens' tale promises to be much more interesting."

She smiled and took the hint to open the book.

"You're much nicer than the Rebs who were on our doorstep that day. Thank you for chasing them off."

"You're quite welcome. And you're much nicer than the cousin who vowed to shoot and poison all of us."

At his conspiratorial wink, she laughed aloud. "Actually, Alexa is one of the kindest people I know. She just doesn't show it much."

An image of her came to mind. He'd seen evidence of that the night he'd come upon her in the battlefield, tending the dying like an angel of mercy. "Tell me, Miss Winters, does your cousin have any suitors?"

The book tumbled from her lap, and she made a wild grab for it. It hit the floor with a thud.

"Sui—she…Alexa, that is. She doesn't…" She picked up the book and refused to meet his gaze, her face rosy in the dim light.

"I know about her divorce."

Her gaze widened. "She *told* you?"

He smiled at the memory of Alexa climbing higher into the willow tree while the old women gossiped about her below. "In a manner of speaking, yes."

"I didn't think she ever told anyone." The young girl dusted the book off with great care. "Well, because of that, she doesn't have gentleman callers. The ones who should call are too timid, and the ones that do are under the impression…well they…"

"They're not gentlemen?"

"Precisely. But she really didn't have many suitors, even before."

He clasped his hands behind his head, ignoring the pain the position caused his healing chest wound and gazed up at the cobweb strewn ceiling. "Are the men of this county blind or merely half-wits?"

"I think a little of both."

He hadn't expected an answer, hadn't even meant to ask the question aloud, but he turned to see Felicity had grown thoughtful.

"It's intimidating, I think, for men to be around someone like Alexa. She's more capable than most of them and twice as smart. I think that scares them off." She drew in a deep breath and met his gaze with a stern look. "It would take a man who was very sure of himself to attract her attention, I think. Someone who wasn't intimidated by her independence or her intelligence." She cleared her throat and opened the book. "Of course, that man would have to be available, not promised to someone else."

Apparently, he'd made his interest too evident. "Of course."

He listened intently as she began to read aloud, but his mind flitted between memories of home and wondering how long Alexa intended to avoid him.

****

Sultry night air enveloped Alexa as she left the home of Georgia McLellan. The young woman's sister, Ginny Wade, had been killed by a stray bullet during the battle, and Alexa had wanted to pay a call on Georgia and her mother to see how they were.

Putrid-smelling air hit her, a quick reminder she'd forgotten to put a hanky over her mouth and nose before stepping outside. At times, it felt like her life would never be normal again.

"Alexa, wait." She stifled a groan as Quentin approached her. He'd insisted on escorting her this evening, though she doubted he was much protection on crutches. "Were you trying to sneak off without me?"

"No, not at all." Despite her best efforts, the words rang false even to her own ears.

He shook his head. "You're still mad about me capturing those Johnnies."

"My brother happens to be a so-called Johnny." She glared at him. "Is that how you think of Nate now?"

Quentin fell into step beside her, and she slowed her pace to match his careful step and thump of the crutches. "I had to do it, Alexa. It was an order. Besides..." He glanced around, as though worried someone might overhear. "I did it for you."

"For me?" She couldn't help a bark of laughter. "Are you saying I should be *thanking* you instead of imagining all the ways I'd like to break your other leg?"

"General Meade is arresting anyone he thinks is anti-abolitionist." He hurried his pace to catch up to her. "And there are rumors, Alexa. About you."

She shook her head in disgust. "Because Nate fights for the south." He was silent for a few moments, and she stopped walking to face him. "Is there something else?"

"You had Rebel guards at your house before the battle. And you were seen in the company of a Reb officer. More than once."

A trickle of fear began to coil through her. Who had seen her? Were Grammy and Felicity in danger because of her? "Those soldiers were guarding my home because a man tried to force his way inside."

"And the officer?"

She swallowed a bitter taste, realizing how

incriminating the truth would sound. "The same officer who posted the guards caught me out after hours when the town was under siege. I was looking for Nate."

"You were *what*?"

She put her hands to her hips. "Quentin Lord, you know me well enough to realize I'd go searching for my brother, just as he would for me."

"But that officer found you instead. What did he do to you, Alexa? If he so much as laid a hand…"

"For heaven's sake, settle down. It wasn't my virtue he was interested in, but rather my skill with a needle. He was injured. He insisted on escorting me home for the sake of my safety and that was it."

"You didn't see him again?"

"Well…" she hedged, wondering who had seen her with Caleb and when. "I mentioned that I was searching for my brother and hadn't heard from him. He promised to let me know if he heard anything about Nate. He stopped by the next evening to let me know what he'd learned."

"And what was that?"

She shook her head and continued walking. "Just that he's missing."

"Well, hell's bells, Alexa, we all knew that much." He shook his head and began to move forward again. "That was just an excuse to see you again."

"Really, Quentin, he was old enough to be my…" She swallowed as an image of how dashing and handsome Caleb looked in his gray coat and hat came to mind. "My father."

"You're lucky he didn't try to press his advantage."

"Advantage? Over a woman with sharp medical instruments at hand? Quentin, you underestimate me."

He grinned. "I guess that's a good reminder for me to remember myself."

"It is."

They continued on in silence, though as every step brought her closer to home, Alexa wondered just who had seen her with Caleb—and how much they had seen.

Ten

Night had stretched into the wee hours of morning by the time Alexa made her way to the fruit cellar. She'd had a bite to eat and taken time to wash her hair and freshen up with a sponge bath. How strange that such a small thing as bathing now seemed like a luxury.

Despite her efforts to be as quiet as possible, the faint light from her candle showed Caleb leaning up on his elbows. "Did I wake you?"

"I wasn't asleep."

She made her way toward him in the semi-darkness and held out the cup she'd brought with her. "This might help."

He shook his head. "No more laudanum. I can tolerate the pain."

She pressed it into his hand. "It's warm milk with honey and whiskey. Grammy Winters' special recipe."

He took it from her, and in the dim light, she saw him sniff and a smile cross his lips before he took a sip.

"My nursemaid, Mimsy, used to make this for us when we were children. To help us sleep."

Alexa shook out the blanket she'd left on the table the last time she'd slept in the cellar and spread it on the floor. "Grammy always did, too."

He took another sip, watching her movements. "You're not sleeping down there tonight."

She didn't miss the authoritative tone of voice, as if

he were giving an order to a soldier. "Oh?"

"I won't allow it." He threw the covers aside. "If anyone is sleeping on the floor, it will be me."

"Don't be ridiculous, you couldn't get down here let alone get back up."

"I'm willing to try if that's what it takes."

"Fine. I'll sleep on the table then. Just pray I don't roll off in my sleep." She grabbed up the blanket and stalked off.

"I don't need to be coddled or watched over, Alexa. You can sleep in your own bed."

She smoothed the blanket on the table. "Grammy and Felicity are using it at the moment. The rest of the house is filled to overflowing, as you know. Sleeping down here isn't simply to keep an eye on you; it's the only place left."

"There's no reason we can't share the cot."

She whirled to face him, though the candle didn't illuminate the room enough for her to see if he were jesting. "I think the whiskey has gone to your head."

"I confess to feeling a bit lightheaded, but it's not the liquor talking. I give you my word as a gentleman that you'd be as safe as a babe in her mother's arms."

"It wouldn't be proper."

He chuckled, the sound washing over her senses and sending a languid warmth through her. "After that bath yesterday, we're a long way past proper."

Her cheeks burned, and she was grateful for the dim light. "I'm fine sleeping on the table."

"I'm not. You looked exhausted the last time I saw you. I can't begin to repay you for saving my life, or risking your own by hiding me here. At least let me offer you a good night's sleep."

"Caleb—" She moved back toward him, intent on tucking the blankets around him and ending the conversation.

"It's not up for discussion." He reached for her hand. "I'm older than you, and I'm fairly certain I outrank you, so consider it an order."

She couldn't help a soft laugh. "Do you miss having men to order around, McKenna?"

Despite her reluctance, the thought of sleeping on a soft, giving surface, even if she only had a tiny portion of it, was far more appealing than she'd care to admit.

Before she could change her mind, his fingers grasped hers and pulled her onto the cot as he scooted closer to the wall. She took care to tuck the blankets around him before lying beside him atop the blankets. "Are you sure this will work?"

"I've slept in places far more cramped than this."

"I don't want to put pressure on your wound."

He raised an arm over his head to make room for her to lie beside him. "My wound is fine. Stop being a doctor and just be an exhausted woman who needs rest."

Beside him, she held herself rigid, determined to maintain some distance between them, however slight. He gently pressed her head toward his chest.

"Rest your head on me or we won't fit side by side. I assure you, I won't fool myself into thinking you're...what was it? *Besotted with affection?*—for me."

Her face heated at his gentle teasing, while at the same time the warmth of his body surrounded her, lulling her into relaxation.

His cheek brushed the top of her head. "Your hair is damp."

"I washed it when I got back tonight."

He inhaled deeply. "You always smell like lilacs."

She smiled and nestled more comfortably into his shoulder. It seemed like another lifetime ago that she'd ground dried flowers and herbs into a powder to scent her soaps. It also seemed like a foolish pastime now.

"Where were you tonight?"

"To visit a girl I know from town. Her sister was killed in the crossfire of the battle. Then I went to the hospital set up by the Sanitary Commission to check on a few of my patients that have been moved there, and to bring my father some dinner."

"You take care of everyone." Sleep slurred his voice. "Who takes care of you, Alexa?"

"I don't need anyone to take care of me."

His arm came around her to squeeze her closer. "That's where you're wrong."

An image of her former husband came to mind, taunting her. "I made that mistake once. I'm happier this way."

"Your husband?"

She nodded, surprised when tears stung her eyes. She thought she'd cried all the tears she had for him; she must be more tired than she realized.

"Why did you leave him?"

She yawned, surprised to be growing tired so soon. "I married too fast—before I realized he wasn't the person I thought he was. By the time I knew, it was too late." Memories she didn't often allow herself to dwell on intruded, and she forced them aside. "I didn't know how to back out of the wedding, I thought I just had cold feet, and it would go away once we were married. But the minute he put that ring on my finger, I felt…"

Her mind went blank as she searched for the right word to describe how she'd felt.

"Trapped."

She raised her head to look at him, though she couldn't actually see him in the dark. "Yes. How did you know?"

A sigh escaped him. "Just a lucky guess." He yawned. "Is he from Adams County?"

"No. I met him when I went away to school. He's a doctor, too."

"I see."

"We were students together. He seemed to admire my determination to become a physician, and appreciated my independent nature. But in the end, we just couldn't overcome our differences."

"I'm sorry." He gently stroked her arm, and instead of pulling away from the sensation, she allowed it to relax her.

"It's for the best." She shrugged. "I was miserable. Homesick for Adams County and my family. And though I'd begun my own practice with my husband, most patients weren't accepting of a woman doctor; they'd die—literally—before seeing me if he wasn't available. I spent all my time looking after a house, cooking meals, assisting at the occasional birth."

"You wouldn't have gone to medical school if you'd wanted to do those things."

"No." The soothing touch of his hands lulled her closer to the edge of sleep, and she yawned. "I shouldn't be telling you any of this."

"Why not?"

"It just doesn't seem that I should."

"Well, as I said, we're quite a ways past proper, so

I don't see the harm in it. We're not strangers. In another time and place we might even be…"

The possibilities of his suggestion flashed through her mind. "What?"

"Lovers."

She shifted on an elbow, attempting to rise, but he held her firmly in place. "Don't get your feathers ruffled, Alexa. I merely said we *might* be. If circumstances were different."

Already missing the comfort she'd found in his arms and the lure of sleep calling to her, she rested her head down again. "As long as you realize that's never going to happen, Caleb."

His deep chuckle rumbled beneath her ear. "I'm in no condition to try and change your mind."

"I suppose not."

She yawned again and gave in to the siren call of slumber. As she drifted off, she felt his cheek rub against her hair.

"Sleep well, sweet Alexa."

****

Light filtering around the doors and the muffled song of morning birds had declared the dawn quite some time ago, but Caleb was reluctant to wake Alexa. Oh, she'd be mad as a wet hen when she finally woke, but he took comfort in having given her several hours of rest, probably the first she'd had since the Confederate army had invaded her little town.

He stared down at her, admiring the sweep of dark lashes against her ivory skin, the gentle parting of her pink lips. Her hand rested just inside the opening of his shirt. He enjoyed the feel of her fingers nestled in the hair on his chest, the warmth of her touch.

Waking beside her made the dark little cellar feel less like a prison. Even if his hip throbbed like hell from the pressure of her body so close all night, he didn't care. He wouldn't mind waking like this every morning.

Well, not quite like this. His cock stood stiff and erect beneath the blankets, hungry as always upon awakening, ravenous from having been denied pleasure far too long. Alexa had that affect on him. But if he wanted her to sleep beside him again, he couldn't give in to the pure lust surging through his veins.

As if she sensed his struggle, her eyelids fluttered open. She stared at the brick wall for a moment, frowning, before looking up at him.

"Good morning."

She shifted, stared at the hand on his chest as though it belonged to someone else and snatched it away as though she'd touched hot coals. "What time is it?"

He reached for the table beside the cot, where his pocket watch lay. The movement brought their bodies in close contact and he purposely took his time with the device. "Six-thirty."

"No. Oh no." She sat up, her hair falling loose about her shoulders. "Grammy will be looking for me."

"Does she know you came back from the hospital?"

"She was asleep when I got home."

"Then she'll think you slept there." He pulled the blankets back to help her untangle herself, and she swung her feet to the floor.

"What are you trying to say, McKenna?"

"That you don't have to rush off."

"The longer I stay, the harder it will be to sneak out of here unseen." She pushed her hair back from her face, glancing from the cot to the floor and back again. "I had something in my hair last night, a ribbon to keep the ends tied."

The ribbon was the least of his worries. "I don't like you taking risks because of me."

"That can't be avoided right now."

She glanced down and resumed her frantic searching, but he couldn't take his eyes from her. With her dark hair falling about her face in carefree waves, she was more beautiful than ever.

A scrap of dark green silk on the blanket caught his eye. He wordlessly offered it to her, watching as she gathered the dark strands back with her fingers.

"Sit," he said. "I can do that for you."

"My hair?"

He nodded. Hesitantly, she sank to the floor, and he pulled her hair back, dividing it into three even sections. "I have younger sisters, you know."

"And you braid their hair?"

He chuckled at her amused tone. "I've done it once or twice. My youngest sisters were always getting into mischief—usually by following me around where they shouldn't. More than once I had to help clean one of them up and fix her hair so she looked like a young lady before Mimsy or Mother saw her."

Alexa half-turned to glance at him over her shoulder. "You must miss your family."

"Every day. Especially now when I have little else to do but think." He tied off the end with the ribbon. "Not perfect, but better than you could do without a comb, I'll bet."

She smiled and checked the braid with her fingers before rising to her feet. "I think you may be right. I'll have Felicity bring you some breakfast and something to read, I have to check my patients."

He wanted to ask if she'd come back tonight, but how could he ask her to sleep beside him again without it seeming like a suggestive invitation?

Before he could think of a way, she'd run up the steps, pushed the doors open and slipped out.

****

Caleb wasn't sure what woke him. He lay there in the darkness, straining to hear.

There it was again. A soft, almost barely audible sound—sniffling? He didn't have to see her to sense Alexa's presence. He'd stayed awake for as long as he could, hoping she'd join him as she had last night, but she hadn't come. But he must have dozed off since he hadn't heard her open the doors.

"Alexa?"

Another sniffle, though muffled as if she didn't want anyone to hear. "Yes."

"You're not planning to sleep on the floor again, are you?"

"No. I—I'm not thinking about sleep right now. I need to check your lungs."

"*Now?*" He sensed an urgency in her voice, enough to pull himself to a seated position and light the candle at his bedside. He picked up his pocket watch and flipped it open. "It's one in the morning."

She came toward the bed, her expression drawn and tired, her nose red even in the candlelight.

"You've been crying."

"It's nothing." She dropped to her knees and

reached for the edge of the blanket.

He placed his hand on hers, ceasing her motions. Was she planning to move him? Hide him somehow? Or had the Federal army discovered his presence and ordered her to turn him over? "What's happened?"

"Nothing, please just let me check your wound and listen to your lungs."

"If it's that important to you." He tugged the blanket back, exposing his hip to her view. She held the lamp close, examining the healing wound with gentle fingers. "Do you feel all right?"

"As well as expected. Why the concern for my welfare at this hour, Alexa?"

"I'm just being thorough. I need to listen to your breathing, Caleb. Would you please remove your shirt?"

She rose from the floor and crossed the room while he swept the nightshirt over his head. Shadows hid her actions, but when she returned, her stethoscope was around her neck. She stood beside him and pressed the cold metal to his back.

"Just breathe normally."

The scent of lilacs and her own uniquely female scent teased his nostrils, making normal breathing nearly impossible. After several moments, she moved to sit beside him on the cot, this time pressing the instrument to his chest.

He studied her face while she listened. Her gaze was focused, intent on her task. She finished and removed the device, leaving it to dangle about her neck. "Would you hand me that lamp, please, so I can examine your chest wound?"

He reached for it, and held it while her fingers

gently explored. He had no idea how long ago she'd removed the shrapnel and stitched him, but it seemed a lifetime had passed since then.

"I lanced this when you were still unconscious. It had become infected. Does it hurt?"

"Not enough to notice." He took up her hand and pressed it against his chest while he set the lamp back on the table. "What's happened, Alexa?"

Her breath hitched. She tugged at her hand, but he raised it to brush his lips over her fingertips. Her gaze flew to his face, her eyes dark with emotion.

She pulled at her hand again, but he held tight. "Your touch is soothing," he explained, pressing their clasped hands to his chest. "I'm alone down here all day and night with very little company, I miss simple human contact." *Especially yours*. He gave her hand a slight squeeze. "Now, are you going to tell me what has you so troubled?"

Her eyes welled, and she swallowed. She looked away for several seconds before facing him again, and he remembered her reluctance to cry in front of him once before.

"I lost a patient."

He'd assumed as much. "Someone you cared about?"

"Not in a romantic sense, no." She drew in a shuddering breath. "Just a young soldier from a Maine regiment. He was transferred to one of the hospitals and was doing much better. Until this morning."

He kept a tight hold on her hand. "Go on."

"He started with a cough and a fever and grew worse throughout the day."

At her next tug, he reluctantly released her hand.

"You've lost patients before. Was there something special about this one?"

She rose and crossed the room. Another sniffle, and in the shadows, he watched her lift a pitcher and fill two cups. "No, not really, he was just…young. Sweet. Eager to go home." She returned to his side and held out one of the cups. "Milk with whiskey and honey. I made enough for two tonight."

He accepted the cup, and she slid down to sit on the dirt floor, leaning back against the cot.

"He was looking forward to getting well enough to go home and marry his sweetheart." She raised the cup to her lips and sipped.

He did the same, savoring the familiar taste, the warmth of the alcohol as it warmed his throat.

"I know he wrote several letters to her with the help of the nurses, but now that he's gone I'd like to write her myself and let her know what happened. I just don't know what to say."

"I've written many such letters, Alexa, I'd be glad to offer my assistance."

She glanced at him over her shoulder. "Thank you."

"Keeping in mind that the letter will probably be saved and passed down through generations to come helps a great deal. No matter the manner of death, it's important his loved ones know he died a hero."

"Did you write to Simon's wife?"

"I did." He swallowed past a sudden thickening in his throat. "If any man ever died a hero, it was most certainly him."

"Yes." She raised the cup to her lips again, and they drank in silence for several minutes. At last, she rose to her feet and set her empty cup on the table at his bedside. "Do you mind if I sleep down here again tonight?"

He inched closer to the wall and patted the spot beside him. "Not at all."

She shook her head. "No, no. I won't do that again. It's not—"

"Proper. We discussed that already. It's no less proper to do it again."

"I don't know that it's wise."

"Why?"

"You're naked, for one thing."

He glanced down at his bare chest. "Only slightly more so than last time. And you still have my word as a gentleman that your virtue is safe."

"Caleb—"

He reached to take her hand and pull her toward him. "I'll stay tucked safely beneath the blankets. And if you'd like, I'll put the nightshirt on."

"It really should be washed." She sat on the edge of the cot. "I found some trousers I think will fit you, but until you're well enough to take them on and off easily when I need to examine you, it's probably best not to wear them."

He pulled her down beside him and tucked her head into his shoulder. "You prefer your male patients undressed from the waist down. I understand."

She gave him a playful swat.

"So, checking my wounds in the middle of the night, listening to my breathing. Are you concerned I'll get sick and die, too?"

"It's damp down here, and you aren't moving around much—pneumonia is always a risk." She tugged the blanket up over his chest before settling her hand there.

"You don't really think I just lie here all day long, do you?" Though he couldn't see her clearly in the darkness, he felt her gaze on him. "I stand for as long as I can, and walk as far as my body will allow."

"You shouldn't do that without someone here in case you fall."

He gave her shoulder a squeeze. "I'm too stubborn to fall. And I don't venture far from the cot or the chair."

"I didn't fight so hard to keep you alive to lose you now."

He pressed a kiss to her head, savoring the familiar scent of lilacs. "You aren't going to lose me anytime soon, Alexa."

Her fingers flexed on the blanket. "I just want you to get well enough to head south. Then I won't have you down here to distract me."

He couldn't help but chuckle. "Caring for me distracts you from your other duties?"

"No. Worrying about you does." She turned to face him. "Worrying someone will discover you. Or that you'll take a turn for the worse, and I won't be here."

He pressed his lips to her temple. "I'm sorry to cause you such worry, but I assure you I'm fine. Weak, sore, a bit shaky when I stand for too long. But otherwise fine."

She said nothing. For a moment, he thought the whisky had worked its magic, and she'd fallen asleep.

"It's more than that, Caleb." Her voice was barely a whisper. "You creep into my mind at the oddest times."

He nuzzled the top of her head with his cheek. "That's the whiskey talking. You'll hate yourself in the morning for telling me that."

She shook her head, a movement he felt rather than saw.

The hand that had been stubbornly atop the blanket moved, and he felt her fingers on his bare skin. Heat rushed through him, and he steeled himself to believe her touch was purely accidental.

Her fingertips grazed his nipple as they explored his chest and coherent thought was difficult as his aching erection pressed against the scratchy wool blanket.

"Alexa, you're making it very difficult for me not to kiss you."

She shifted up on an elbow, her hand still on his chest. "Then I'll kiss you."

He slipped a hand to the nape of her neck, holding her in place. "I vowed to be a gentleman."

"Yes, but I didn't."

She leaned over him, her breasts pressing against his chest, bringing an involuntary groan from him. Her lips brushed his, soft, hesitant. Oh this would be no tentative kiss, not if he had anything to say about it. He moved his hand to the back of her head, holding her in place when she would have moved away. He urged her lips to part and let him inside, tasting the whiskey that lingered on her tongue. The effect of the liquor was even more intoxicating this way.

Her fingers mindlessly stroked his nipple, which had grown taut and sensitive beneath her touch.

She lay half atop him on the small confines of the cot, and though pain throbbed in his hip, it was nothing compared to the pain throbbing elsewhere. He shifted her, slid her atop him. The movement caused a pleasant friction across his aching manhood and dragged a moan of pleasure from her. Rather than allow her to linger there, where he'd surely lose his head and come like an inexperienced boy, he shifted her closer to the wall, so he could lie on his uninjured left side.

She didn't protest, merely wrapped her arms about his neck and kissed him with the same fevered desperation he felt.

Unwilling to go another moment without tasting her sweet skin, he nuzzled her neck, stroked the hollow behind her earlobe with his tongue.

She moaned as he filled his palm with her breast and thumbed the delicate bud, enjoying the bittersweet torture of touching her, the moans and sighs that came from deep in her throat.

Her fingers curled into the hair at his nape and she arched toward him. "We shouldn't be doing this."

"We're not doing anything wrong," he whispered against her neck.

"Your fiancée—"

He leaned up on an elbow to peer down into her face. "Our parents are friends. We were promised to each other before we were even born. I have great fondness for Melody, but I don't love her. I never have."

As he spoke, he unfastened the buttons down the front of her blouse, fingers skimming the swells beneath.

"Then why…"

"Shhh…" He bent to nuzzle the skin he had bared. A shiver moved through her. He dragged his lips across her collarbone, trailing openmouthed kisses over her skin, tugging the material down her shoulders, pulling it lower until he freed one breast. He shuddered when her bare flesh filled his hand, and he bent to taste the sweet bud, circling the rosy nipple with his tongue, drawing it between his lips.

Alexa cried out, her fingers threading into his hair. Soft moans and sighs filled his ears until he could focus on nothing but pleasuring her.

She slid a hand down his bare back, and somewhere in the dim recess of his mind, Caleb realized he'd lost the blanket when he'd rolled over. Her hand continued down his spine to slide over his buttocks.

He lifted his head from her breast and met her gaze in the darkness. "I want you, Alexa. God knows I've never wanted anyone more. But not like this. Not with so much unspoken between us."

"What is there that needs to be said?"

She squeezed his buttocks with one hand, urging him closer, her body arching against him in invitation. The scratchy wool blanket bunched around his cock while she writhed against him, and he wished he wasn't such a gentleman.

He rolled away, giving her room to come to her senses. "That even though I don't love Melody—and don't for a moment believe she loves me—I'm obligated to marry her."

Silence. Never a good thing from a woman.

Blast the damn darkness, he couldn't see her, but felt her gaze on him, sensed the anger directed at him.

He cleared his throat, feeling the need to break the silence. "I asked her formally. We even had a date set.

151

And then the war began. And I asked her to wait. And then one of her brothers died in battle, so we waited again. Then my brother died. I've left her to wait all this time. If I don't marry her, it will bring dishonor and shame to both our families."

"Let me up."

"Alexa, listen to me."

"I've heard enough, let me up."

He didn't move.

With an exasperated sigh, she crawled to the end of the cot and climbed off. "I don't know what I was thinking."

He sighed again. "We *weren't* thinking. That's why we had to stop before—" He raked a hand through his hair. "I'm sorry if I led you to believe…"

She let out a huff of indignation. "I'm old enough to know that kisses aren't marriage proposals, Caleb." She moved away and the lamp on the table in the center of the room was turned up, casting a dim glow. "When my marriage grew sour, my husband thought nothing of turning to other women." She began to button her shirt with shaky hands. "When I confronted him, he invited me to do the same—he said an open marriage was our best chance at happiness." With angry motions she tucked her shirt and adjusted her clothes. "I was never unfaithful to him, but I knew of several women in town he was involved with. I won't do to another woman what was done to me."

"Alexa, wait."

"I'll be back to check on you tomorrow."

Caleb swung his feet toward the floor, wrapped the blanket around his waist and carefully rose to his feet.

He'd never felt more helpless, more damn

frustrated by his injury than he did while watching her stalk toward the doors.

"Dammit, Alexa, would you let me expl—"

"Good night, McKenna."

Eleven

Alexa lay on her back, staring up at the ceiling in the darkness. For the first time in nearly a week she chose not to sleep at the hospital, but in her own bed. Felicity snored softly beside her, and the added warmth of her slight form in the stuffy room made sleep impossible.

Why hadn't it been hard to sleep beside Caleb?

Avoiding him the past several days had been easy, she simply sent Grammy to check on him each morning, and Felicity took down his dinner and spent time reading or playing checkers with him each evening.

Avoiding thinking about him, however, was far more difficult. Every time she closed her eyes, he was there. The memory of his kisses beneath the willow tree were nothing compared to the memory of his tongue circling her nipple.

A moan escaped her as heat flared into her belly and spread lower, leaving an uncomfortable ache between her legs.

Lovemaking had never felt like that with Percival.

Beside her, Felicity sat up and considered her with sleepy eyes.

Much to her surprise, the girl suddenly embraced her. "You're home!"

She laughed and returned the hug. "I've been here;

you were just asleep at the time."

"I missed you, Alexa. I love Grammy, and Uncle Edwin is wonderful, but when you're here, I feel like I have the big sister I always wanted."

Alexa swallowed. Guilt stabbed at her. She hadn't considered Felicity's need for female companionship. The poor girl hadn't asked to spend her summer caring for wounded men.

"I'm sorry. I've been occupied elsewhere."

"Is that why you haven't been down to visit Caleb?" Felicity climbed from the bed and hurried across the room to where her dress hung on a door. She took a folded piece of writing paper from the pocket and offered it to Alexa. "He said to give you this."

Alexa unfolded the paper and glanced at the contents.

…slipped the bonds of this earth to gaze upon the face of his Creator…

She frowned. It was the letter he'd promised to help her write.

"We've written a lot of letters this week. To his family, to his fiancée, his friend." Alexa continued to stare at the words on the page.

…though he died not on the battlefield, but in battle for his life, his sacrifice is no less honorable…

She could never have come up with anything so eloquent, yet it somehow seemed typical of Caleb to take ordinary words and make them anything but.

At the bottom was a note she assumed was for her.

If you won't come to me, I'll come to you.

C.

Alarm skittered through her, and she turned to Felicity. "When did he give you this?"

"The day before yesterday. I think he's really sorry about whatever you two quarreled over."

"He said we argued?"

Felicity crawled onto the bed and curled her legs beneath her. "He said you had a misunderstanding." She flopped onto the pillows, a dreamy expression on her face. "What did he do? I'll bet he tried to steal a kiss, didn't he? He's *so* handsome. Don't you think he's handsome, Alexa?"

She glanced back down at the letter. "Umm... I can't say that I've noticed."

A purely feminine giggle escaped her cousin, and she sat up again, brown curls bouncing, eyes shining. "How could you not?"

"I'm beginning to suspect you're spending entirely too much time with him, Felicity."

Another laugh. "Silly Alexa, I could spend a hundred years with him and it wouldn't matter. He's in love with *you*."

Her breath hitched. If only that were true. His feelings for her were of a physical nature, nothing more. "Don't be a ninny, Felicity. He has a fiancée."

"Yes, but he's not married yet."

Alexa sighed and rose from the bed, wondering what Caleb meant by threatening to come to her. Was he pushing himself to walk when his body wasn't fully healed yet? What if he became dizzy and fell? "Well, if he's so wonderful, perhaps you should marry him." She dipped her hands in the water basin and rubbed them over her face.

"I can't marry Caleb. I'm going to marry Captain Carter."

Alexa froze in place, water dripping from her face

back into the bowl. Had Will been inappropriate with Felicity? She reached behind her for a towel to blot her face before straightening. "I beg your pardon, young lady?"

Her cousin rolled her eyes and another laugh bubbled forth. "Oh he hasn't asked me, and he doesn't know it yet. He still thinks of me as a little girl. But one day I'm going to marry Will Carter."

****

Juggling shaving supplies and wash water, Alexa glanced around to make sure no one was about, then nodded for Felicity to open the doors to the fruit cellar. She stepped inside, and the doors closed behind her with a soft thunk. It took several seconds for her eyes to adjust to the change in light, and she squeezed them tightly shut to help things along.

"Hello, Alexa."

Her stomach catapulted at the sound of that deep voice saying her name as only he could, vowels so soft as to be liquid, the first letter of her name rolling into the second. She opened her eyes to make out the shape of him, seated in a chair he'd pulled up to the table, writing paper in front of him.

The sound of the chair scraping back sent alarm skittering through her. "Don't get up." Blast the man for not abandoning such formalities even when injured. "How did you get from the cot to the table?"

"I wouldn't call it walking, but it's a close description."

She mentally calculated the distance. How had he managed it alone? "You didn't tear your stitches…"

"No."

Relief washed over her. It was nearly time to

remove them, the last thing she needed was for him to rupture them. Realizing she had yet to move, she forced her feet forward and set her things on one end of the table.

"What brings you here this morning?"

He sounded as though he were greeting a neighbor, rather than a woman he had nearly made love to when last he'd seen her.

"I wanted to check on you."

He didn't glance up from the paper in front of him or set the pen aside. "I see."

She arranged her supplies on the table, the cup of shaving foam, razor, wash cloth and soap. "I've been very busy…"

"I'm well aware why you stayed away."

Her cheeks burned. "I saw the letter. It's…far more eloquent than anything I could have come up with. Thank you for doing that."

"You're quite welcome."

God she hated this tension between them, the stiffness in his voice. "I…saw your note. I wondered how you'd manage to come and see me, but now…"

He glanced up. The faint light from the lamp on the table illuminated his maple hair and flawless face. Oh how she longed to press her fingertip to the cleft in his chin.

"I was beginning to think that was the only way I'd see you again."

"I meant to come. But I—"

"Staying away is childish, wouldn't you say?"

Annoyance prickled at her spine. She wasn't a child, and she wasn't under his command. "I needed time to think."

He pushed the paper aside and sat back in the chair. "Something I have far too much time for, I'm afraid."

"Are we cranky, McKenna? Restlessness and bad temper are among the first signs of healing. I've several soldiers upstairs who are irritable as well." *And one kind, sweet man whose affection I wish I could return. If it wasn't for you.*

He wiped his hands down his face, and God help her, her stomach somersaulted again at the sight of his long, lean fingers. "I'm merely frustrated with how long it's taking to heal. And weary of being held like a prisoner."

Apparently, if they weren't kissing and touching, they could only argue with one another. She gestured to the door. "Then by all means, head outside. But if the stench from the battlefield that comes in on the breeze doesn't sicken you, the annoying presence of some very well fed flies surely will. And if neither of those bother you, there's a strong Federal presence in town, any of whom would undoubtedly be delighted to find a Rebel officer in their midst."

Sympathy dawned in his twilight gaze. "I wasn't complaining, at least not about the care or the risks you're taking on my behalf." He sighed. "I take it the dead aren't buried yet, hence the stench and the flies?"

She strode to the opposite side of the room, feeling the need to put distance between them. "They're working on it. But every time it rains some of the more hastily dug graves wash away and the bodies are unearthed."

"I'm sorry you have to witness such gruesome sights."

"Everyone in town is angry and in ill temper at

how slow the army has been to clean up after itself. And every day more people arrive to seek the gravesite of their lost loved ones." She sank onto the cot, surprised at how weary she was so early in the day.

"I'm sure it's a recipe for disorder."

"You're actually quite lucky to be down here away from it."

A half-smile crossed his face. "I'll try to remember that."

"How are you feeling?"

"Stiff and sore. Frustrated with how long it's taking to heal, as I said, but better nonetheless."

"Good. There's a cane in my father's study, I think it will help you in moving about. I'll bring that to you tonight after dark. I'm not sure I could easily explain myself should anyone find me about to enter the fruit cellar with it."

Still gazing at her, he tipped his head. "Do you have an escape plan, Alexa?"

She yawned and stretched and rose to her feet. "Escape from what?"

"Should the Federal army question you about harboring Confederates."

Moving toward him, she picked up the brush and dipped it into the shave cup. "I have no intention of leaving others to shoulder the blame for my decisions. If it happens, I'll admit to nothing."

"And if my presence is discovered?" He allowed her to wrap a towel about his shoulders.

"McKenna, no one knows you're here. I think you're right—you have entirely too much time alone down here to think."

"You mentioned a strong Federal presence in town.

I think you need to prepare for how to save yourself and your family in the event I'm discovered."

Pausing in the middle of applying the foam to his face, she met his gaze. "I already told you, I'm not going anywhere. And as for you, there's only one way out of here, Caleb, and it's through those doors, so if you're discovered..." She allowed the words to trail off.

"Then I'd like my revolver returned to me. I don't care for the idea of being a sitting duck, as it were. Surely you'll allow me some means of defending myself."

Alexa resumed spreading the foam across his cheeks, upper lip and chin. "You're not a prisoner here. I didn't take your revolver to keep you from leaving." She bent to rummage through the basket that held her medical supplies. "Here." She set the heavy gun on the table beside him. "It didn't occur to me that you'd need it before you were well enough to leave. Now, you may shoot your way out to your heart's content."

"I have no intention of shooting anyone, but I prefer not to be taken without a fight, should it come to that."

"Of course. Shoot—get yourself shot—whatever you please. But I won't be able to help you if you get injured while being captured."

He reached to pick up the gun, checking the chamber in an action that seemed more automatic than curious. "I don't intend to be taken alive."

She shook off the image of him blood-soaked and half dead just a few weeks ago. A momentary panic strangled her at the though of it happening again. Dear God, what if Will or Quentin or any of the men upstairs discovered him? Forcing the thought aside, she let out a small huff of annoyance lest he realize how his bold statement truly affected her. "Then you'd better hope you don't get taken at all, so I won't have wasted my time saving you only to see you killed."

"I'll keep that in mind." A slight grin crossed his face. "Ahh, Alexa, you *do* care."

Ignoring the playful twinkle in his blue eyes, she leaned in to continue shaving. "Be still so I don't miss and slit your throat."

****

The afternoon wore on with a visit from Father who was still working with the wounded at the hospital, but after a change of clothes and a bite to eat, he left to return to his duties.

Alexa had just finished with a recuperating soldier and sent Felicity to help Grammy with the breakfast dishes from feeding more than a dozen men when she answered a knock at the front door.

"Samuel," she said, recognizing one of the free colored men who lived in town. "How is Mrs. Butler?" During the earliest days of the Rebel occupation, Samuel's wife, Old Liz, had been taken captive by the Confederates to be sold back into slavery. But she'd escaped her captors and returned home.

"Oh, she's feelin' fine, Miz Alexa," he replied, giving a slight bow. "Ma'am, some of the men in town are helpin' the Federal army with buryin' the bodies that been gettin' washed out by all the rain."

"Is someone hurt?" She held the door open wider. "Please, come in so I can take a look at you."

"Oh no, ma'am, I ain't hurt. But one of the boys was helpin' to bury some Confederate fellow and noticed an envelope in his coat. He cain't read none, so he brung it to my shop." He held out a tattered, mud splattered envelope to her. "The ink is smeared like it got wet, but that look like your name on the envelope."

Though she didn't recognize the handwriting, it certainly seemed to be her name and town. Chill bumps broke out along her skin. "It...it might be from my brother."

"I hope so, ma'am." He nodded his head. "Maybe that poor fellow knew your brother and was bringing you good news."

She reached out to impulsively squeeze his hand. "Samuel, thank you for going out of your way to bring this to me. Please come in and let me get you something to eat."

"Thank you, ma'am, but I'd best get back to the wagon shop."

"All right then." She watched him walk away, then stared at the envelope again. The handwriting looked feminine. Was it possible that Nate, much like Caleb, had been injured and was being cared for by a woman in the south? She and Felicity had written many such letters for soldiers in recent weeks.

A frightening thought struck her. They'd written other letters, too, letters of sympathy and condolence. What if...

"Did I hear the door?" Grammy asked.

She turned to her grandmother. If possible, Grammy had aged these past couple of weeks, the exhaustion of caring for dozens of wounded men taking its toll. Worry nagged at Alexa's heart. If there was bad news in the envelope, she'd tell it when she knew for sure.

She slipped her hand behind her back, and tucked

the envelope into the rear pocket of her trousers. "Oh, just a neighbor, checking to see if we needed anything." She placed an arm around Grammy's stooped shoulders and pressed a kiss to her wrinkled cheek. "Let me pour you a cup of coffee. You look exhausted."

Good or bad, the news would have to wait.

Twelve

Day crept forward into evening. More than once, Alexa was tempted to find a quiet place to read the letter she hoped held news about Nate.

Each and every time, however, she was distracted either by someone needing her assistance or the thought that once she opened the envelope, there would be no turning back. And she wasn't sure she could manage to care for the men relying on her if she were upset by bad news.

Not that it was going to be *bad* news. Nate was alive. He had to be. If he weren't, she'd feel it somehow. They were too close.

"You're not yourself today, Doctor Alexa," Will Carter commented when she'd finished wrapping his ribs. "It's like you're a million miles from here."

Caught gathering wool, Alexa offered him a reassuring smile. "I suppose I am a little distracted. Just a lot on my mind."

"Must be hard for you, caring for all of us plus them at the hospitals around town. A body needs rest now and again."

His concern touched her, and the warmth in his hound dog gaze didn't go unnoticed. Ever since Caleb had referred to Will as her admirer, she'd been aware of the way his gaze sought her across the room, or how he went out of his way to ask about her day or how she felt. Most of her patients talked of home or their injuries. Not Will, he was genuinely interested in her. With all her heart, she wished she felt something for him besides simple affection.

"You'll be on your way home in no time, Will."

"I'd rather go back to fighting."

She wasn't sure that would ever happen. "Let's see how that shoulder is healing. Raise your right arm for me."

He did as she asked, but only managed to get the arm about half as high as he should. "Are you exercising it every day like I showed you? Pushing beyond where it's comfortable every time?"

"Yes, ma'am. Every day for as long as I can stand it and then some more."

"You'll get there, Will." She gave him an encouraging pat on the arm. "Just keep trying."

"Doctor Alexa, do you…" He paused and his ears turned bright red.

A knot of dread coiled into her stomach. He seemed nervous, so whatever he was about to ask was probably personal.

"Yes?" She made a show of checking that the bindings about his ribs were secure.

"I know you're busy, and you got lots to do but… Well, it's like I said, a body's gotta rest now and then. You got time to sit and have a cup of coffee with me out on the porch?"

Her jaw went slack. She didn't have time. She hadn't had time for the luxury of a social visit since war had come to Gettysburg. But just as he was right that she needed to rest now and then, he needed the distraction from his injuries as well. And she could certainly use something to take her mind off that letter. "That would be lovely, Will."

His eyes brightened, and a broad smile broke out across his face. "You go out there and sit, I'll get the coffee. Your Grammy's been letting me help out here and there, and I've come to know my way around the kitchen pretty well."

Surprised and pleased by his offer, she headed to the porch. Wounded men no longer littered the house and yard, but blood stained the floor and steps. Taking a seat in Grammy's favorite wooden rocker, she glanced upward, the hole in the porch ceiling reminding her of Caleb standing on her porch just a couple of weeks back. She couldn't help but smile at the memory of him, so handsome in his uniform, hat and shoulders covered in woodchips and white wash, looking angry enough to wring her neck.

The door whined on its hinges and the aroma of hot coffee wafted toward her.

"See now? You're smilin' already, Doctor Alexa. The break is doing you some good after all."

A flush of remorse came over her.

He took a seat in the rocker beside hers and handed her the coffee. "Extra cream, and a little sugar, just the way you like it."

She smiled. "You notice everything."

"Nah, your Grammy told me," he admitted with a sheepish grin.

The friendly chirp of a cardinal calling its mate echoed on the early evening air, and she closed her eyes, enjoying the gentle breeze. Today it seemed the wind was their friend, carrying the rancid stench from the battlefield away from town, rather than toward them.

"Do you have family near here, Will?" she asked, realizing she knew very little about him.

"No, ma'am," he said. "Well, I got a sister in Bethlehem, she's married and has kids. But my folks have passed on." He took a sip of the coffee and swallowed. "I wasn't home to see 'em before they passed, what with the war and all."

"I'm sorry."

"I appreciate that, Doctor Alexa."

"You don't have to keep calling me that, Will. Alexa is fine."

"Oh, that don't feel right," he said, his ears turning a deep pink. "I couldn't call you by your given name. It wouldn't be proper."

"We're a long ways past…" She frowned, recalling where she'd heard those exact words before and darted a glance toward the fruit cellar. Guilt stabbed at her. Caleb should be out here enjoying this lovely summer evening instead of locked up. Perhaps the cane she'd mentioned would make it possible for him to come outside now and again after dark.

Sensing Will's questioning look, she forced a smile. "Past that," she said, realizing she'd never finished her sentence. "With all we've been through, it seems I've known you forever."

"I know what you mean." He stopped rocking and leaned forward, elbows on his knees. "Miss Alexa, I know it probably seems sudden, but I'd like to keep company with you now and then while I'm here."

She could only stare at him. Had she misled him all these weeks? It wasn't uncommon for patients to develop emotional attachments to doctors; she'd seen it happen too often to dismiss it. He was so sweet, so kind…he was exactly the type of man she should want to come calling.

He shrugged, and she realized her silence made him uncomfortable. "I know you're divorced and all, your Grammy told me. Don't you worry about that, it don't bother me none."

Grammy told him, had she? The same Grammy who told him how she liked her coffee? The same Grammy who was apparently playing matchmaker?

"I …" She searched her mind for any possible reason to turn him down. Dare she agree to spend time with Will knowing Felicity had developed tender feelings? It didn't seem right, but as her cousin had already pointed out, she was far too young; Will barely noticed her.

Caleb came to mind again, the funny way he turned her stomach inside out and made her insides quiver with just a glance. Caleb…who frustrated and infuriated her. Caleb…who was bound and determined to marry a fiancée he didn't love out of a sense of duty and honor.

There was no future with him, no point in dwelling on the feelings he inspired.

"I'd like that." The words were out before she could stop them.

He smiled and brushed a hand across his brow. "Whew. You don't know how hard that was, Doc— *Miss* Alexa."

"Not at all, Will. I enjoy your company." She took a sip of the coffee, wincing as it burned her tongue. Perhaps more time spent in the company of a kind and gentle man like Will Carter would do her some good.

And rid her of the futile attraction to Caleb.

****

The watch on his bedside table read a little after midnight, and Alexa had yet to come see him. Caleb sighed and rose from the cot, hating that the one bright spot in his entire day was engaging in a battle of wits with the doctor. So much so that when she didn't come, the disappointment was keen.

He'd long missed the company of females during the long years at war. Visits to the upscale bordellos in Atlanta when home on leave had taken the edge off his physical needs, but Alexa's company provided both mental and physical stimulation. Whether it was the verbal sparring they engaged in or merely the physical attraction they both tried to ignore, he couldn't help feeling his spirits soar when she came through those doors.

Felicity had brought the cane Alexa promised, and he'd spent much of the evening practicing with it. He was still weak and tired more quickly than he'd like, but the cane meant he could get around more easily.

One door was pulled open, and for a moment, the heavenly smell of night air wafted through the stale little room. His heart lifted at the sight of Alexa coming down the steps.

Dressed in a night dress and wrapper, her hair was unbound and hung in dark velvety waves down her back. For a split second, his breath caught at the image of the ethereal beauty before him holding a pitcher and two cups. Like a school boy with his first crush, his heart leapt at the realization she had come to him.

"I thought I was being punished again."

"I couldn't get away earlier, Father was home for dinner. I had to wait until everyone was asleep." She set the cups down and filled two mugs. The familiar aroma of whiskey and milk met his nostrils. "I wasn't sure you'd be awake."

"Your company is worth a little lost sleep. I get entirely too much rest."

"I see you've made good use of the cane." She set one cup on the table near him and raised the other to her lips.

"It helps a great deal."

He couldn't help but smile at the sight of her small, feminine bare feet.

"I'd very much like to take you outside one of these nights, Caleb. I think the fresh air would do you some good."

It was the warmth of the sun he missed most, but he'd settle for moonlight if he had to. "I'd like that."

She took a seat at the table. "I wrote that letter tonight, the one you helped me with."

"Good." He sensed there was more on her mind and carefully made his way to the center of the room to join her, leaning heavily on the cane.

"It's much more sympathetic than what I'd have come up with on my own. And certainly more eloquent."

"Alexa, you're not here to talk about a letter. Why did you really come here tonight?" He lowered himself into the chair, hoping she didn't notice how stiffly he moved.

"To check on you, as I promised." She pulled an envelope from the pocket of her wrapper and handed it to him across the table. "And because of this. So you see, I really am here to talk about a letter."

Alexa's name and town written with a feminine

flourish of loops and curlicues crossed the front of the missive. Caleb glanced from the envelope to her worried expression.

"One of the men who is helping to re-bury the dead found it on the body of a Confederate soldier who'd come unearthed. I know no one in the south, Caleb, and this isn't Nate's handwriting."

"I see." He took a sip of the drink while she paced across the room.

"I want to open it, but…"

"You're afraid."

She whirled at that, as though admitting to fear was a weakness. Her shoulders slumped. "Yes. I pray it's good news, but if it isn't…"

As he watched her, she wrapped her arms protectively over herself. He'd never seen her so vulnerable.

"You don't want to read the letter in front of your grandmother or cousin, in case it's bad news."

"And I don't want to be alone when I read it." She crossed the room to stand before him, then dropped to her knees so they were more evenly matched for height. "In fact, I was hoping…Caleb, would you read it for me? If I have to hear bad news, I'd rather it came from you."

The pleading in her vibrant green eyes reminded him of the night she'd begged to care for the dying soldiers left on the battle field. It had been difficult to deny her then, but he'd reacted as an officer. As her friend—and much as it pained him to admit it, that was the true nature of their relationship—he could refuse her nothing.

Clearing his throat to rid the lump of emotion that

had lodged there, he tore open the letter. It was dated October 10, 1862. Well aware of Alexa's frantic gaze, he read it quickly to himself.

Dear Alexa,

A dear acquaintance is writing this letter for me, and if you receive it, I am gone from this world. I was injured in a battle outside of Richmond and this kind family has taken me in to care for me like I was one of their own. I lost a leg, but that doesn't bother me much. Now pneumonia has settled in, and I'm weak like a newborn kitten.

Before I leave this world, little sister, I want to beg you not to blame yourself. You encouraged me to follow my belief in state's rights, and I know you well enough to guess you'll find a way to blame yourself for my passing. In the end, I made my own decision, I hope you'll remember that. Tell Pa I asked for his forgiveness. We said some pretty awful things to one another last time we spoke.

I sure wish Grammy was here with one of her smelly concoctions to smear on my chest or force down my throat. I know she'd kick this illness right out of me. Tell her I love her and she was the best grandmother a man could ask for.

I hope this letter finds its way to you, my sweet baby sister, and I hope it brings you peace to know I'm watching over you from a better place.

All I ask now, Alexa, is for you to be happy. Find a good man to love and have a whole passel of kids—preferably a boy or two with my good looks. And now and then, when you look toward the sky on a warm summer morning, look for me and know I'm looking back.

I hope you'll think of me often and remember me fondly.

Yours with great affection,

Nate.

Caleb forced his eyes to linger on the letter until he was sure he could face her. He wished she'd never asked him to read it, wished he had better news to give her. But one thing lacking in this damn war was good news.

He folded the letter and placed it back in the envelope. Clearing his throat, he forced his gaze to meet hers. "I'm truly sorry, Alexa."

He'd expected her to scream or cry, but instead her face remained impassive. Though emotion darkened her eyes, she said nothing.

"The letter is from your brother, written on his death bed."

She rose to her feet and folded her arms over her stomach, walking slowly across the room.

"It's a very heartfelt letter. Maybe reading it for yourself will help." With effort, he rose from the chair, leaning heavily on the cane.

"I...I will. Thank you. I should probably let you get some sleep."

She started toward the steps, but he blocked her path.

"Wh—what are you doing?"

"You aren't leaving this room until you talk to me."

"There's nothing to say. I feared the worst and it...happened."

"You don't have to bear this alone."

She pulled in a deep breath. "I won't be. At

daybreak I have to wake Grammy and find Father and tell them—"

Her voice wavered, and he breathed a small sigh of relief at the hint of emotion.

"Tell them what?" He wouldn't allow her to pretend it wasn't real. He'd seen men receive bad news from home and choose not to acknowledge it, only to lose their head over some minor upset weeks later. He couldn't let her slip into a state of denial.

"That Nate…that he isn't…"

She stepped around him, and he wasn't fast enough to stop her this time. She rushed up the steps, but stopped when she reached the top. Her shoulders slumped, and she put her face in her hands.

A lump of emotion wedged in his throat. "Alexa."

"How is it possible I've laughed or enjoyed the sun on my face when my brother has been dead for almost a year?" She turned to look at him. "How is it possible I went on living as though nothing had changed when Nate…"

"You couldn't have known."

"I *should* have." She came down one step, then another and abruptly sat.

He stepped slowly across the room. Pain throbbed in his right side, and his right leg trembled from standing so long, but the need to touch her, to hold her and offer what comfort he could propelled him.

She looked up as he approached. "You don't look well, McKenna. You shouldn't be on your feet."

"This isn't about me." Reaching her side, he bent to take her hand and lead her down the last step. He tugged her closer, slipping a hand to the small of her back. To hell with the trembling in his limbs. He'd had

175

to hold her to get her to cry the last time he'd comforted her, as well. "Dammit, Alexa. Let me hold you."

"No." The sound was a high pitched squeak. "Because if you do…"

Her cheek met his chest, and he wrapped his arms around her, pinning her in place. A strangled sob escaped her, and her arms came around him, hands splaying over his back.

"I…I don't know what to do."

"Hold onto me." He rubbed his cheek against the dark head at his shoulder. "That's all you have to do."

Another sob came followed by another until her entire body quivered with the force of her emotions. Her fingers curled into the material at his back, and she clung to him as if sapped of all her strength. Her grief brought to mind the anguish he'd felt at the loss of his father, and learning of his brother's death months after it had happened.

Caleb had no idea how long he held her, stroking her hair, whispering soothing nonsense, pressing comforting kisses to her hair and face until the storm passed. But at some point, her sobs became hiccoughs and the tears that soaked his shirtfront ceased until all that remained were sniffles and shakily drawn breaths.

"I've never felt so alone," she whispered.

"You're not alone, sweet Alexa." He flexed his arms, squeezing her a little tighter. "You're right here with me."

She made no attempt to pull away, and though sheer force of will was all that kept him upright, he couldn't release her. Long, silent moments passed, only the sound of an occasional sniffle from her interrupted the thudding of his heart in his ears. Burning pain seared him as nerve endings protested being disturbed and healing tissue pulled against stitches.

But there was something so vulnerable about her right now, so at odds with the confident, capable woman she showed the world. The need to protect her, comfort her, was more important than any pain. And truth be known, the warmth of her body against his after so many nights alone was too intoxicating to give up.

Thirteen

A loud rumble overhead stirred Alexa from sleep. She raised her head from the warmth of Caleb's chest and tried to focus in the pitch dark. How had they come to be on the floor of the fruit cellar? Her wrapper was draped over her legs to keep her warm, but she had only a distant memory of sliding down to rest on the floor.

A brilliant flash of light lit the edges of the doors and rain pelted them without mercy, bringing the smell of damp earth into the little room.

Caleb stirred and murmured. His arm, still around her waist, twitched as though he were reaching for something.

She felt his forehead for any sign of fever, relieved to find it cool. Thunder boomed again, and he called out something that sounded like an order. Perhaps in his dreams the thunder was cannon fire, rather than a summer storm. She gently shook his arm.

He stirred, and though she couldn't see his face in the dark, she sensed when he woke. "You were calling out in your sleep."

"I'm sorry, did I wake you?"

"No, the storm did." Light briefly lit the edges of the room enough for her to make out the white of his shirt and mussed hair. "I was worried you were having a bad dream."

"I don't have any other kind these days." He

shifted, and she moved to allow him to flex his arm. "Are you all right?"

"I'm fine, just worried how we'll get you up and about."

"We'll find a way, but not until morning. I'm comfortable enough."

"Me, too."

He readjusted his arm around her, and the warmth of it seeped through her nightgown at her back. Another crash that sounded as though the heavens had fallen from the sky rumbled outside.

"That's some storm."

Alexa swallowed, remembering how much Nate had liked thunderstorms. And rain. A shudder moved through her as the pain of his loss pierced her all over again.

"Are you cold?"

She shook her head, but realized he couldn't see the movement. "No."

"You're not afraid of a little thunder storm are you?"

"I used to be. When I was little. I would put my hands over my ears and hide my head in Nate's shoulder so I didn't have to see the flash and he…" Emotion clogged her throat, strangling any further words.

Caleb caught the tear that slipped past her lashes, smoothing it away with his thumb.

She pulled in a ragged breath. "He would hum so I didn't have to hear the booms." The floodgates opened and hot tears coursed down her cheeks. "I haven't thought of that in years, why would I think of it now?"

He gathered her closer. "Shh…"

She pressed her face to his chest. "I never got to say goodbye."

"Sweet, sweet Alexa. I'd give anything if you didn't have to go through this." He rocked her gently and stroked her hair. "I've lost my father, my brother and countless friends to this damn war. It never gets any easier."

More tears scorched her cheeks. And then…kisses. Gentle, soft kisses. In her hair, at her temple, her cheek. She raised her head to speak, and Caleb's lips briefly brushed hers. She couldn't breathe, couldn't form a coherent thought as his breath mingled with hers just a hairsbreadth from her mouth.

His fingertips stroked her jaw, leaving shivers in their wake. She didn't dare speak and break the spell that held them captive.

With a growl of defeat, he closed the slight distance between them. Warm, soft lips met hers with the assurance of a man well acquainted with her mouth. He urged her lips to part, and with a ragged sigh, she surrendered, knowing as she did, she tumbled headlong into the abyss.

Her body craved the warmth of his, and she sank against him as his tongue stroked hers. Her hands met his chest where the nightshirt lay open and her fingertips tangled in the soft hair. God she loved the feel of his chest, so hard and solid. She grazed his healing wound, slipped her fingers over it to check, only to have him take her hand and squeeze her fingers.

He slid one hand into her hair at the nape and pulled back just far enough to stare into her face. "Stop thinking like a doctor."

"I was just—"

"For God's sake, Alexa, not now."

He released her hand and continued his thorough exploration of her mouth. Her mind whirled with all the reasons why she couldn't allow this to continue. But her body craved more contact, and the nagging attraction that had been her constant companion for weeks thirsted for him.

She moved her hand down his stomach, guided by memory rather than sight of his flat abdomen and the strip of soft golden hair that led from his naval to a thick patch of dark curls. She brushed something hard and warm, and heard Caleb suck in a breath.

"I didn't realize…I'm so—" She swallowed. Men became aroused more easily than she realized.

"Don't ever apologize for causing that reaction. It's the only way I know I'm still alive."

His mouth, warm and moist, returned to the curve of her neck, his fingers sliding over her breast until he found her swollen, overly sensitive nipple.

"You can touch me, Alexa. I promise I won't turn into an ogre and demand to be sated."

His moist breath against her skin sent shivers through her, and without thought, she arched into his touch, offering her entire breast.

Hesitantly, she reached between them again, wanting to touch that mysterious part of him. Warm steel encased in velvet met her fingers.

He shuddered and sucked in another ragged breath.

Shyly, she explored the length of him with her fingertips. She'd never touched Percival like this, had never even seen him naked since they'd only made love in the dark. But she was well acquainted with the sight of Caleb's member, and now that it stood pleasingly erect, she wanted to familiarize herself with it.

Feeling bolder, she wrapped her hand around him. A moan tore from Caleb's throat.

He arched back, and she pulled her hand away. "I hurt you, didn't I?"

A shaky laugh escaped him. "Not a bit."

He found her mouth again, and as thunder continued to rumble in the distance, he unfastened the tiny row of buttons down the front of her nightdress. Damp night air met her bare skin and she shivered, both from chill and the thrill of anticipation. He bent his head, nuzzling her flesh. Fingertips grazed sensitive skin followed by the sweet, wet heat of his mouth on her nipple.

Shivers of pleasure shot through her, and for long moments, she couldn't move, could only feel.

"Alexa," he whispered. "I don't want this to—"

Instead of listening, she returned to her exploration of him, exploring every warm, silken inch from the rounded tip to the base, fascinated by the gasps and moans her touch elicited.

He sat up and shrugged out of the nightshirt, placing it on the floor behind her.

"What are you doing?"

With his body, he eased her down until she felt the warmth of the shirt beneath her.

"I won't have you lying on a dirt floor like an animal, but I'm in no shape to carry you to a softer place."

His hand stroked the length of her thigh, carrying her nightdress with it. He eased the material higher, past her hips. She ached with need, and though she'd never enjoyed her marriage bed, this was different, and she desperately wanted to feel the hard, thick length of him inside her.

A scraping at the doors, and a gust of wet night air shot into Alexa's senses. She jumped guiltily away at the same time Caleb straightened.

"Alexa?" came Felicity's frantic whisper. "Are you down here?"

She grabbed Caleb's nightshirt from the floor and threw it over his lap. Scrambling to her feet, she rushed to the table, putting as much distance between them as possible. "Y-yes. I'm here."

She turned her back to the doorway and buttoned her nightdress as fast as her trembling fingers would allow.

"I…I can't see." Felicity stepped inside and pulled the door closed behind her, plunging the room into pitch blackness again.

Relief flooded her.

"Can you light a lamp?"

"J-just a moment." There was no time to get Caleb to his feet, let alone abed. She hurried over to the cot, pulled a blanket from it and tossed it to him to cover himself with. She'd think of something to tell her cousin later.

"Were you sleeping?"

Felicity sounded concerned, and Alexa cursed herself for worrying the girl.

She fumbled on the table for the matches to light the lamp. "I…I was." At last she succeeded and a warm glow filled the area around her, though shadows kept Caleb more or less hidden.

The girl hurried down the steps. "I'm sorry, it's just—" Her gaze fastened on Alexa's bodice, and she frowned. "Quentin is here, demanding to see you."

Alarm prickled her skin. "Is he alone?"

"Yes. He's hurt. He shot himself somehow and wants you to take care of the wound." She glanced toward Caleb's bed, then back to Alexa. "He's been waiting for a while, I told him I didn't know where you were and didn't think you'd be walking home in this storm, but he's had some brandy for the pain, and he's getting a bit...insistent."

"He thinks I'm not at home?"

Felicity nodded.

"Oh, this is a fine kettle of fish. Where is he?"

"In the kitchen."

Alexa bit her lip. "I can't go in the front door to slip upstairs and dress without being seen, and I can't change clothes to make it look as though I was out if I go in through the kitchen in my night clothes."

"I can give him some more brandy. Maybe if he's drunk, he won't notice what you're wearing."

Alexa's jaw went slack. "I should scold you for being so devious, and yet, I've never been more proud of you."

Felicity smiled. She turned to leave and pulled up short at the sight of Caleb. "Why are you on the floor?"

He cleared his throat. "Your cousin thought it would be good for me."

Alexa's brows rose at how easily the lie rolled off his tongue.

"To sleep on the floor?" Felicity turned a confused gaze to Alexa. Her gaze once again fell to Alexa's buttons, and then back to Caleb.

She winced. "Felicity, I—"

"You might want to...straighten yourself up before

you come upstairs." She gestured toward the nightdress. "I'll go get that brandy. Good night, Caleb." She turned and rushed up the stairs as if the hounds of hell snapped at her heels.

As the door closed with a quick thunk, Alexa sank into a chair at the table. Sure enough, a glance down showed she'd missed a few buttons. She groaned. Now, not only would she have to tell Felicity about Nate's death, she'd have to find a way to explain why Caleb was on the floor and she was disheveled.

****

On the porch outside the kitchen, Alexa paused to pull in a calming breath and tried to quiet the thoughts racing about her mind. Caleb had tried to apologize for what had nearly happened between them. But she felt just as guilty—mortified at her behavior after so recently losing her brother. How could she ever face him again and yet...

Heat spilled into her stomach at the memory of what they'd nearly done, filling her with restless longing.

Forcing the unfamiliar feelings aside, she pulled open the door. Quentin sat at the table, his foot propped on a chair, a blood soaked rag wrapped around it. He turned a drowsy gaze in her direction as the door whined on its hinges. A half-empty glass of brandy sat before him, and she suppressed a smile to see Felicity's plan had worked.

"I didn't think you were ever comin', 'Lexa."

"What have you done, Quentin?"

He started to swing his leg off the chair. Instead, he grimaced and picked up the brandy again, taking a hearty gulp, not bothering to wipe the liquid that dribbled down his chin. "Shot m'self inna damn foot."

She walked around the chair and cautiously unwrapped the bloody rag and bent in to examine what remained of his two middle toes. "That's not very wise."

"I was cleanin' my—" He belched unapologetically. "R'volver."

"You didn't damage the large toe. You're very lucky."

"I don't feel ver' damn lucky." Quentin tipped the glass up again. "Where's Fuh...lissy? I need her to gimme some more brandy."

"I'll get you some, but only because you'll be wishing you were drunker yet before I'm done cleaning and stitching that foot."

She rose and headed across the kitchen, intent on getting the brandy from her father's study.

"'Lexa?"

Pausing in the doorway, she resisted the urge to roll her eyes impatiently. "Yes?"

"I miss Nate."

Tears burned her eyes, and her throat thickened with emotion. Quentin was yet another person she'd have to share the news with. "Me, too." She prayed he was too drunk to notice how her voice quivered with emotion.

"He's my bes' friend, and I'll ne'r forgive him makin' me go to war by m'self."

She started to answer him, but his chin had already met his chest and a nasal snoring came from his direction.

With a sigh, Alexa stepped through the dining room doors headed for her father's study. She'd just taken the bottle from the sideboard when Will appeared in the doorway.

His face lit with pleasure, those hound dog eyes of his brightening at the sight of her.

"I didn't know you'd come in, Miss Alexa."

Guilt, heavy and leaden dropped into her stomach. She had agreed to keep company with this man, and yet minutes ago, she'd been ready to give herself, body and soul, to a man who had asked no such thing of her.

Will deserved better than that.

He stepped into the room and nodded toward the brandy. "Is that for Lieutenant Lord?"

"Yes, he's in quite a bit of pain, and it's going to get worse before I'm done with him."

He scowled. "I know it ain't my place, but injured or not, I don't think you or your cousin should be alone with him."

She'd never seen Will so annoyed.

"He's been dulling his pain with spirits most of the night. I don't trust him."

"I've known Quentin for years, I hardly think—"

"Family friend or not, he ain't a boy, and he's drunk, Miss Alexa." Will stepped in front of her. "I'm going in there with you, and I'm stayin' until he's gone."

Warmth moved through her at his noble intentions. Why couldn't she feel the same yearning for him that she did for Caleb?

"Very well. You don't get faint at the sight of blood, do you?"

He chuckled and stepped aside, gesturing for her to go ahead of him. "I wouldn't be much of a soldier if I did."

For some reason, the mention of the word soldier brought to mind thoughts of Nate. Tears burned her eyes, blurring her vision until she managed to get hold of herself.

"Your little cousin there just about wore herself out takin' care of him earlier," Will commented as they stepped back into the kitchen. "Back and forth for brandy and food or another cloth to wrap his foot. It was all I could do not to throw him out the door."

She held her breath, wondering if he'd ask where she was or comment on her absence. But he didn't.

Quentin looked blearily at them. "'Bout time you came back. Thought I'd bleed to death waitin' for that brandy."

"That's no way to talk to the lady whose gonna fix you up," Will scolded.

"And tha's no way to talk to a soo...per'yer off'cer."

"You ain't a superior anything yet, Lord. You got a few more arses to kiss before you out rank me."

"That's quite enough from both of you." Alexa stepped forward and placed the brandy in front of Quentin. "Take a few sips as you need to, this is going to be painful." She took a seat and, as gently as possible, propped the foot in her lap.

He took a hearty sip from the bottle, then fixed his drunken gaze on her. "How come you're not wet?"

She nearly dropped his foot. "Wh—what?"

"You came in from o—owww—" Quentin howled as she gently examined one of the bloody digits. He gestured toward the door with the brandy bottle. "It's rainin' ca's and dogs and you...you were out there. But...you're not all wet."

With more pressure than necessary, she probed one toe for fragments, hoping to distract him. He shouted and tried to rise, but Will stepped around to press him down into the chair.

"So…" Quentin persisted. "Where were you?"

"In my room. Asleep." She threaded the needle and studied one toe for the best place to begin suturing.

"Tha's not wha' Fuh…lissy said."

Guilt nagged at her once again as she took the bottle from him.

"And you did'n come in from there," he pointed over his shoulder toward the dining room and parlor. "You came in from ow'side. So where—"

She tipped the bottle, pouring a generous amount of brandy over the wound. Sputtering a string of foul curses, he jerked his foot away.

Alexa sighed. This was proving to be a very long night.

Will took up the brandy bottle and set it before Quentin with a thunk. "Drink up. It'll be easier on all of us if you're out cold."

****

By dawn's first light, Quentin snored a loud, drunken snore on the kitchen floor, where Will had helped Alexa to settle him when she'd finished with his foot.

The early birds of morning were singing a pleasant song despite the destruction and decay around them as she headed for the chicken coop for eggs to begin breakfast. She paused outside the doors to the fruit cellar, wondering if she should slip in to check on Caleb.

Heat flushed through her at the memory of how

intimate things had become last night. No, she'd do well to avoid being alone with him until she got her feelings under control again. First the grief of losing Nate, then the security she'd found in Caleb's arms as he comforted her. No wonder she'd all but thrown herself at him during the thunderstorm.

"Miss Alexa?"

She nearly jumped out of her skin at Will's voice behind her.

"Did I startle you?"

"A little."

"Aww, I'm sorry. I was just...well I was hoping to talk to you alone for a minute, and this is probably the only chance I'll get."

"Are you well? Does something hurt?" Out of habit, she quickly looked him over from head to toe.

"I'm healing just fine. I have a good doctor." A teasing twinkle lit his gaze. "But that's part of what I need to talk to you about."

She darted another glance at the doors that stood between Caleb and the sounds of their voices and gestured toward the barn. "Why don't we go in here?"

The large doors were open, and she felt him at her back as she stepped just inside, within view of the house. The town gossips were most likely not out at this early hour, but she wasn't about to take the chance. "What was it you needed to tell me?"

"My ribs are healing. And so is my shoulder. It still ain't right, and I know it's probably not ever gonna be the same again, but..." He glanced away, as if choosing his words. "I gotta get back to my division."

"You know I don't think that's wise. A little more time, a bit more exercise and it could be much improved."

"I'll keep moving it like you showed me, but that ain't what I wanted to talk to you about."

A warning chill trickled through her. "Y-yes?"

"I muster out early next year. I got nothing left to go home to. I like this little town, Miss Alexa, and nothing would make me happier than knowing you were here waiting for me." His soft, hound dog brown gaze met hers hopefully. "I want to come back and build a life here. With you."

Oh God, that's exactly what she'd feared he was going to say. Unable to face him and allow him to see the indecision in her face, she turned and stepped into the barn. "W-we hardly know one another."

"I know it seems sudden, and if it weren't war time, I'd agree with you. I'd gladly marry you right here and now, but I know without even askin' that you'd say it was too soon."

"Will, you deserve better." She glanced at the hay-strewn floor beneath her feet, wishing with all her heart that his words filled her with joy and excitement, cursing her own fickle heart for pining after a man she couldn't have, instead of this thoughtful, sincere gentleman. "Wouldn't you rather have a woman who isn't tainted with the scandal of divorce?"

Warm hands settled on her shoulders and turned her to face him. "Not unless she's you."

Swallowing the lump that had lodged in her throat, Alexa chanced a glance into his face. "Will, as tempted as I am to accept—"

"But—"

She took both his large, calloused hands in hers. "My whole life, I've witnessed something remarkable that happens when a doctor heals someone. Widows older than my grandmother have come courting my father with preserves, pies and all manner of baked goods after he's cared for them or their loved ones. Girls Felicity's age stare at him like lovesick ninny's after he's seen them through an illness." She laughed. "And you've seen my father, so you know he's not the most handsome man in town."

He frowned. "I…I don't follow."

"What I'm trying to say is…while I know your feelings are sincere, I'm not so sure they aren't the result of my caring for you these last few weeks."

His hands flexed in hers and she allowed him to pull them away.

"I don't think that's possible." He walked farther into the barn, as if he needed to put distance between them.

Alexa forced her feet to remain in place rather than follow him. "If after you return to town, you find your feelings for me haven't changed, then I'd be honored to consider your proposal, Will. You're a kind and wonderful man whom any woman would be proud to call her husband. But I simply cannot take advantage of your feelings for me until you've had time to sort them out."

He turned to her, hurt and confusion evident in his eyes. "Can I at least…write to you?"

She forced a smile she was too exhausted to truly feel. "I'd like that very much."

His broad shoulders filled her vision, and she wished again that she felt even half of what she felt for Caleb. Perhaps when he returned to town, she'd be over her distraction and able to focus on what a wonderful and caring husband Will Carter would be.

"There's nothing I can say that would change your mind?"

"No." And it was true.

Before she could utter another word, he bent to kiss her. Her heart fluttered for a brief moment and then...nothing. Warm lips lingered on hers and she waited, desperately wanting him to pull her against him, deepen the kiss, stir her soul with unexpected longing.

She might as well have kissed the barn wall.

Will pulled away, a puzzled frown creasing his brow as if he, too, had expected something more. "Maybe with practice we'll get better at that."

She forced an encouraging smile. "Maybe."

He reached out, brushing her cheek in a tender gesture. "Your heart is already taken, isn't it?"

The air left her lungs in a whoosh. "Wh-what?"

His voice was whisper soft. "You get kind of a dreamy far off look sometimes, and your eyes kind of shine. I seen that look before, when my sister first met her husband."

"Don't be a goose." Guilt stabbed at her, and she forced herself to look away, lest he read the deception in her eyes.

He took a step back from her, but his gaze remained on her face. "I'm perfectly willing to wait until you've made up your mind, Miss Alexa. I'm coming back to Gettysburg next spring, and if you'll have me then, I intend to marry you."

Fourteen

The cloying stench of the dye pot began filtering into Caleb's hiding place just after sunrise. That could only mean Alexa had shared the sad news with her loved ones, and they'd begun the task of dying their clothing black for mourning.

He'd noticed the distinctive odor many times as the Southern army marched through small towns, and it never failed to bring painful memories of his father's death, the sound of his mother and sisters' weeping, the horrid smell of the dye as the house workers toiled to get all the clothes tinted black before Father's burial.

He shook off the thought and, with the aid of the cane, paced restlessly about the small room. He'd done it so many times he knew exactly how many steps from one side to the next, as well as how many steps it took to go from end to end.

Alexa would surely say it was all in his mind, but his injury felt better after moving around than it did if he sat still.

Alexa. His stomach clenched and his cock tugged with interest at the thought of her. He'd been tormented most of the night by how close they'd come to making love, haunted by the thought of leaving her behind to give birth to his illegitimate child, especially after the way the two "pea hens" had spoken of her that night they'd hidden in the tree. If Felicity hadn't come through those doors… A vision of exactly what would have occurred flashed through his mind like an image on a French postcard.

"Dammit." He shoved a hand through his hair. He'd always believed passion had its time and place, and until meeting Alexa, it had. Now, he understood why he'd never felt the fevered yearnings for Melody that other men spoke of for their wives or sweethearts; it wasn't rigid self control keeping his romantic fervor in check, but rather a lack of passionate feelings for her.

Why had it never occurred to him before?

The cellar doors opened, and as if summoned by his thoughts, Alexa stepped inside.

He met her gaze and was about to speak when his jaw went momentarily slack. "Y-you're wearing a dress."

Her brows arched in surprise. "That's an unusual greeting."

"I…" Caleb winced, hearing how he stammered and stuttered like a boy in knee pants. "I don't think I've ever…" But she was a vision. While most women looked pale and drawn in black, the shade seemed to emphasize her dark hair and brows and bring out the roses in her creamy complexion. She'd never looked lovelier.

A pink stain spread over her cheeks, and he realized his intense stare made her uncomfortable.

"It's just a dress." She smoothed a hand down the front. "And damn hard to walk in at that."

"Why are you wearing it?" He forced his gaze away from her tiny waist and the flare of her hips that had his loins tightening already.

Alexa moved across the room, her steps made

careful by the heavy skirts, and set a tray on the table. "Grammy is dyeing my clothes. This is all I have left that isn't blood stained. I wore it when my uncle, Felicity's father, was laid to rest."

"I see." He marveled that something so simple as a change in her clothing could distract him so. "Your grandmother is dyeing the clothes…then you've told everyone."

Her face fell, and the shadows he'd noticed beneath her eyes on so many occasions seemed more pronounced.

"The news wasn't entirely unexpected, of course. Father is taking it hard, given the way he and Nate quarreled when last they saw one another. But I think he found Nate's letter soothing. At least I hope he will in time."

"And you?"

"I…I don't know. I haven't had much time to think about it."

"Did you sleep after we… parted?" The memory of what they'd nearly done before parting returned to taunt him.

She placed a hand to her forehead and frowned, as though trying to remember. "No. Quentin's foot… He needed…" She swayed and gripped the table for support.

"Alexa?"

Caleb reached her side a moment before she slumped to the floor. He hoisted her in his arms, wincing as the added weight tugged at his healing wound. Though she'd likely lost weight caring for everyone in recent weeks, she felt heavier than the last time he'd held her like this. By the time he reached the cot, just a few short steps away, his breathing was labored and his arms trembled from exertion.

"Put me down. Dammit, your—"

"Say the word 'sutures' and I'll drop you right here on the floor." With great care, he placed her on the cot. She immediately tried to sit, but he pressed her down. "Stay put."

"I can't. I have to…"

"What? Exhaust yourself caring for others?"

"I was just a little dizzy. It's better now."

He took the pitcher of water from his nightstand and poured a glass for her. "If something happens to you, what do you think will become of the soldiers who depend on you? They need you well enough to care for them."

She eyed him over the rim of the cup before taking a dutiful sip. "I'm not thirsty."

"Well then, Doctor Winters, let me ask you. You have a patient who has not had sleep, who becomes dizzy and nearly faints. What would you do for her?"

"If she wasn't feeling ill, or wasn't in a family way, I'd ask when she last had something to eat or drink."

"And?"

She pulled a face and drained the contents of the cup. "There. Satisfied?"

"Hardly." He rose, walked over to his breakfast tray and picked up the thick slice of buttered bread with honey that sat beside a plate of cold eggs. "Eat this."

"No, that's—"

"I can miss a meal or two. I suspect you've missed more than that."

Brows furrowed, she rested her head on the pillow

and closed her eyes. "I don't remember. I haven't sat down to an actual meal since before the battle. I've just sort of grabbed something on my way to doing something else."

"Then you'll eat now and rest for a few hours."

She leaned up on her elbows and shook her head. "I can't."

"You will." He pressed the bread toward her.

With a huff of resignation, she accepted it and dutifully chewed and swallowed. He handed her another cup of water.

"Are you feverish, McKenna, or have you forgotten this is not a battlefield, and I don't take orders from you?"

"It's not an order. But I should warn you, if you walk out those doors anytime soon, I'll follow. Just so there's someone around to catch you should you faint again."

Her eyes widened. "You've taken leave of your senses."

He chuckled and pulled the blankets up over her. "There is nothing so urgent it can't wait a few hours."

"You don't know that..." Her eyes drifted closed, and in a matter of moments, her chest began to rise and fall steadily.

Caleb watched her sleep for a few moments, then rose and set the half-finished cup of water aside.

Across the room, the letters he'd spent most of the night writing sat on the table where he'd left them. One for Alexa, Felicity and their grandmother thanking them for their care and hospitality, and another for his loved ones that he would ask Alexa to post once hostilities between north and south were resolved—just in case he didn't make it back to them.

He couldn't allow Alexa and her family to continue risking their safety caring for him, and he couldn't stay here another day without telling Alexa he'd fallen in love with her. There was a war to be fought; he'd have to save his tender feelings for another day.

If that day ever came.

He gazed at Alexa, still soundly sleeping. The sweep of her dark lashes against her pale skin, the softly parted raspberry lips—the dark hair he loved to caress. God's teeth, the woman had thoroughly bewitched him. The thought of never seeing her again took his breath away.

When night fell, he planned to leave the safety of the fruit cellar and head south.

****

Alexa opened her eyes with a start. One moment she'd been talking to Nate, the next...

Her gaze came to rest on the gray stone walls of the fruit cellar. How had she come to be here? The memory of how exhausted she'd been this morning struck her with brutal clarity—had Caleb really carried her to the cot?

She leaned up on an elbow. Caleb sat beside the cot, a book in his lap, one ankle resting on his knee. Warmth spread through her at the sight of him keeping vigil beside her. The faint light from a nearby candle painted shades of gold and light brown in his hair, and cast shadows on his cheek from his lashes. For a moment, she allowed herself to imagine they were a happily married couple, alone in their own little home... But it would never happen. Sorrow pushed aside the warm glow that had filled her moments ago.

He glanced up from the book and met her gaze. A warm smile spread across his face and her heart belly-flopped into her stomach.

"I thought you planned to sleep the day away."

With a groan she sat up, and her stomach loudly mimicked the sound.

"Stay where you are. Felicity brought some food down a while ago."

"Please don't say she saw me sleeping in your bed."

He rose with a chuckle and stepped across the room. With much less effort than he'd walked previously, she noted. Just how often had he been practicing?

He glanced at her over his shoulder before picking up the tray. "As much as I like your implication, she thinks nothing of the sort. She was worried that she hadn't seen you and came looking." He set the tray at one end of the cot and resumed his seat. "She was pleased you were getting some rest."

Alexa bit into the corn muffin he handed her.

"Your young cousin cares about you a great deal."

"I…I know. We've become quite close these last few weeks. I'll miss her when she goes back home."

Caleb picked up a tea pot wrapped in towels to keep it warm and poured out two cups. "I don't think she intends to leave you any time soon."

Alexa sipped the tea, lukewarm despite the towels; she must have been out for quite some time. "Just how long did the two of you talk?"

"Oh, we talk most days when she stops down to visit. Sometimes we talk about the war, or the weather." He glanced up, a meaningful mischief twinkling in his eyes. "Or you."

"Me?" Heat flushed her cheeks at the thought of the two of them discussing her. "I can't imagine what the two of you find to discuss about *me*."

He sat back in the chair, still staring at her with amusement. "Apparently Will Carter and Quentin Lord have nearly come to fisticuffs over you a time or two." He winked at her before raising the tea cup to his lips. "Including last night."

"Quentin had quite a bit of brandy under his belt. He…he took the news of Nate's passing very hard and said some things he would never have said if he were sober." She winced as she recalled the way he'd shouted that Nate's death was entirely her fault. A lump of emotion lodged in her throat, and she quickly gulped more of the lukewarm beverage.

"You know better than to think that way, Alexa."

"Yes, I supp—" She glanced down and noticed for the first time the dark boots he wore. In near panic, she took in the sight of his trousers and crisp white shirt. She frowned, had she been so tired she hadn't notice his attire this morning? A tingle of warning rushed over her, leaving gooseflesh in its wake. "Why are you dressed like that?"

He sighed and set his cup aside. "It's time for me to be on my way, Alexa."

"What?" The words struck her like a bolt of lightning. "You're not strong enough to make your way south, let alone avoid the Federal presence in town. Why now?"

"I can think of several reasons. But most important is my concern for your safety."

She stared at him, waiting for him to continue, her

mind rushing to sort out when her safety had been compromised. "That was only one. You said *several*. Is there something more?"

His gaze met hers, and his expression softened. "You mean other than the single-minded fascination I have for a certain raven-haired temptress who haunts my mind night and day?"

The empty cup tumbled from her suddenly trembling hands. "Y-you're leaving because of me?"

"I'm leaving before you and I do something we'll both regret."

"Because of last night?" She straightened, face heating at the reminder of just how close she'd come to giving herself to him. How much she'd *wanted* to give herself to him.

"Perhaps. But it's something I've been thinking about for a while. I'm a soldier, and I need to resume my duties. Instead, I read about the movements of the Southern army in the papers, while here I sit like a caged animal." He rose from the chair. "Or worse, a deserter."

"Caleb, don't do this. I understand your reasons, but until you're stronger, you shouldn't take the chance. And please don't leave because of me. I'll see to it only Grammy and Felicity look after you, if that's the problem."

He paced across the small room. "I couldn't bear being here and not seeing you, Alexa. And I couldn't see you without touching you. Sooner or later we'd—"

"*No.*" She crossed her arms over herself. "We wouldn't. I told you, I won't allow that to happen, not as long as you belong to Melody."

"It nearly happened last night." His tone was soft,

gentle. Far more in control than she felt. "And I don't belong to anyone. Except you."

Her jaw went slack. A slow anger began to brew inside her. How dare he say he belonged only to her when for weeks she'd heard of nothing but his obligation to Melody? "How can you say that when you're promised to someone else?"

His gaze met hers, blue eyes tortured. "How can I *not* say it when my every waking moment is spent thinking about you? Wanting *you?*" He shoved a hand through his hair and pulled in a ragged breath. "Believe me, even sleep offers no reprieve."

"Caleb, I don't know what to say..." She couldn't find the right words, but at the same time, couldn't take her eyes from him. Caleb wanted her? Dreamed of her? "Then for God's sake why are you marrying Melody?"

"Why are *you* keeping company with Will Carter?"

The blood drained from her face so quickly she had to grip the table to remain upright. "How did you know that?"

"I told you, Felicity and I talk." His stare pinned her in place. "Good God, Alexa. Do you even love him?"

"Do you love Melody?"

He winced. "I deserve that. But...Alexa, how many times will you marry a man you don't love?"

She pulled in a shaky breath. "I can't marry the man I love. He's promised to another, and too damn honorable to break her heart." Tears slipped freely down her cheeks. She swiped at them, hating the weakness they represented. "Will is a good man, and I know I could love him if not for..."

"Me. You could love him if not for *me*." A look of

utter anguish crossed his face. "I won't stand in the way, Alexa, but I won't pretend to like knowing you're forcing yourself to feel something that isn't there."

"You mean like you?" She clenched her fists, wishing she could slap his arrogant face, yell, scream at him for shredding her emotions like this.

He flinched as though she'd actually struck him. "Exactly like me." He strode across the room to the cot. "I'll pack what few belongings I have and be gone as soon as it's dark."

"No..." The thought of losing him so soon after losing Nate was too much. She reached for him, hating the pleading tone in her voice. "Please, Caleb, wait until you're—"

A familiar scratching came at the doors as someone began to open them.

And then a shriek.

"Oh!" Felicity cried out. "Quentin, you startled me."

Alexa met Caleb's gaze, her heart hammering.

"Where you goin' with that tray?" Quentin demanded.

"Grammy asked me to put some things down in the fruit cellar."

"I've known your Grammy a long time, Miss Felicity, and I've never known her to store a tray of food in the fruit cellar."

Alexa bit her lower lip, frantically searching her mind for some way to rush to Felicity's aid.

"I… Well, she asked, and I'm not one to question my elders." Felicity's voice wavered.

"I saw you goin' in there this morning, too. What are you hiding down there?"

"Nothing. I just like to be alone sometimes."

"Well then, allow me to be your escort." The doors tugged open. Alexa motioned for Caleb to step into the shadows near the cot.

He shook his head, stubbornly refusing to cooperate.

"Please! Just go away." Felicity's voice rose in panic.

"Afraid I'll try to steal a kiss? Or maybe you want me to?"

Daylight flooded the room as the doors opened and Quentin thumped onto the top step with his crutches.

Alexa rushed up the steps, nearly bumping into them. "She was bringing the tray to me. I'm the one who needs to be alone."

Quentin pulled up short. His gaze swept the length of her, then narrowed shrewdly. "What the hell for?"

"For privacy. When the house was so overrun with men to care for, I slept down here. I find myself rather accustomed to it now."

Alexa took the tray from Felicity and remained in the doorway, blocking Quentin's descent. And hopefully preventing him from spying Caleb.

"You expect me to believe you like sleeping in the fruit cellar."

It sounded more like an accusation than a question. "It's quiet. It's cooler for sleeping than the house." She raised her chin defiantly, daring him to pursue this ridiculous inquiry.

"This is where you were last night, when Felicity couldn't find you?"

"Yes. I was asleep."

"I don't believe you." He attempted to step past

her, but she moved to the side, obstructing him.

Too late, she realized he'd been testing her.

"You're hiding something."

She narrowed her gaze on him, daring him to question her again "No. I just want to be alone."

As though she hadn't spoken, he continued. "I think you meet someone down here. Question is, why would you involve your little cousin—and your Grammy, too, since she fixed that food."

"Why indeed? So, you see, it's as I told you, there's no one here but me."

"Wait a minute." He snapped his fingers as if making a decision. "Your cousin and your Grammy have been helping you care for—oh no. You wouldn't."

With a shove that nearly sent her sprawling, he pushed past her and thumped his way down the few steps.

The sound of a revolver being cocked sent a chill through Alexa.

"I must object, sir, to the way you're speaking to the lady."

Alexa groaned at the Southern drawl and deadly cold tone.

Ignoring Caleb, Quentin turned to glare at Alexa, eyes glimmering with triumph. "I'll bet this is that Confederate officer you were seen about town with. I knew there was more to it than you said."

Grabbing up her skirts in one hand, silently damning the bulky dress, Alexa scrambled down the steps and thrust the tray on the table. "Caleb, it's all right. Quentin is Nate's friend, and he's grieving at the news we all received yesterday. That's what's made him so—"

"Grieving or not, he owes you and Felicity an apology."

"He's your lover, isn't he?" Quentin challenged as if Caleb hadn't spoke. "Just like a divorced woman, once you've gotten used to the marriage bed, you can't live without—"

Caleb's fist met Quentin's jaw with a punch that knocked him off his feet. Felicity shrieked, and Alexa jumped back as Quentin landed with a thud in front of her.

"Dammit, McKenna. I had things under control."

Ignoring her, he leaned over Quentin, who lay on the floor, fingers gingerly touching his bloody lip.

"Doctor Winters' conduct has been nothing but ladylike. She saved my life not to mention—"

"That's too bad then, isn't it?" Quentin sneered. "'Cause the only good Reb...is a dead one."

Had he pierced her heart with an arrow, he couldn't have caused Alexa more pain. "How can you say that?"

Caleb hauled him up by the collar. "Apologize to these ladies for your foul mouth, soldier."

"Or you'll do what, Reb?"

A movement at the top of the steps drew Alexa's gaze. Her stomach dropped and a cold chill invaded her bones. Will Carter thundered down the cement steps, pulling up short at the sight of Caleb and Quentin. He stopped so abruptly Grammy, who was at his heels, stumbled into him.

And right behind Grammy, wearing an expression like a thundercloud, was Father.

Fifteen

Will glanced around the room as if assessing the situation, then his familiar brown gaze came to rest on Alexa. "I heard a woman scream."

Caleb released his hold on Quentin, and the smaller man slumped to the floor.

Words seemed to have deserted her, and though she opened her mouth to speak, nothing came out.

"It...it was me." Felicity stepped forward, her voice barely above a whisper. "I was...startled. I'm all right."

"What's going on here?" Father demanded.

"Uh...we..." Alexa winced at the jumble of words coming from her lips. "That is, I..."

"Your daughter's been harboring a Reb down here," Quentin spat the words.

Father stumbled backward, as if the news had knocked the wind out of him. "Alexandra! Is this true?"

Caleb stepped forward. "Sir, if I may—"

"*Yes*." She shot a warning glare at Caleb. "I treated him, and since he wasn't well enough to be moved or to return to his men, I've continued to care for him." She swallowed, scarcely daring to meet either her father or Will's gaze. "If he'd been found, they'd have imprisoned him at Fort McHenry. He'd have surely died there."

"Well, he's gonna die there now," Quentin

snickered.

"Oh, you hush up," Grammy hissed.

Confusion and disappointment furrowed Father's brow. "And you dragged your Grandmother and Felicity into this?"

Her cousin slipped her arm about Alexa's waist. "She didn't drag us into anything, Uncle. She saved his life, Grammy and I helped her with the surgery."

Frowning, Father turned. "Mother?"

Nose in the air, Grammy shuffled forward until she, too, stood beside Alexa. "A man bleeds red whether he's from the north or south, and she saved a lot of lives here this summer. She's a fine doctor, Edwin. I don't expect you could 'a done any better."

Alexa shrugged off Grammy and Felicity's hold. If Father was going to be angry, he could direct his anger at her, not them.

"Father, Will, this is Maj—*Colonel* Caleb McKenna. And while it may be true that I saved his life, I should point out he saved mine first."

"He saved all of us," Felicity insisted. "The first day Confederate troops rode into town, a bunch of foot soldiers set up camp on our lawn. One of the Reb— *Confederate*—soldiers tried to force his way into the house. Colonel McKenna came to our aid."

Alexa glanced over at Caleb, then at her father. "Later that night I...I wanted to see if I could find Nate. Colonel McKenna found me and insisted on seeing me home safely."

Father's gaze narrowed on her. "Searching for Nathaniel *where* Alexandra?"

"I found her in a field where some of our men lay, sir. She was administering to the gravely wounded and dying."

Father put his hands to his balding head. "Good Heavens, you could have been—" He crossed the room and sank into one of the chairs at the table.

Alexa hurried to his side. "Father, I'm sorry I defied you. But when I saw all those men suffering—"

"I'm not upset about you caring for wounded men. When I told you not to let any Rebs in the house, I…I couldn't have imagined anything like that happening in Gettysburg." He shook his head "But I never realized until this moment what a headstrong, foolhardy girl I raised. Sneaking out at night when the Rebs were in control of the town to go find your brother—"

"Precisely my sentiment at the time, sir," Caleb added.

Alexa shot a sideways glance at him. With hands clasped behind his back, he looked every inch the officer he was. Had she been close enough, she might have smacked him.

"If I'd'a known what she was up to," Grammy spoke up, "I'd have taken a wooden spoon to her,"

Father glanced up at Caleb, his face still registering shock. "And you brought her home?"

"Yes, sir. And though we were without escort, I assure you her virtue was not compromised."

Alexa closed her eyes as memories of that night sped through her mind. Had she been falling in love with him even then?

When she finally opened them, Will still stared at her, but something in his expression had changed. Understanding dawned in his eyes.

"Well, a hell of a lot of good it did him," Quentin said, still on the floor with his crutch out of reach.

"'Cause I'm placing you and your Reb lover under arrest, Alexa."

Grammy let out a strangled cry. "If you arrest her, Quentin Lord, you'd better arrest me right along with her."

"And me," Felicity disentangled herself from Alexa and stepped forward.

"There's no need for these ladies to sacrifice themselves," Caleb spoke up. "If you allow them to remain free, I'll surrender like a gentleman."

"Now, wait just a damn minute." At last, Will spoke up. "In the first place, I outrank you *Lieutenant* Lord, so you won't be arresting anyone unless it's on *my* orders. And the way I see it, Colonel McKenna, you're in no position to negotiate."

"Understood." Caleb nodded and gave a slight bow. "But I must warn you, if you intend to arrest these ladies, you'll have to go through me."

"Stop it," Alexa couldn't tolerate another moment of male bravado. "Dammit, McKenna, I won't let your Southern honor make things worse for you. I knew the risks." She stepped forward, wrists extended toward Will. "Arrest me. Go ahead."

Reaching his crutch at last, Quentin struggled to his feet. "Carter, if you don't do it, I'll turn you over to General Meade."

Without a word, Will stepped over to Quentin, pulled back a fist and socked him in the jaw. Quentin fell to the ground unconscious.

"I can't think with him talkin' so much," Will admitted somewhat sheepishly. He glanced at Alexa again, this time with something of a wounded calf expression. "Look, I don't want to arrest any of you ladies, and I won't if I can help it. But him…" He glanced at Caleb. "I'm sorry, Miss Alexa, but I have to take him to Fort McHenry."

"No," Felicity cried, rushing over to grab hold of Caleb's arm. "Can't you let him go, Will? Please?"

"I wouldn't be much of a soldier if I did. And even if I could, your friend over there would make sure everyone knew about it." He sighed and scratched his head. "Doctor Winters, could you find some rope so I can bind his hands?"

With a somber expression, Father rose from the table. "Of course, son."

Tears stung at Alexa's eyes, and she turned away. She'd stubbornly refused to admit this could happen, and now that it had, was helpless to stop it

Caleb came up behind her, the familiar smell of him, bay rum and lye soap, surrounding her.

"Alexa." Warm hands settled on her shoulders. "I won't ask you to wait for me, because I can't promise I'll return."

She wrenched around to face him. "Don't say that."

He lifted her chin on a finger, forcing her to look into his eyes. Fear clenched her insides, but in his gaze she saw only calm resolve and determination.

"When the war ends I intend to return home and tell Melody I can't marry her."

Her breath hitched painfully in her chest, and his image blurred as tears filled her vision. "Now? You decide this *now?*"

He took her hands between his and dropped to one knee. "Marry me, Alexa."

A sob tore from her throat. Head spinning, she

could only shake her head. "Caleb, you're not thinking clearly right now. What about the shame…the disgrace to your family? The years Melody has waited for you?"

"Right now, faced with losing you forever, I realize I can live with that far more easily than I can face a lifetime of never seeing you again."

She tried to tug her hands from his, but he held tight.

"And you tell me this now—when you're about to become a prisoner of war?"

He pressed his lips to her fingers. "*Now*, because fate may not grant me the opportunity to say it later."

"You've taken leave of your senses. This isn't love, Caleb, it's gratitude for saving your life."

"God willing, I'll spend the rest of my life proving you wrong."

Across the room, Will cleared his throat. "Uh…Miss Alexa, might I have a word with you?"

Guilt stabbed at her to realize Will had witnessed their exchange. She glanced at him across the room, looking somewhat embarrassed, then back to Caleb, who waited patiently for her answer. Reluctantly, she pulled her hands from his grasp.

Granny and Felicity joined Caleb near the cot, laughing and crying and assuring him that Alexa was stubborn, but would come around.

Will motioned her over toward the steps, out of earshot of the others. "It's him, isn't it? He's the reason for that dreamy expression."

She couldn't bear to wound him, couldn't bring herself to look him in the eyes. Feigning a sudden interest in his feet, she frantically searched her mind for a way to avoid hurting him.

"What he said gave me an idea."

Frowning, she peered up into his face. Instead of the wounded puppy expression she'd expected, he appeared resigned, in control and every bit the Federal officer. This was a Will she hadn't seen before.

"I'm still trying to figure a way to get you out of this without you being thrown in prison. The General doesn't like citizens harboring the enemy but…he'd be a lot more lenient if you were…" He swallowed, Adam's apple bobbing. "I don't think he'd imprison a woman for hiding her husband."

Chill bumps broke out along her skin and a tingle of trepidation threaded through her. "I'm not sure I understand."

"Look, it's up to you, but like I said, the General probably would go easy on a woman hiding her husband." He shoved his hands in his trouser pockets and shrugged. "He'd probably also understand a soldier not wanting to arrest his wife. So, the way I see it, you got two choices." He nodded toward Caleb. "You can accept his proposal…or you can accept mine."

****

The rhythmic tick tock of the grandfather clock in the parlor of the Winters' residence soothed Caleb's nerves. After all that had taken place, he could scarcely believe only an hour had passed since he had proposed to Alexa.

The preacher, who had been pulled from his supper to perform a hasty wedding, paced across the room, his boots barely making a sound on the wood floors. Caleb had all but memorized the blood patterns on the floors, following a line from the front door through the dining room, to others that soaked the parlor floor. His heart ached to realize how much suffering had occurred here, and how valiantly Alexa had fought to keep wounded soldiers alive.

Beautiful, brave Alexa. He could scarcely believe they were about to be wed.

The creak of a door opening drew his attention up the stairs. A short time ago, Felicity headed up there with a handful of wildflowers, but after much whispering and opening and closing of doors, the second floor had gone silent. Now he felt a fleeing stab of disappointment as Grammy Winters, rather than Alexa, exited the room. With slow, careful steps, she shuffled down the stairs.

Caleb met her at the bottom step, offering his arm to assist her, shortening his pace to match hers as he helped her toward a chair. Once she was settled, she reached for his hand, pressing something into his palm. A glance down revealed two gold bands, warm from her grasp. She touched the larger ring. "This was her grandfather's. We were married thirty years before he passed away. I was saving it for Nate but..." Her voice cracked and she swallowed. "I think he'd want you to have it."

Caleb watched her, feeling a flood of affection as her small, dark eyes welled with tears.

She pointed to the second ring. "This was her mother's. She left before Alexa could even walk, ran off with some peddler man who promised to show her the world. Head full of fanciful notions, that one." She gave her head a disgusted shake. "I don't think she's comin' back for it." She closed his hand around them and gave a weak squeeze.

A ball of emotion wedged in his throat. He'd likely

never live to wear the ring as long as Alexa's grandfather had. He opened his hand to study the rings, staring at the one that had belonged to her mother. She'd never mentioned her mother's leaving; he'd assumed the woman had passed on. So many things he didn't know about the woman he was about to marry; so many things they hadn't had time to say to one another or talk about. Would they ever get the chance?

Beside him, standing in as best man, Will Carter cleared his throat. "I'll see to it that you and Miss Alexa get a proper wedding night," he said. "I got nothing to gain by taking you to the General tonight."

Surprised at that information, Caleb frowned. "What about Lieutenant Lord? I think he'd feel otherwise."

Staring up the stairs toward the closed bedroom door, Will shrugged. "He's in the fruit cellar, tied up. He won't be goin' anywhere before morning. After I take you to the prison camp, I'll come back and take him before the General. He needs to answer for his conduct."

Caleb suppressed a smile at that. No one had been more surprised than he when the Union Captain had used the requested rope on Quentin Lord rather than him.

"You're a good man, Captain Carter."

"I ain't doing it for you; I'm doing it for Miss Alexa. You're a lucky man, you know." Will slid him a glance. "But I'll have sentries posted near the house, and they'll have orders to shoot first and ask questions later, so don't try anything foolish."

"You have my word as a gentleman." He wouldn't insult Alexa's family by trying to escape immediately after their wedding, nor would he force his new wife to watch her husband get shot trying to escape. "Will, I know you have fond feelings for her…"

The other man's jaw tightened. "That's beside the point."

"If I don't make it back…look after her for me."

The captain turned a startled gaze on him. "You really do love her."

Caleb cleared his throat past a sudden thickening of emotion. Unable to speak, he nodded.

Another sound came from upstairs. Felicity exited the room this time. She'd changed her dress and pinned wildflowers in her hair. Glancing over the railing at Caleb, she smiled a broad cat-that-ate-the-canary smile. Affection for the young girl so reminiscent of his sister flooded him. He wished his family were here, his mother and sisters would be so excited... Or would they? He *was* marrying a Yankee girl, after all.

Alexa's father was next to exit the room. His jaw was set, his expression drawn. His gaze met Caleb's over the railing, studying him. Curious about Alexa's father, he studied him back. Doctor Winters had reluctantly given his blessing for the marriage, adding that days ago, he would have never allowed it. Now, after losing his son, he realized life was too short for bitter feelings.

A sound behind him pulled the elder doctor's attention, and Alexa stepped out.

Caleb's breath caught at the sight of her. She still wore the mourning dress, but her long, dark hair was pulled to one side of her face, loosely braided with purple, pink and blue wildflowers twined through it.

As she took her father's arm and started down the

stairs, she met his stare. If he'd expected to feel nervous or trapped at this moment, as he had when he thought of marrying Melody, no such feeling came. Instead, warmth swept over him, security in the knowledge he was exactly where he wanted to be. Alexa may not possess the generations-long Southern heritage so prized by his family and neighbors, nor the sheltered, pampered upbringing of a coastal Georgian belle, but *this* was the woman he wanted to pledge his life to.

After what seemed an eternity, she reached his side. He took her hand, unwilling to wait another moment to touch her.

Icy cold fingers met his grasp, and he leaned in close to her ear. "Are you all right?"

"Scared to death," she whispered. "I can't believe this is happening."

"Look at me." When she turned to face him, he clasped both her hands in his. "If you'd rather not do this…"

"I want to." She met his gaze and her lower lip quivered. Tears slipped down her cheeks. This time she wasn't trying to stop them. "*Very* much."

The preacher began to speak, but Caleb couldn't look away from Alexa. A delicate pink flush stained her cheeks, and the moisture shimmering in her eyes only deepened their bewitching green color. How was it possible she had so completely captured his heart and mind in just a few weeks. Or had she had them all along? Looking back, he couldn't recall when his feelings for her had begun, it seemed as though they'd been there all along.

Minutes later, he slipped a ring on her cold, trembling finger and recited the vows that would bind them for life.

****

The bed had been freshened with clean sheets and blankets, candles lit around the room cast a soft, inviting glow and the windows were open to let the evening breeze spill into the room. Alexa couldn't help but smile. Her romantic-minded cousin obviously wanted to give them a special night.

Grammy was of much the same mind, having given orders to the soldiers guarding the house for the night to bring the tub and plenty of water inside so the couple could freshen up.

The few recovering soldiers at the Winters' home had been relocated to the hospital in town. Father had gone to help them settle in and Grammy and Felicity were on their way there to help him.

She was completely alone with her new husband. But plans for helping him escape, rather than romance, occupied her mind.

"Alexa?"

Heat bathed her insides at the sound of his voice from below stairs. No one said her name quite like Caleb.

Reminded her new husband was unfamiliar with the house, she stepped into the hallway and peered over the banister. "Up here."

He began a slow climb up the stairs, and she had to bite her tongue to keep from scolding him for not using the cane. She stepped back into the bedroom before he reached her, nervous flutters in her stomach making her almost queasy.

She stood before the wardrobe, pondering the contents when she felt him in the doorway.

"Were you planning to hide in there?"

Despite the humor in his tone, Alexa found no reason to laugh. "I was wondering which of these old dresses might fit you."

"I see."

She glanced over at him, cursing herself when her insides fluttered at the sight of him leaning in the doorway, one blond brow cocked in amusement.

"I thought if we dressed you in women's clothing, we could slip past the guards—" She reached inside to pull out one of her old dresses, then with a frown, tossed it aside.

"You want me to wear a dress?"

The laughter in his tone raked over nerves already stretched taut by the day's events. "It's not my best plan, I'll admit. But it's too late to cover you with a sheet and say I'm taking you to the undertaker." She bit her lip. "Maybe one of Grammy's dresses…" She turned to move past him, but he caught her elbow as she started through the doorway.

"No."

Frustrated, she met his gaze, wishing her body would stop reacting to his nearness. But try as she might, she couldn't forget this was their wedding night. Well, they wouldn't be spending it the way most newlywed couples did, so there was no point in dwelling on the exciting sensations rioting inside her. "Do you have a better idea?"

"As a matter of fact, I do."

Something in the languid, honeyed way he spoke made the hair at the nape of her neck prickle. She backed up a step and caught her foot in one of the dresses she'd tossed on the floor. She bent to retrieve it, well aware of Caleb right behind her.

When she righted herself, he stood so close, his warm breath fanned the back of her neck. Gooseflesh broke out along her skin.

"What…" She licked her lips, forced herself to swallow. "What is this idea of yours?"

Warm lips brushed the curve of her neck. "Would you prefer I tell you…or show you?"

"Caleb…" She needed to move away, to break the spell that held her in place. But as if he read her mind, his hands came to rest on her shoulders, then slid down her arms in a slow caress.

"Do you think I married you simply to buy time to plan an escape?"

Moist heat met her skin again, and an involuntary moan escaped her when his lips met the curve of her jaw.

"Y-you married me because you were too much of a gentleman not to."

She felt as well as heard the chuckle that rumbled in his chest.

"My reasons are anything but gentlemanly." His hands moved to her waist, and he bent to rest his chin on her shoulder. "I gave my word that I wouldn't try to escape. And I won't. Not tonight."

"But you *must*." She wrenched around to face him, anger and sorrow churning her insides. "You'll never survive prison."

He dropped a kiss to the top of her head. "I can survive anything knowing I have you to come home to."

"*No*." The need to scream built up inside her, but she squelched it, knowing it would bring the guards posted outside. "I won't listen to any of your Old South romantic nonsense. Surviving has nothing to do with will, it has to do with physical strength—and you're still recovering."

"For a doctor, you know very little about life." One corner of his mouth lifted in a half-smile. "And you'd make a lousy soldier. A few months ago, I didn't care if I survived when I went into battle. What others might have called bravery was merely indifference on my part." He shrugged. "I was simply doing my job. And when that job was over, I would go home to a life I didn't want—to a *marriage* I didn't want. So, whether I lived or died made no difference to me."

Alexa swallowed past a sudden lump of emotion and gazed up into his face. "I've never heard you talk like that."

"I don't think I was aware of it. Until I met you, I only knew how to act, how to say and do what was proper in any given situation. But I didn't know how to *feel*." He shook his head. "I won't be so cavalier again, Alexa. Not with so much to lose."

"Which is why you need to leave *now*." She turned back to the wardrobe, hands trembling as she yanked aside one dress after another. "There must be some way to disguise you, to keep you from being discovered."

"And miss our wedding night?"

"I'm more concerned with getting you safely back south."

"Not tonight." He hooked an arm about her waist and tugged her toward him until her body collided pleasantly with his. "I gave my word as a gentleman that I wouldn't repay Captain Carter's charity by escaping. It's because of him that we have this night together, and I won't cause him to regret giving it to us."

"Damn you!" She struggled to remove herself from his arms. "Your chivalry is going to be the death of you; I won't let you do this." Unable to contain her emotions any longer, an anguished sob bubbled forth.

Caleb turned her and pulled her tighter to his chest, holding her in place until she stopped struggling. "I promise you, if an opportunity for escape comes, I'll take it. Whether it's tomorrow, or the next day or six months from now." He pressed his lips to her hair. "And with God as my witness, I swear I'll come back to you."

She curled her fingers into the warm linen covering his chest. Six months. How on earth was she to exist that long—or longer—not knowing whether he was alive or dead? Only one thing was certain, she knew Caleb well enough to know this debate was pointless; he was just as stubborn as she, perhaps even more so. Arguing would get her nowhere and waste what precious few hours they had left.

Lifting her head from his chest, she met his gaze through the watery haze blurring her vision. In an instant, the rioting emotions fled. Unwilling to wait another moment, she reached up to feather her fingers into his maple sugar hair, tugging his mouth closer to hers. "Love me."

"Sweeter words have never met my ears, Mrs. McKenna."

She smiled at the sound of her new name for the first time.

Caleb scooped her into his arms, silencing her objection with a stern look as he carried her to the bed.

He deposited her gently upon it, and then began to unbutton his shirt. A warm breeze stole into the room, and candles around the room flickered. Though the smell and feel of fresh air after being locked up for so long soothed his senses, he wondered if the candles cast shadows that could be seen from outside.

Rather than close the windows and pull the curtains, he chose to extinguish the candles one by one. Just as he finished, Alexa slipped up behind him, wrapping her arms about his waist. She pressed her lips to his bare back. The feel of her soft breasts pressed against him, the sight of her small, pale hands on his skin was nearly his undoing. The urge to throw her onto the bed nearly overtook him, but they had all night, there was no need to rush.

He unhooked her arms from his waist enough to allow him to turn and face her. "I wonder how long it will be until I see you in a dress again."

A smile played over her lips. "A long, long time."

"Then allow me to remove it for you."

She turned and presented him with her back, and he realized she had no idea of his intent. With the painstaking slowness reserved for unwrapping the last gift on Christmas morning, Caleb unfastened the row of buttons down her back, pausing to press his lips to each bit of milky white flesh he exposed.

When half the buttons were open, he eased the dress down; it fell to the floor with a gentle swish of material. She rested her head against his shoulder, and he bent to kiss her. He slipped his fingers over her collar bone, stroking, skimming until he brushed the ribbon at the front of her camisole. He swallowed her gasp of pleasure as he slid his hand purposefully inside, lifting and stroking one velvety breast. Dragging his mouth from hers, he glanced down at the sight of her creamy, pale flesh filling his palm and realized that the chemise, too, had fallen to the floor. "You're not wearing a corset."

"There should be a law against them." She pulled his head back toward hers, mouth seeking his.

His fingers sought and found a plump, ripe nipple, and he rolled it gently between his fingers, squeezing slightly when she moaned in pleasure. Then he dragged his mouth from hers and branded the curve of her neck with his tongue.

"As your husband, I really must insist you dress like a proper lady."

A soft laugh escaped her. "Insist all you like, it'll do no good."

He turned her to face him and lifted both her breasts in his hands. "You might *pretend* to obey now and then, just to humor me."

Caleb bent to stroke his tongue over one rosy nipple. Enraptured by the taste of her, he lingered, circling the swollen bud with his tongue. He drew the peak into his mouth and suckled. Soft moans came from her throat, reminding him of the purring of a kitten as she threw her head back and arched toward him. His hands strayed lower, splaying over the curve of her hip, to her waist, seeking the ribbon that tied her pantaloons. He tugged at it, and with a brush of his hand, they soon joined the dress and chemise on the floor at her feet.

He tore his mouth from her breast only long enough to seek her lips again. Their mouths fused together in a hot, openmouthed kiss that left no doubt in his mind she was every bit as eager as he.

But it had been so long since he had been with a woman, and he'd dreamed of Alexa so many nights, he wasn't sure he could last long enough to give her the pleasure she deserved on her wedding night.

With a mind of its own, his hand stole between her thighs, finding the moist heat at her center. She cried out as he brushed the damp curls at her opening, his finger slipping inside. The moist, slick heat was nearly his undoing.

Her gasp turned to a cry as he found and stroked the sensitive bud. "Caleb, what are you…"

Her knees buckled and he lifted her, carrying her to the bed where he set her gently on the edge. When she would have scooted to the other side to make room for him, he placed a hand on her thigh. "Lie back."

She did as he asked, and he knelt before her. Pressing a kiss to the inside of one knee, he slid his hand up the length of her thigh. He stroked the dark curls, finger delving inside to tease as he kissed and nipped his way up the inside of her thigh, the musky, feminine scent of her filling his senses.

He glanced up at the incredible sight of her nude skin bathed in the rosy glow of the waning evening twilight, legs parted for him. God above, she was a vision of Venus.

"Alexa, when I mentioned sleep giving no respite from my thoughts of you…"

A sound, half-sigh, half-question came from her.

"This is what we did in my dreams."

Before she could ask, he dipped his head to taste of the sweet nectar between her legs. A startled cry escaped her and she shifted, trying to bring her legs together, but Caleb held them open, stroking, caressing her with his tongue until she began to moan and writhe.

Alexa cried out, and he felt the spasm that shook her, tasted the honey that flowed from her as he lifted her buttocks to hold her closer until her cries faded.

Something powerful and instinctive surged through him, not just the primal need to pound his chest with his accomplishment, but the need to gather her in his arms and shelter her. He joined her on the bed, kissing her, stroking her. Despite his own aching, throbbing need, he felt an immense satisfaction at having pleasured her.

She wrapped her arms around his neck and pressed her face to his bare chest. "What was that?"

"That never happened with your first husband?" He dropped a kiss to her forehead.

"Heavens no." She frowned up at him. "Should it have?"

A relieved grin came over him. "Not as far as I'm concerned."

She splayed a hand over his bare chest, fingers trailing down over his stomach. Her fingers stilled when they reached the waistband of his trousers. "Caleb, I…"

He held his breath, waiting to see if she'd venture lower.

"I want to touch you."

He grit his teeth as a wave of need swept over him so strong he nearly came right then and there. God's nightshirt, the woman knew how to turn him inside out. Unable to speak over a sudden thickening in his throat, he took her hand and moved it to where his erection strained for freedom against his trousers.

Her fingers slid over the length of him, exploring even as he unfastened the buttons that would free him.

He sprang free, and she closed a hand around him. She leaned up on an elbow, her mouth seeking his lips as she trailed her fingers over his cock, familiarizing herself with the feel of him.

This time, it was he who moaned when she closed her palm around him. He reached up to fist a hand into her hair, holding on as she turned him inside out with her innocent touch. When he could stand no more of her pleasant torture, he pulled his mouth from hers. "Alexa, if you don't stop, we're going to have to start over again."

She gazed at him with heavy lidded eyes. "I don't understand."

"You will."

He grabbed her about the waist and swept her beneath him. She gave a playful shriek, her legs parting as she arched against him in invitation.

The moist heat of her entrance touched the tip of his shaft. The urge to plunge forward nagged at him, but he wanted to savor this moment before passion completely took them away. After weeks of longing for this, of wanting her from afar, being tormented by dreams of her, they were finally free to make love.

He eased forward. Tight, slick warmth surrounded him as her body at first resisted and then gave way to the size of him. With painstaking slowness, he retreated, pleasure skittering along his spine, then moved forward with the same languid care.

A whimper tore from Alexa's throat. Her hands moved restlessly over his back, sliding over his buttocks, urging him closer. He rocked against her, lifting her hips to meet his next thrust and the next. She cried out, muscles clenching around him, squeezing.

At last he let go his own rigid control. Despite having pleasured her earlier, he wanted to give her so much more than that one moment to remember their wedding night. A tremor moved through him, and as his seed spilled forth, he sent up a desperate plea that it would take hold, giving Alexa his child to keep her company through the years in case he never returned.

White-hot heat seared his brain as wave after wave of ecstasy consumed him, sapping him of every last bit of strength. It was all he could do to keep from collapsing atop her.

Chest heaving with exertion, Caleb rolled to one side and pulled her against him. Never had he experienced something so primal. This had been far more than sating carnal desires, it was as though she'd crawled inside him to touch his soul.

Alexa's head rested on his chest. She, too, was silent, as though she needed time to recover from what they had just experienced. He stroked her arm, admiring the silken feel of her skin, and was reminded of the many times she'd accused him of confusing his true feelings for her.

"Do you still think this is merely gratitude?"

She laughed. "If it is, then I'm the luckiest woman alive."

He pressed her close, nuzzling her dark hair. "I intend to spend the rest of our lives making you feel that way."

She was silent for several moments. He thought she'd fallen asleep, but then she raised her head to stare into his face.

"Caleb, what are we going to do about Melody?"

He trailed a finger over her nose, touched by her

concern for a woman she'd never met. "When the time comes, I'll tell her in person. I owe her that much."

She frowned. "And your family? Will they…accept our marriage?"

"You are my family, now, Alexa. We belong to one another. I know your father doesn't wholly approve of having a Southern son-in-law, and I'm sure my mother and sisters will be suitably shocked, as well." He rolled to one side, staring into her face, willing himself to memorize every detail before the dawn came and they were torn apart. "Whatever comes, we'll face it together."

Sixteen

Never had the pre-dawn chirping of a songbird been such a hateful sound.

Alexa stirred from restless sleep haunted by images of young men bleeding to death. For a moment, she couldn't comprehend why her cheek was pressed against Caleb's bare chest, or why they were undressed. Memories of making love well into the night flashed through her mind, and a familiar longing began to pulse at her very core.

And then cold realization dawned.

"Good morning, Mrs. McKenna," came a sleepy drawl from beside her. "Did you sleep well?"

"Get up," she whispered. "Now. We need to get you out of here before they come for you."

"We talked about this last night. I told you, I won't go back on my word."

"Then I'll go back on it for you." She tossed the blankets aside and sat up.

He grabbed her about the waist, hauling her back toward him. "I'd rather make love to you again."

"Caleb—"

He settled her pleasantly atop him. His thick erection pressed against her as his hands stole up to lift both her breasts, thumbs plying her nipples until they swelled and grew tender.

She moaned, almost embarrassed to be wet for him

so quickly, and eased herself onto his thick shaft. He shifted and leaned up, taking the peak of one breast into his mouth, tongue sliding over her nipple.

The now familiar sensations began, and she threw back her head, riding him as he thrust deeper. A guttural cry tore from her throat as heat swelled inside her, spiraling through her until she felt her muscles clench around him, felt the warmth of his seed spilling into her.

In the back of her mind, Alexa uttered a silent prayer that his seed would take root, that when he returned she'd present him with their son.

She'd barely begun to come back to herself when an insistent pounding came at the front door.

Her breath hitched and a panicked sensation engulfed her. She stared frantically into Caleb's face, hoping for some sign that he had changed his mind, that he had a plan for escape. She saw only calm resolve.

Emotion clogged her throat, and she fought against it. The last thing he'd want to see was tears.

He placed his hands to either side of her face. "We knew this moment would come." He kissed her, then rolled away from her to sit up.

While he dressed, she rose and gathered her clothes. She quickly threw on the dress she'd worn yesterday, scrubbed her teeth and pulled her hair back with a ribbon. By the time she'd finished, Caleb was fully dressed and waiting for her.

Alexa descended the stairs woodenly, frightened to allow herself to feel, to think beyond putting one foot in front of the other. She wasn't the first woman to send her husband off to war, and she likely wouldn't be the last. That thought gave her strength even as her knees wobbled and threatened to collapse.

The pounding on the door came again, then it opened, and Will stepped inside, his face set in a grim line

At the bottom of the stairs, Caleb turned and placed his hands on her waist, gazing down into her face as though he intended to memorize every detail of it. A warm smile came over him. "You are the bravest woman I know, Alexandra McKenna. Stay strong for me."

"Caleb, when the war ends..." She swallowed, allowing the words to trail off lest he hear the crack of emotion.

"I promise I'll come back to you. Meanwhile..." He pressed something warm into her palm. His wedding ring. "Hold onto this for me. I'd hate for anything to happen to it."

Her husband bent to kiss her, his lips lingering on hers for only a moment. It wasn't long enough. A million years wouldn't be long enough.

Then he stepped out the door.

Seventeen

May, 1865

Golden sunshine warmed Alexa's back as she pressed dirt at the base of the flowers she'd planted on the freshly dug grave.

A tear slipped down her cheek. "It's over now, the war is finally over. General Lee has surrendered and some insane fool has gone and killed poor President Lincoln. They'll be freeing the men from the prison camps most any day now."

The glint of her wedding band caught her eye and tears poured more freely. "I'm so glad you were here to see me through the worst of it. I'd have never gotten through any of it if you hadn't kept reminding me not to think a moment beyond the present one."

A butterfly flitted past and a delighted gurgle followed. She glanced up and laughed at the sight of pudgy little legs crawling determinedly after the insect. Pressing a kiss to her fingertips, she pressed them to the cross that bore the name Mabel Winters and the date of her passing in March. "I miss you every day, Grammy, but your great grandchild is here, reminding me that life goes on, just as you said."

Rising to her feet, she hurried after her daughter, scooping her up. The child let out a disappointed shriek.

"Liberty Hope McKenna, you're going to be the

death of me now that you've finally mastered crawling," She kissed the fine, dark curls. Blue eyes, the same exact shape and shade as Caleb's regarded her with a stubbornness Alexa knew too well. Liberty's legs and arms pumped in a wordless demand to be let down.

Felicity finished with the flowers she'd planted on Grandfather's grave next to Grammy's and rose, brushing the dirt from her skirts. "It's hard to believe the war is finally over. How long do you think it will take Caleb to reach you?"

Alexa raised the complaining tot over her head, twirling with her until she stopped complaining and smiled, then swung her back onto her shoulder. "It's hard to say. If he was released before General Grant ended the prisoner exchanges early last year, then he's probably somewhere south. It will take time to work his way north since the Union army destroyed most of the railroads when General Sherman marched through Georgia last year."

Felicity bent to pluck a handful of dandelions. "Do you think he was exchanged?"

Heaviness settled on Alexa's heart. Nearly two years had passed since she'd last seen her husband. She'd had no word of his whereabouts or even a way to know if he was still alive. She didn't allow herself to dwell on dark thoughts. "I've asked Will many times, but he just doesn't know, or else won't tell me." True to his word, early last year, Will had returned to Gettysburg and purchased a farm just outside of town. He'd worked hard to make it successful and was now one of the most eligible bachelors in Adams County. "I'm honestly not sure which way to hope."

"I've read terrible things about those prisons, Alexa." Her young cousin, no longer a girl but now a young woman, bent to gather more dandelions and began to weave the stems together. "Men freezing to death during the winter, sickness, overcrowding. Why on earth did they ever stop exchanging the prisoners?"

Bouncing and jostling her daughter to keep her happy, Alexa shrugged. "Will said it was a calculated effort to end the war. That if they kept exchanging like numbers of Confederate soldiers for Union, then the South would always have men ready to fight. The war might have dragged on for years and years."

Liberty began to babble, sing-songing nonsensical sounds that Alexa hoped would soon become words. She glanced at her cousin and laughed. "I guess that's what she thinks of our conversation."

Felicity plopped the dandelion chain on the baby's head and reached for her. "You go on into town and check on Mrs. McCorkindale. I'll take this young lady home for her nap."

At the very mention of such a foul word, the baby's face screwed up and an angry howl poured forth.

Alexa handed her daughter to Felicity, wondering for the millionth time what Caleb would think of his daughter. *If. When.*

Those two words were her constant companions now.

****

August, 1865

It was a sight he thought he'd never see again. When Caleb had heard about Sherman's march through Georgia, he'd feared there'd be nothing left by the time the Union general was finished. As much as he grudgingly understood the need for the harsh military tactics deployed by Union Generals Grant and Sherman to end the war, he'd been angry at the rumors of rampant destruction, and worried for his home.

Of course, in a prison camp, any news he heard was months old, if not older. Now, after weeks of walking, a few wagon rides from well meaning strangers and the unbelievable kindness of many fellow soldiers from both sides of the war, he was home. Not the home he longed for—that was anyplace Alexa happened to be. But Georgia was where he needed to be right now.

Years of fear and worry for the safety of his loved ones, coupled with the toll life in prison had taken on him, made it necessary to head south the moment the prison gates had been thrown open, rather than travel the shorter distance to Pennsylvania.

More than vanity kept him from seeking out his wife. Though his hair hung well past his shoulders and his beard nearly as long, the meager food and rank conditions of prison camp had whittled so many pounds from his frame he resembled a walking skeleton. He looked nothing like the Southern officer Alexa had fallen in love with. He wouldn't return to her until he had recovered, never again did he want her to see him as an invalid or a patient. And while he recovered, he needed to see Melody, to apologize and tell her he'd married another.

Now, shaded by what remained of the grand old oak trees that lined the curved path to Belle Claire, his family home, he could scarcely believe his eyes. It still stood. Weeds overflowed the place where once beautiful peonies and roses so lovingly tended by his mother had grown, shutters hung half off their hinges in some places. Chipped and peeling white wash dotted the grand structure, yet never had a more beautiful sight met his eyes.

Memories teased the edges of his brain as he continued down the path, and his mind's eye recalled the sight of a small child—usually a boy, but sometimes a girl—whose sole job it was to keep the chickens from getting into the garden. The child would sit there day after day, only stirring when one of the chickens strayed near the porch.

He stood still and for a moment, imagined Mimsy, his nanny, running from the front door to give chase at the sight of him when he'd strayed too far or been gone too long. "*Massa Caleb, you c'mon back here now!*"

Closing his eyes, he inhaled the piney smell of home, and recalled the feel of Mimsy's plump arms and bosom as she rocked him to sleep. Mother always said there wasn't a babe in the county so fussy that a few moments in Mimsy's arms couldn't calm it.

For a moment, he could almost hear the songs and chatter of the field workers, the clink of fine china as the table was set, the nasal "*yas suh*" of Elijah, his father's valet.

He opened his eyes to face the stark reality before him.

Gone. They were all gone now. He forced his feet forward, despite the exhaustion of his body that begged him to rest a while longer in the shade.

As he drew closer, a woman carrying a basket of vegetables came around the corner from the back of the house. No hat covered her fair hair. She stopped to look at him and her shoulders sagged. "Here comes another one, Mother."

Undoubtedly many men returning home had come this way seeking food or a night's shelter, but didn't they recognize their own?

Just as he reached the stone path that led to the porch, the front door opened. His mother stepped out— careworn and far older than when he'd last seen her. Beside her was a man he almost didn't recognize as his best friend, Ty Chandler. He had only one arm, but he held a rifle in the one remaining and looked more than ready to use it should the need arise.

The woman in the yard stepped closer, and he noticed her protruding belly—she was well into pregnancy. His gaze fled back to her face. Was that his sister? Had Tyler and Aurora finally wed? His friend had been sweet on her for years.

Her gaze locked with his, and her face lit with recognition. "Caleb!" A cry escaped her, and dropping the basket, she ran toward him. "Mama, it's Caleb!"

Tyler set the rifle aside and hurried down the steps. "Savannah, you'll hurt yourself."

Savannah? The woman so heavy with child was his *baby* sister?

She didn't stop until she'd thrown herself at him. Caleb nearly toppled from the sheer force of her embrace and tried not to hold on too tight, lest she realize how close he was to collapse.

Tears burned at the back of his throat. The young woman in his arms looked nothing like the girl, barely out of pigtails, he'd kissed goodbye when he'd ridden off to war. He held her for long moments, her tears soaking his shirt front, as she sobbed nearly incoherent words.

When at last she released him, he gazed from her face up at his startled best friend, and Melody's brother, once to be his future brother-in-law. Never had Ty indicated an interest in his youngest sister, he'd only ever had eyes for Aurora.

"*You're* responsible for this?"

Savannah beamed happily up at him. "Yes, we—"

With every last ounce of strength Caleb could muster, he socked his friend in the jaw.

His sister screamed. Ty stumbled, but stayed upright while the momentum carried Caleb's weakened body forward until fine red Georgia dirt met his cheek with a smack that rattled his teeth.

Alexa's face swam before him and then sweet, heavenly blackness engulfed him.

****

A warm breeze stole over Caleb in a gentle caress. He stirred, his mind unwilling to wake from the most pleasant dreams he'd experienced in a long, long time. Soft down pillows cradled his head and cool sheets— not a thin scratchy blanket—covered him. The moans of the dying and insane were silent. In fact, the only sounds were the buzz of insects and the distant sweet song of birds. The damp, piney smell of home tickled his nose.

His eyes snapped open. *Am I dead?*

In an instant, it all flooded back, as it had every morning for close to a week. He'd slept most of the time away, his body exhausted from years of disjointed sleep and too little food. He pulled back the covers and swung his feet to the floor. Weary of his mother and sister tiptoeing around him, not answering his questions and generally treating him like an invalid, he was determined to get out of bed today. He much preferred Alexa's no-nonsense method of doctoring.

Alexa.

At the very thought of her, a wave of something much like homesickness washed over him. He missed her—no, more than that, *craved* her. Her nearness, her touch, the sound of her voice. The taste of her. The passion in her eyes when he argued with her, the way she never hesitated to challenge him. Despite having returned to the place he considered home, he wouldn't truly be home until he was reunited with her.

There was no doubt in his mind she would be mad as a hornet when she learned he'd gone to Georgia after the war ended instead of immediately to Pennsylvania to find her. But hopefully, she would understand once he explained his reasons.

Since being freed from Union captivity, he'd yet to write her a letter. He'd tried; he'd begun half-a-dozen or more. But the words he came up with weren't what he longed to say. The right words eluded him. He wanted to tell her how desperately he missed her, how much he loved her; that thoughts of her were what had gotten him through being surrounded by disease and death and near starvation.

More than anything, he wanted to ask if she'd waited for him. Had she given him up for dead long ago and married someone else? Somewhere deep inside, he feared she hadn't waited. Perhaps if they'd had a real courtship, and time to say all the things he'd wanted to say to her, he'd feel more secure.

Barefoot, he walked to the wash basin, enjoying the feel of the cool hardwood floors beneath his feet. It was the sort of small, every day pleasure one didn't expect to miss while at war, but he had.

He splashed water on his face, glad to finally be rid of the scraggly beard that had grown during his captivity. He avoided looking directly at himself as he lathered and shaved; the hollows beneath his cheeks and the sunken appearance of his eyes unsettled him—the image in the mirror wasn't what he was accustomed to seeing reflected back. It would take a few more weeks of rest and food before he looked anything like himself again.

He knew from what little his mother had shared that the Union army had taken every last bit of meat from the smokehouse and any livestock they could find during their march through Georgia last fall. A few root vegetables and whatever was in season were all that remained now.

A movement in the doorway reflected in the mirror caught his gaze as he bent to rinse the last of the shave soap from his face. The top of a blonde head was visible over his shoulder. At first, he assumed it was Savannah, but as she moved into the room, he saw it was his mother.

She held a folded bundle of clothing. "I found these old shirts of yours and washed and mended them." She smoothed a hand over the material. "Some of the buttons were loose."

"Thank you."

Her gaze met his, and a haunted look came into her soft blue eyes.

"I'm sorry I wasn't home sooner, Mother."

"If you had been, it would have been because you were injured, like poor Tyler." A tremulous smile touched her lips. "You've suffered a great deal, but at least you're home and in one piece."

"Mother, where is Aurora?" He'd yet to see his other sister and wondered why she hadn't come to visit with him. He had a vague recollection of asking Savannah the same question, but he'd been sleeping so much he couldn't recall whether it was a few days or a few hours ago. But he recalled she hadn't answered the question.

"I thought Melody would be first on your mind when you got home." She moved to the bed and began to straighten the covers. He'd never seen her do that before, a house servant had always seen to the task, yet she did it now as though it were second nature to her. The war had changed so many things.

"I plan to speak with her soon. Preferably when I look less like a scarecrow and more like a human being."

She straightened. "I don't think that matters to her, she just wants to see you."

"Soon. You still haven't told me where Aurora is. I'm not going to stop asking, so you may as well tell me."

"When the army marched through last fall, they used our home for a few nights." Mother put a hand to her heart. "Your father would turn over in his grave at the notion of Yankees sleeping at Belle Claire." She sank onto the bed, a worried frown creasing her brow.

"Father passed away before the war," he reminded her gently. "And he was opposed to the secession talk, so I highly doubt he'd react as strongly as you think. Now, where is my sister?"

"Oh, Caleb, she…" Mother pressed a hand to her mouth, stifling a sob.

Chills skittered down his spine. Had a Yankee soldier harmed her? "Tell me."

Another sob. "*She married a Yankee.*"

A sigh of relief escaped him in a rush.

"The same Yankees who took our food and livestock, who burned their way through town. And your sister up and married one of them." Genuine anguish tinged her voice.

He stepped closer. "Mother, as long as she's happy—"

She reached for his hand. "Thank Heaven for dear sweet Melody. She's been a pillar of strength for me through all of this. And now that you're home, we have something to look forward to. The sooner you two are married, the happier I'll be."

He stared at her, and in those moments, he realized just how much the war had changed them all. How was he going to tell her that the sweet, lovely girl from the neighboring plantation whom she loved like a daughter would never be his wife?

If she was this distraught over Aurora having wed a Yankee soldier, how on earth would she react when he told her about Alexa?

****

While Liberty played nearby, Alexa worked in the garden pulling weeds from around the herbs and vegetables. Doing it without Grammy nearby felt strange, but the happy gurgles and coos coming from her daughter helped relieve the sadness.

Nothing, it seemed, would ease the lonely ache that settled more deeply in her heart each day that no word came of Caleb. Had he survived the war, she should have heard from him by now. At times, she tried to convince herself that when news of General Sherman's march through Savannah reached him, he would head for home first, to see to his loved ones. He'd told her more than once that his mother and sisters had no one left but him, so it made sense that he would head south before seeking her out. And with the railroads in that part of the country still under repair, it would take him a long, long time to get there and back.

But surely he'd have sent word to her by now if he were able.

She sat back on her heels, wiping a trickle of sweat from her brow. In the distance, a man approached, and she recognized Will's familiar loping gait.

Liberty giggled with happiness at the sight and rose to her feet to toddle toward him, running when walking didn't get her there fast enough.

"Hey, little lady." Will bent to scoop her up, and she shrieked with happiness as he swept her onto his shoulders. "Mornin', Miss Alexa."

The sound of her daughter's laughter gladdened her heart even as it saddened her to think that Liberty should be running to greet Caleb with such enthusiasm. "How are you, Will?"

"I'm all right, I reckon." He stepped closer and swayed back and forth to entertain the wiggly toddler still perched on his shoulders. "I was in town picking up some supplies and thought I'd stop by and see how you and Miss Felicity were doing."

Alexa rose and brushed the dirt from her trousers. "I was looking for an excuse to take a break. How do you feel about joining me for a glass of lemonade?"

His soft brown eyes lit with pleasure. "I'd like that."

"I'll just get this messy girl tidied up and meet you on the porch in a few minutes."

Will chuckled. "Dirty hands ain't gonna hurt her none, but I remember what a stickler you are for hand washing." He bent low enough to allow Alexa to pluck the child from his shoulders.

A short time later, she met the former soldier on the porch with a pitcher of lemonade and a plate of cookies Felicity had baked earlier in the day.

Will settled into a chair and helped himself to a cookie. His gaze strayed toward the house. "So, is Miss Felicity planning to go back home anytime soon?"

Alexa poured a glass for him and a partial glass for herself, knowing Liberty would insist on sampling whatever she had. "No, she plans to stay here to help me with the baby. She wants to be a nurse, but she's too young to work in one of the hospitals in the city. So she's learning what she can by working with me or with Father."

"Nice about your father and the Widow Thompson."

Alexa laughed. "After twenty five years, it's about time he gave up on my mother ever returning and started seeing someone."

Will set his glass aside and fidgeted a bit, then sat forward with his elbows on his knees. "Miss Alexa, are you goin' to the church picnic next week?"

For lack of something else to do, she helped her daughter bring the glass of lemonade to her mouth. Ever stubborn and independent, Liberty moved out of her reach, content to let the sticky drink dribble down her chin. "You know the town biddies would be scandalized if a fallen woman like me darkened the door of a place of worship."

"Don't talk like that." His tone was gentle, and a little frustrated.

"Well, it's the truth." She succeeded in pulling the empty glass from the tiny hands and swapped it with half a cookie. Effectively distracted, Liberty turned her focus back to her friend, grinning at Will with delight.

Alexa poured a bit of lemonade for herself. "They never saw Caleb, so I don't blame them for not believing I was ever wed to Liberty's father. You know how they love to gossip."

Will stretched out his long legs, gaze intent on the baby. "Not in front of me they don't. I won't stand for them talking that way about you, not after all you do for the people of this town."

"I appreciate that, Will."

"There's still no word from Caleb, then?"

A familiar pang of sadness pierced her. "No."

"I'm sorry, Miss Alexa." He straightened so Liberty could climb onto his lap. "You must hate me for the role I played in all this."

"I could never be angry with you, Will. You were duty-bound—Caleb would have done the same had he been in your position. And it's *because* of your generosity in allowing us to have a wedding night that I have my beautiful daughter." His ears had turned bright red, and she reached to place a hand on his. "No matter what comes, I'm grateful for that."

He glanced down at her hand on his. "How long do you plan to wait for him?"

"I'm in no hurry to declare myself a widow." She shrugged, and decided to pull her hand back, in case anyone happened by and got the wrong impression.

Liberty turned to look at Will and he pulled a face and tickled her. "Have you written to his family?"

"Not yet, but I plan to." As soon as she figured out how to explain who she was and why she was writing for news of her husband. "Will, why don't you ask Felicity to the picnic? She spends far too much time looking after Liberty and me and no time at all having fun."

That familiar hound dog gaze landed on her with a look somewhere between hurt and surprise. "You know why."

"I'm not sure I do. Will, I'm a married woman. You'll only make yourself fodder for gossip if you're seen talking with me."

"I don't care what those old pea hens think." Nonetheless, he seemed to take her suggestion to heart and rose to his feet. "I owe you my life, and you're the only real friend I got in this town." He set Liberty down, pausing to tweak her cookie-smeared nose. "Besides, they won't gossip much about me, they're still hopin' I'll marry one of their horse-faced daughters."

She laughed as he placed his hat on his head and smiled warmly.

"That's a sound I haven't heard lately."

"Please think about asking Felicity to the picnic. She's a wonderful cook, and I know she'd enjoy a day out."

He glanced toward the house again, as if fearing someone would overhear. "Don't you think she's a bit young for me?"

"She'll be eighteen this month." Alexa wished she dared tell Will that her young cousin had been sweet on him since caring for him after the battle.

"And I'm twenty seven, a lot closer to your age than hers. I'll think on it. But it seems to me you need a father for that baby, and if your husband doesn't come home soon, I'd like you to reconsider my proposal."

Genuine affection warmed her at his sincere words. Dear, sweet Will; she could always depend on him.

But her heart wasn't ready to give up on Caleb.

Eighteen

My Dearest Alexa,

Mere words cannot describe the depth of my longing for you. My fondest wish is that we'll be reunited soon.

Caleb rubbed a hand over his jaw and re-read the lines for what felt like the thousandth time. Never in his life had the right words been so elusive. He'd written other letters since returning home, including one to Aurora, letting her know he had returned and to congratulate her on her marriage. So why wouldn't the words he needed to say to Alexa come to him?

Sighing, he leaned his head back against the trunk of the tree whose shade had beckoned him a short time ago, and closed his eyes in the hope that bringing her image to mind would help.

"Caleb?"

Even after all these years, he recognized that sweet voice.

He opened his eyes. Sun blocked his vision but lit the dark golden hair with an angelic glow. "Melody."

Caleb rose to his feet. Undoubtedly his mother was behind this unexpected visit; she'd been in a hurry to put them together again.

Melody reached out, and he took her hands, bowing gracefully over them in greeting.

"I haven't seen anyone do that in a long, long

time."

Her laughter, as always, reminded him of the tinkling of wind chimes. "It's good to see you." He searched her face, wondering if he'd feel something he hadn't before. But nothing had changed. She was as lovely as ever, the hard years of war may have aged her, but she was easily still the most beautiful girl in the county.

"Are you well?" she asked. "Your mother says those awful Yankees had you prisoner for two years."

He pulled away, clasped his hands behind his back and began to walk. "I'm getting stronger every day."

She fell into step beside him. "I wondered when I didn't hear from you if…" Her voice trailed off. "So many of our young men were lost, and so much has changed since I last saw you. I wasn't sure you were even alive."

He sighed, realizing that as much as he'd dreaded this conversation, she had presented him the opportunity. "A great deal has changed."

As briefly as he could, he told her about being wounded in Pennsylvania and the female doctor who had saved his life and risked her own safety to keep him hidden until he was well.

"Only to turn you over to the Yankees?" Melody asked, an expression of horror crossing her lovely face.

"No, not willingly. She would have defied Abe Lincoln himself to keep me from being taken prisoner, but she had others depending on her."

"She sounds like an amazing woman." Her tone was thoughtful.

"She is." He stopped walking and turned to face her. "If I hadn't been injured, if things had turned out differently, I'd have been home on Christmas furlough that year and we'd have wed."

Her gaze searched his, as though she sensed what he was about to say. "Caleb, it's not your fault."

"Melody, did you ever truly love me?"

Her golden brown eyes widened. "Did I... Of course I did."

But her slight hesitation gave him hope.

"I've had a great deal of time to think—far too much of it, really. Melody, your face never lit up around me the way it did around Matthew." It seemed odd to say his brother's name aloud again. Taking her arm, he began to walk again. "It was him you loved. Not me."

She pulled in a shaky breath. "My promise was to *you*, Caleb."

"Promises were made for us, but they were never *our* promises." They walked on a bit farther, and he stopped and took her hands in his. "I want you to marry someone you love. Someone who makes you happy— not someone you're *obligated* to wed."

Tears welled in her eyes. "I don't understand."

"Forgive me, Melody, for being too young and naïve to realize what you and I had was not love. Respect, admiration, friendship. But not love." He pulled in a deep breath. "I didn't know...until I felt it for someone else."

Her jaw dropped. "You, too?"

Relief swept over him. "You love someone else?"

"I do." A bubble of laughter escaped her. "You know him—Stephen Wilson. He followed you and Ty around like a shadow."

"That little pup? He was barely knee high to a

grasshopper when I left for war."

Her cheeks pinkened. "He's only two years younger than us. But he remembers you fondly. He was hurt in the war. I've helped to care for him since he came home and it just...*happened*." Tears spilled down her cheeks. "One day I was faithfully awaiting your return, and the next I realized I loved Stephen. I'm not even sure when it began."

Memories of the time spent in Alexa's care flashed through his mind. He squeezed her hand. "I understand. More than you could ever realize."

"But Caleb—who? Where did you have time to meet—" She gazed into his face, her eyes shining with happiness. "It's the lady doctor, isn't it? I thought I heard something in your voice when you mentioned her."

He couldn't help the smile that came over him. "Her name is Alexandra Winters—well, she's Alexandra McKenna now."

"You're *married*?"

It felt so good to finally tell someone, to share the news that he'd kept to himself for nearly two years. He nodded. "It wasn't planned, but yes, before I was taken prisoner, we were married."

To his great surprise, she punched him in the arm. "Then why in God's name are you *here*?"

Caleb laughed at her playfulness, not having seen this side of his old friend since they were children. "I needed to make things right with you, and to see my family. I wasn't here for spring planting, but I feel obligated to stay and help Tyler with the harvest." Guilt nagged at him at the thought of leaving his family again. "But I hope to head up North soon, to see my wife, and sort out how I'll support us and where we'll spend the rest of our lives together."

He tucked her arm in the crook of his elbow and began to walk again. "Now, tell me about this county boy who has stolen your heart."

****

Telling Mother and Savannah had been more difficult than Caleb had imagined. He'd had two long years—from injury and recovery to imprisonment—to get over any bitter feelings about the war and Yankees. And time spent with Alexa had helped him see things differently.

But for his family, the wounds were still fresh; they still suffered the devastation of ravaged homes and farmland, lost livestock and the destruction of their way of life. The damage that had been done and the angry, bitter feelings would take time to heal.

Nearly a month had passed since he'd come home, and though it would be months before he was anywhere near recovered, his strength returned a bit each day, and he was eager to return to his wife.

Caleb glanced around the dining room where he'd gathered his family to tell them his news. The fine velvet draperies that had hung at the windows were gone. Most of the furniture in the house had been destroyed, cut up for firewood as his family had needed it, or carted off by greedy Union soldiers.

Though the mahogany table they'd dined at every meal remained, most of the chairs were missing.

Now, his mother had turned completely away from him, and Savannah silently cried beside him while cradling her newborn son.

"A Yankee, Caleb?" Mother sobbed. "The same

people who held you prisoner and nearly starved you to death? The same ones who ruined our crops and burned our cities?"

He moved to stand at his sister's side, sensing she would be the one most likely to come around to his way of thinking. "Alexa did none of those things. She exhausted herself caring for men from *both* sides of the war."

"You might have mentioned your marriage before now." This from mother, who dabbed a lace handkerchief to her eyes.

"I had to tell Melody first. She needed to hear it from me."

At the mention of his former fiancée's name, Mother sobbed anew.

"She's still part of your family," Caleb offered with a hopeful glance at Tyler. "You'll always be related to Melody by marriage."

"No." Mother stamped her foot, appearing in that moment the spoiled, coddled belle she'd once been. "I refuse to listen to this nonsense. You may be married to some Yankee girl, but I don't have to accept it." She turned in her chair to face him with angry tears. "And I won't. No more than I have to accept your sister's traitorous marriage."

"He's not a traitor, Mama," Savannah spoke up. "He fell in love. There's no crime in that." She glanced up at Tyler, who shifted from foot to foot as if uncomfortable with the entire conversation. "Melody loves someone else, too. They're getting married next month."

Rising from her chair, Mother hurried off, sobbing as though her heart were breaking.

"Take Matthew. I'll go after her." As Savannah handed the baby to Tyler, she met Caleb's gaze. "It's been hardest on Mother. This war has taken everything from her."

Caleb raked a hand through his hair. "And now I've taken away the hope that I would come home and make everything better."

"It's not your fault." She rushed off in the direction their mother had gone.

An awkward silence descended as he stood there with the man who had once been his best friend.

Cradling his tiny son with his one good arm, Tyler turned to stare out the window. "My mother's the same. Their whole way of life is gone—husbands, sons, their homes. It's not easy to accept that it'll never be like it was."

"Not for any of us." Caleb sighed and moved around to sit at the table. He was no closer to getting home to Alexa than he had been before telling Melody and his mother about his marriage.

"It's funny how things work out." Ty spoke up, still staring out the window. "If the war hadn't come, you'd be married to Melody, I'd probably have married Aurora. We'd be living completely different lives than what we are."

"Melody would never have been happy being wed to a military man, and that's all I ever wanted to be." He pinched the bridge of his nose between his thumb and finger, wondering, not for the first time, how he would support his wife when he returned north to claim her.

"She's happy here. Or at least she was." Ty glanced over his shoulder. "It's going to take a lot of time to rebuild. Folks are beaten down, the old are weak and the young are injured or sick."

"Sick?" The word snapped Caleb out of his musings. "I never thought about that. Tyler, is there even a doctor left in the county?"

His friend shrugged. "Ol Doc Macintosh is still around, far as I know. But he must be older than the hills by now."

Filled with energy and a renewed sense of purpose, Caleb sprang to his feet.

Ty stared at him with a look of amusement. "Where are you off to?"

He couldn't help the grin that came over him. "To prepare for the trip north. I know just the doctor who would relish a chance to work with the sick and downtrodden." Especially when the county folk weren't in a position to care if that doctor was female—or a Yankee. He started out of the room, then stopped and grinned back at his friend. "One of these days, I may even forgive you for marrying my little sister."

Ty's chuckle followed him into the hall. "And I may forgive you for *not* marrying mine."

Nineteen

Alexa finished drying the last of the dishes from supper and put them away—all with a fussy toddler on her hip.

She glanced at her daughter, and out of habit, swiped a towel over her wet chin. A wave of tenderness washed over her at the sight of the little face set in a scowl. Cutting teeth had poor Liberty cranky and unable to sleep. A spoonful of brandy sweetened with a little honey would help, though, if tonight was anything like last, she wouldn't sleep long at all.

The door groaned on its hinges as Felicity came in from the backyard with a pail of water. "I know you didn't get much rest last night, so I thought I'd give Liberty a bath and get her settled for bed."

"If you can get her to cooperate." Alexa bounced the tot on her hip. "She's been stuck to me like this for most of the day."

"Oh, I'm sure she'll put up a fuss, but she loves her Aunt Felicity. She'll be fine." Felicity laughed and reached her arms out to take the baby. "Why don't you take your coffee out onto the porch and enjoy it before it gets dark. It won't be long until the nights are too cold to sit outside after dinner."

Despite her daughter's protests and whimpering, Alexa did as Felicity suggested. One thing she'd learned since becoming a mother was a little rest went a long way toward saving her sanity.

She pulled Grammy's shawl around her shoulders for a bit of warmth, taking a moment to press the soft material to her face and inhale the scent of her grandmother, then settled into her favorite rocker and gazed out across the yard.

Visible scars remained on the landscape, damaged or missing trees, houses with cannon holes, all reminders of what the town had gone through two summers ago. She often wondered if things would ever return to any kind of normalcy.

For two years now, visitors arrived from surrounding states, seeking their loved one's remains or simply wishing to see the land on which their son or father perished. Now that the war was over, Southerners were also making the journey, paying respect to their lost loved ones. *Normal*, it seemed, would have to be redefined.

Alexa sipped her coffee, smiling slightly at the fussing coming from inside where Felicity did her best to soothe and entertain Liberty. She'd come to truly love her young cousin these past two years and wondered how she'd have gotten through the shame of pregnancy with no husband in sight—and no way to prove she'd ever had one when the Reverend passed away—or Liberty's birth and Grammy's death without Felicity beside her.

The door groaned on its hinges. Father stepped out, bringing with him the familiar smell of witch hazel. The sight of his best trousers caught her eye. "You're all dressed up."

He adjusted his suit coat. "Just my Sunday clothes."

"Off to visit Adelaide?"

"*Missus* Thompson, to you, young lady."

Alexa rose to her feet and brushed a bit of lint from his shoulder. "Yes, but I've examined her many times, and it's hard not to call a woman by first name when you know her so intimately." To anyone else, the words would be shocking, but Father understood. "When do you plan to bring her over for supper?"

"We're keeping things quiet."

"Yes, expect every wagging tongue in town has seen you sitting on her front porch all summer long."

The twitch of a smile touched his lips. "I suppose they have." He gazed out across the yard, and a sadness crossed his face. "The same wagging tongues who call my daughter a Jezebel and say my granddaughter was born on the wrong side of the sheets."

Anger nipped at her, but she'd long ago realized the town pea hens would gossip about her whether she gave them reason or not. But she prayed their sharp tongues wouldn't harm her daughter as she grew up. She smoothed his lapel and leaned in to kiss his cheek. "They can say it all they want, we know it's not true, and that's all that matters."

He looked at her, his pale eyes misty. "I wish I could spare you having to listen to it, that's all."

"One of these days, Caleb will show up, and I'll be able to prove them all wrong." She returned to her seat in the rocker. Her heart fell at the thought of him and the months without a word from him. A familiar ache began deep inside her.

"Daughter, don't you think if that young man was still alive, he'd have sent word by now?"

His words echoed the thoughts that had been

whispering through her mind for weeks now.

What if he never returned? What if he'd died in prison—how would she live never knowing what had become of him? The sight of him before her blurred as tears filled her eyes.

Father pulled out his hanky and pressed it into her hand, then bent to hug her. "There now, I didn't mean to upset you, sweetheart." He pulled back, removing his spectacles and wiping them on his shirt. "You're a mother now, so you know how important it is to a parent to know their child is happy. And when I see you with that far off look on your face…"

"I know." She swiped at the moisture on her cheeks, then reached to smooth the shirt he'd wrinkled with his spectacles. "Your daughter wants to see you happy, too. So don't keep Miss Adelaide waiting or she may throw you over for some other eligible doctor."

He chuckled, placed his hat on his head and was off. As she watched him stroll out the gate and down the street, a heaviness settled on her heart.

Before Caleb had left, he had written letters to be opened in the event he didn't return. She had long ago read the one he'd left for her and Grammy, thanking them for taking such excellent care of him, but he had written it before they'd made love, before they'd married, so it wasn't so much an expression of love as it was gratitude.

He'd also given her a letter to send to his family. She had never opened it, not wanting to intrude on his privacy. But she had never mailed the letter—doing so would be the same as admitting she believed he was dead. Holding onto the letter was a way of holding onto the hope that he'd return.

She pulled in a ragged breath, inhaling the early autumn smells of moldering leaves and the tang of the cooler night air. Six months since the war ended and she'd still had no word from him.

Was Father right? Was it time to let Caleb go?

****

Melody's wedding was not the society event it would have been four years earlier, when Caleb was to marry her. But small ceremony or not, he thought she made a beautiful bride. Joy radiated from her and Steven both and anyone could see they were in love. He almost felt guilty for the months he'd insisted on holding onto their engagement. His stubborn refusal to let go of their betrothal out of a sense of duty would have cost them both the loves of a lifetime. And in the long run, they would have been miserable.

As he celebrated with a glass of port, his sister approached him. He smiled at her, still trying to reconcile the image of his baby sister that had existed in his mind all these years, with the young mother before him.

"They both look so happy. Don't you think?"

"They do. And so do you."

A flush of pink stained her cheeks. "I am."

He glanced across the room, where Tyler stood with his sister and her new husband. "You've loved him your whole life, haven't you?"

Emotion welled in Savannah's cornflower blue eyes. "Yes."

He took hold of her arm and began to walk with her. "But as I recall, he only had eyes for Aurora. How did you manage to steal him away?"

A delicate flush stained her cheeks. "I wrote him

letters nearly every day while he was away. By the time he came home to recuperate from his injury, we were in love."

Caleb sensed there was much more to it, but didn't want to push. All that mattered was Savannah's happiness.

She smiled up at him. "And you? What was your wedding to the Yankee girl like?"

An image of Alexa in her mourning dress came to mind, closely followed by memories of the carnal delights they'd enjoyed the entire night afterward. He cleared his throat. "Every bit as nice as this one."

"Do you love her?"

He met his sister's sincere gaze. "With all my heart. I resisted for a long time, not wanting to dishonor my promise to Melody, but in the end, it was just too powerful for either of us to ignore."

"I'm so glad to hear that." She leaned up to kiss his cheek. "Are you heading north to see her soon?"

"Early next week." He'd made the decision just today. It was time. Whether his family was ready to get by without him or not, it was time. Alexa was his family now, and he couldn't bear to be away from her any longer. Especially since he'd yet to find a way to let her know he was still alive and planning to return to her.

"Caleb, don't you think you should send a wire or write her that you're coming?"

"I've thought of that." In truth, he'd thought of little else. But the longer he went without sending her a letter, the harder it seemed to be. And to wire her now to say he was coming would be nothing short of a shock. "I promised her I'd come back. I know Alexa;

she'll wait for me."

"I can't wait to meet her." Savannah said with a dreamy sigh. "A real lady doctor *and* the woman who stole my big brother's heart. All in one package."

He chuckled. "She'll need to make arrangements to return with me. It may take several weeks. And I want to travel to Maine to visit Aurora while I'm up north. So it may be some time before you get to meet her."

"Quite the contrary," she scoffed. "Didn't mother tell you? We all want to meet her. We're going with you."

"*Mother* is planning to go?" He glanced across the room to where his mother, cradling her grandson, beamed with pride while chatting with Mrs. Chamberlain.

"I've convinced her she'll need to help me with the baby," Savannah added in a conspiratorial whisper.

He allowed his gaze to travel the length of her. She seemed fine, but he knew little Matthew didn't allow her much rest. "Savannah, you just had a baby; you shouldn't travel."

She put a hand to her hip, and he recognized the stubborn set of her chin when she gazed up into his face.

"Maybe I'm not quite ready to part with my big brother yet. I only just got you back; I'm not ready for another farewell. And I haven't seen my sister in over a year, if you're going to visit Aurora, I'm going, too."

"What about Mother?"

"It's high time she got over this nonsense about Yankees. Besides, if Alexa is as amazing as you say, I know Mother will come to love her."

"I hope you're right." More than that, he hoped *he*

was right about Alexa waiting for him. He reached into his coat pocket and felt the envelope he'd placed there earlier. When he'd gone into town yesterday there had been a letter waiting for him. Not for him directly—it was for his mother and sisters, written in his own hand. He still remembered the day he'd written it, the last day they were together, when he'd made plans to leave Gettysburg.

He'd asked Alexa to mail it if he didn't return, but then they had been discovered in the fruit cellar and so much happened afterward he'd forgotten about the letter.

Apparently she hadn't forgotten it. He had only himself to blame, for waiting so long to contact her. But the fact that she'd finally mailed it could only mean one thing.

My wife thinks I'm dead.

Twenty

Stepping off the train in Gettysburg was a little like stepping into another world. The town appeared very different from the one Caleb had surveyed with the Confederate army nearly three years ago.

Then, it had been a quiet, sleepy town. Now, it bustled with the busyness of people coming and going, and despite the chill in the air of early November, they were far from the only Southerners making the journey. Several other southern families were there as well, hoping to find the remains of a loved one, or to thank someone who had cared for their brother or son after the battle. Veterans from both north and south were also traveling to the town, wanting to revisit the battlefields.

Though he was in a hurry to get settled into the hotel and be on his way, his mother and sister had other ideas.

As they passed the different store fronts, Savannah and Mother, so long denied the purely feminine pleasure of browsing window displays, lagged behind. At last, seeing an arrangement of hats and shoes in the window of one store, they pleaded with Caleb and Tyler for a few moments to browse inside.

In truth, he was more than a bit nervous to find Alexa again. Thoughts that she'd changed her mind plagued him, as did the memory of his request that Will Carter look after her should he fail to return. No doubt the Union Captain who had been Alexa's most ardent admirer waited in the wings to take Caleb's place at her side.

As Savannah cooed over a bonnet, a snippet of conversation stopped him cold.

"Last week she wore those Turkish pantaloons in town. Did you see her?"

"I did, indeed, Clara. And she can call them whatever she pleases, they're still trousers."

A prickling sensation crept along his spine. He knew those voices. And he had an odd feeling he knew who they were discussing.

Caleb turned to see two middle aged women browsing the hat selection alongside his mother and sister. He didn't recognize them, but their voices were definitely familiar.

"My Carol Ann just adores that Mister Carter, but he won't even look at her. Because of *that woman*."

The other woman tsked. "It's disgraceful. Claiming herself a widow when the whole town knows she was never married except to that fellow from Syracuse."

"I heard it was a Rebel soldier who fathered that baby."

The word slammed into Caleb like a brick wall. *A baby?* So many times he wondered if a child had been created from their love that night, but he'd never allowed himself to dwell on the hope.

"Oh, there was never any Rebel. I'll bet poor Mr. Carter fathered that child. He *was* right there in her house recuperating for months. They were alone for hours at a time."

By now, Mother and Savannah had moved away, and Caleb wondered if the gossip had made them uncomfortable.

The shorter woman finished fondling the hat and set it back on the display with the others.

"And now this wedding—if that isn't a mockery of all that's decent."

Caleb could remain a silent observer no more. He cleared his throat, effectively attracting their attention.

"Good morning, ladies." He swept his hat from his head and bowed in the fashion of a true Southern gentleman.

Both tittered like school girls. "Good Morning, sir."

"Pardon me, but I couldn't help overhearing your conversation."

The two exchanged guilty glances.

"That wouldn't happen to be Doctor Alexandra Winters you were discussing?"

The taller woman's hand fluttered to her throat to fumble with a broach. "Well, she calls herself Doctor McKenna now, but yes."

"I was injured here after the battle in sixty three, and it was Doctor Winters—er, *McKenna*, as you say, who cared for me."

The smaller woman backed up a step. "A great many women from town cared for injured soldiers, sir."

Annoyance prickled as the two, undoubtedly Alexa's dreaded "pea hens," tried to discredit her contribution and hard work. "She did a great deal more than that, she saved my life." He gestured to his mother and sister, who had stopped browsing when he'd spoken. "My family and I are here to thank her. Did I hear you mention a wedding?"

"Y-yes. At the Winters' place today."

God's Nightshirt, was she preparing to re-marry? He couldn't bring himself to ask, not with his family standing right there.

"You've been most kind." He bowed gracefully, and once again they simpered like young girls. Caleb turned to leave, his feet suddenly in a hurry to move, but forced himself to stop. "Oh, and ladies? I'll thank you not to speak ill of Doctor McKenna. She happens to be my wife."

****

In one of the upstairs bedrooms, Alexa reached to adjust Father's tie, then brush a bit of lint from his lapels. "You look very handsome."

He smiled. "Almost as nervous as I was at the last wedding we had here."

At the reminder, Alexa felt a familiar wave of sadness. "That feels like a long time ago."

"I'm sorry, honey, I didn't mean to upset you."

"You did nothing of the sort. After all, weddings are happy occasions, right? And today is a happy day, not one for dwelling on the past."

He chuckled at her ministrations. "Stop fussing over this old man and go get dressed."

Alexa kissed his cheek, inhaling the smells of peppermint and tobacco, smells she would always associate with her father, and hurried into her own room.

She bent to check on her sleeping daughter, smiling at the sight of the little cherub with a thumb in her mouth, soundly asleep.

As she changed her clothes, the sounds of raised voices floated in through the window.

"I don't care what you say, Will Carter." Felicity's

angry voice came from outside. "I can write whomever I want."

Tiptoeing closer, Alexa peeked out the window. One of the soldiers they had cared for after the war, a young man from Ohio, had been writing to Felicity. For some reason, once Will had gotten wind of the news, he'd made his disapproval known.

"He's coming here to visit next summer, and you have no say whatsoever in it." Felicity stalked off in a huff. Will stalked off in a different direction.

Alexa smiled. Whether he knew it or not, the day was fast coming when Will would realize Felicity was no longer a little girl.

The front door closed with a bang and Liberty wailed her dismay. Alexa scooped her up as her cousin rushed up the stairs and stomped into the room. She pulled up short at the sight of the angry toddler.

"I'm sorry. I forgot she was sleeping."

"It's all right. She'd have woken soon anyway. I don't want her to miss the wedding."

Felicity flopped onto the bed with a huff of indignation. "Oh, that Will Carter makes me so angry."

Smiling, Alexa went about changing the baby. "He certainly doesn't like to hear you speak about Robert."

"It's not as if it's his place to be concerned." Her young cousin stared up at the ceiling, a frown furrowing her brow.

"Did you ever consider that he might be jealous?"

A bark of laughter escaped the girl. "I sincerely doubt it." She rolled to one side and smiled at the sight of the baby. "You've got enough to do today without worrying about silly things such as that."

"Nonsense."

"I don't need to get dressed just yet, but you do. Why don't I take Liberty outside for some fresh air while you get ready?"

"I appreciate that. Felicity...I really don't know what I'd have done without you here, especially since Grammy's been gone."

Her cousin beamed, her eyes misting. "Weddings always make you nostalgic, don't they?" She took the baby into her arms. "But thank you. I'll make sure she doesn't get her dress dirty."

Alexa laughed at the absurd notion of keeping her daughter out of mischief. After the two left, she washed up and changed into her black dress—a bit somber for a wedding, but she was in mourning, after all, both for Grammy...and for Caleb.

At the thought of him, sadness descended on her. This was the very dress she'd worn when they'd taken their wedding vows. She never wanted to give up on him, especially since he'd promised to return. But he hadn't been far enough into the recovery process, his body still weak...

She brushed away the tears that trickled down her cheeks. She wouldn't allow sadness to overshadow things today. Finishing with her hair, she smoothed her dress and headed for the stairs. A few fall flowers would be just the thing to brighten her up.

Outside, she searched the yard for Felicity and Liberty. After walking the full length and not finding them, she headed into the barn.

No sign of either of them.

Most likely her daughter had insisted on trying out her new walking skills and taken Felicity farther than planned. Guests would be arriving for the wedding soon, so she would have to choose flowers without them. October had been pleasantly warm, so many of Grammy's beloved fall flowers were still in bloom.

Alexa had just gathered a handful of zinnia's, black-eyed Susan's and chrysanthemum when a prickling along her spine alerted her to the presence of someone else.

"I've come to pay my respects to the Widow McKenna."

Her inner core stirred at that voice. Liquid vowels and smooth as brandy. Her heart leapt to her throat, and the breath left her lungs in a whoosh. She whirled around, scarcely able to believe her eyes.

Caleb!

He stood before her, looking every inch the gentleman in a brown frock coat, vest and ascot, and thinner than when she'd last seen him, with a weariness about his eyes that hadn't been there before. But it was him.

The flowers slipped from her fingers. "Y-you're alive."

"Very much so." He stepped toward her. "News you apparently find surprising."

She could only stare as he moved closer, his steps never faltering as he closed the distance between them.

Caleb was alive and healthy and—*here*.

He pulled her against him, bending his head toward hers. "Allow me to congratulate the bride."

"The wh—" Her words were cut off as his mouth claimed hers. At first his kiss was harsh, angry, but after her initial resistance fled and she softened, parting her lips beneath his, it changed. His mouth gentled on hers, until the years that had passed existed no more.

The sorrow she'd felt, the worry, the joy, all spilled forth, and she kissed him with abandon, reveling in the familiar taste of him, the warmth of his tongue seeking a response from hers, the smell of his skin so close to her nostrils.

Feelings that had lain dormant sprang to life, igniting within her, consuming her until nothing existed but this moment.

When at last he pulled back, dark blue eyes, the dusky color of twilight, met hers in an anguished stare. "For God's sake, couldn't you wait?"

The words barely registered in her pleasure-hazed brain. "Wait? For what?"

"I understand there's a wedding here today." Sarcasm tinged his voice. "I'd certainly hate to miss it."

The warm, pleasant emotions swelling in her came to a dead halt. She pushed away from him. Did he really think she would re-marry so quickly?

"Will must be the happiest man alive to finally—"

"Bastard!" Her hand met his cheek with a loud crack. "That's for leaving me to wonder for six months whether you were alive or dead...or in Melody's arms. And *this*—" She swung again, this time meeting her target with less force. "Is for being such an ass!"

She bent to scoop up the flowers, moaning in dismay to see that in their passion they'd shifted enough to trample some of the buds.

He bent to help her retrieve the flowers. "How could you think I'd go back to Melody?"

"And how could you think I'd marry someone else not knowing..." She hated how her voice broke. "My *father* is getting married today. And you have a lot of explaining to do."

Straightening, she stalked across the yard, resisting the urge to run before an onslaught of tears could overcome her. Caleb was alive! It was the news she'd waited on pins and needles to learn since he'd been marched off to prison over two years ago. So why was she angry?

Damn him, he always affected her this way. But she hadn't waited all this time to bicker with him the moment he returned.

She stopped so abruptly she nearly ran into Felicity, who came rushing around the corner with Liberty in her arms. "The reverend is here, and I think guests are starting to arrive, there's a carriage—*oh*!" She halted in her tracks, eyes going wide. The young face lit with pleasure, but fell as she glanced from Alexa back to Caleb.

The anger Alexa had felt faded at the sight of Liberty staring up at Caleb.

Flowers fell forgotten to the ground as she took the toddler from Felicity's arms and turned. "Caleb, this..." A ball of emotion lodged in her throat. She'd waited so long to tell him about his daughter, had dreamed of this moment. Somehow, in her dreams it had been a more joyous reunion.

His eyes welled as the baby studied him with open curiosity. He reached to take her, and the toddler went cautiously into his arms, staring at him with the same inquisitiveness she normally reserved for new experiences.

He ran a hand over her head, twining one dark curl about his finger. "My God. Alexa, she's the perfect image of you."

"I see more of her father in her. She's quite bossy."

"Her name is Liberty," Felicity offered. "Liberty Hope McKenna."

"It's a beautiful name." A broad grin crossed Caleb's face, and he glanced at Felicity. "Speaking of beautiful, look who's all grown up."

Her cousin blushed. "I was beginning to think we'd never see you again."

He glanced at Alexa, his eyes darkening with emotion. "So I've been told."

Liberty whimpered, her face crumpling into a pout and reached for her mother.

"What did I do?" Caleb asked, relinquishing her to Alexa.

"Nothing at all," Felicity assured him. "She just needs time to get acquainted with you."

The first strains of piano music filtered out the door, causing a panic to rise in Alexa. "The wedding is about to start. Felicity, can you take the baby and give us a few moments alone?"

Without waiting for Caleb to object, Alexa took hold of his hand and half dragged him toward the house.

A smile twitched at Caleb's lips as she pulled him along. Had any other woman tried to lead him about, he'd find it amusing. But not Alexa. Her take-charge manner was part of what he'd first fallen in love with two summers ago. She tugged him past the willow tree where they had first kissed, then onto the porch that still bore the scar from the bullet she'd fired into the ceiling. Hurrying past the front door, she all but dragged him over to the side entrance where he'd seen her come out the night he'd come to tell her about Nate.

When he stepped into the kitchen behind her, he

spied Will Carter chatting with Alexa's father. Both turned startled expressions on him. Carter's jaw all but hit the floor, but Alexa didn't give any of them time to speak, simply tossing an, "I'll explain it all later," as she pulled him through the dining room.

She didn't give him time to speak to any of the people gathered in the room as she tugged his hand hard, urging him into what appeared to be a study.

At last, she released his hand and hurried across the room to the large desk that sat opposite the door.

Unsure of her intent, but unwilling to allow her to control things a moment longer, Caleb closed the door behind him, taking care to slide the bolt in place for added privacy, then leaned against it.

"So, was that disappointment or relief on Will's face just now? He clearly wasn't expecting to see me."

She frowned, rummaging through a drawer in search of something. "Will's in love with Felicity and she with him. They haven't figured it out yet, but they will."

"Some people are stubborn that way."

Her gaze flitted from him to the closed door, to the desk between them. Was she nervous to be alone with him again? The thought brought a smile to his face, recalling all the times they'd been alone in the past. "This is the second time I've seen you in a dress. I rather like it."

"I certainly don't make a habit of wearing them."

"I know." He stepped forward, beginning to close the distance between them. "When I was in town earlier this morning, I overheard your pea hens discussing your latest attire. Turkish pantaloons, I believe?"

She flushed. "I…thought it was a fair compromise

to wearing britches everywhere. I don't want Liberty to grow up hearing people speaking about her mother's attire." She closed her eyes for a second. "But no matter what I do, the tongues wag."

"Liberty will grow up to be exactly like her mother, if I have any say in it." He stepped closer. "And I do."

"Y-yes."

As he drew closer, she backed up a step. Sunlight from a window behind the desk glinted off something gold clutched in her hand.

He continued closing the distance between them with predatory purpose, and she continued backing up until she could go no farther.

"Why are you retreating? That's not the Alexa I recall."

"Because…" She crossed her arms over herself. "Because I'm not the Alexa you knew, my entire world has changed. And you're… You feel different. *This* feels different."

"It will take time to get used to one another again. We had a rather unusual courtship."

She met his gaze with a challenging look. "If by *unusual* you mean you were planning to marry someone else until minutes before we were wed, then I suppose we did."

A grin twitched at the corner of his mouth at the jealousy dripping from her voice. Had she really thought he'd decided to stay with Melody?

"Alexa, I've waited more than two years to be near you again. The kiss we shared earlier wasn't nearly enough to satisfy that yearning."

Without waiting for her to answer, he took hold of

her wrist and pulled her closer. Lilacs wafted around him, surrounding his senses with the smell of her. Whatever she'd held in her hand tumbled to the floor with a metallic sound, but he was too concerned with how close her mouth was to worry about it. He slid his hands into her hair, not caring if he scattered hair pins and mussed the carefully arranged style.

A whimper escaped her as he bent to kiss her, halting when their lips were a hairsbreadth apart. "Whatever else the war may have changed, I'm still the same man who fell in love with you, Alexandra McKenna."

He took great pains to be tender, reacquainting himself with the taste of her, the softness of her. Her arms twined around his neck and she moaned, pressing into him. What he'd intended as a sweet kiss between reunited lovers quickly engulfed them both.

Where moments ago he'd been exhausted and world weary, now his body surged to life. Their lips had always fit so well together. He savored the familiar feel of her body against his, soft in all the places he was hard—and Heaven help him he *was* hard, aching with need for her.

Before all sense of reason left him, he pulled back slightly, breaking the kiss.

Anguished green eyes met his. "Dammit, Caleb, where were you?"

He pressed his forehead to hers. "You have every right to be angry."

"I had no way to know if you—"

"Shhh." Finding the desk chair behind him, he sat, pulling her with him. Her buttocks rested against the bulge in his trousers that so desperately wanted to take command. But for now, it would have to be enough.

Her hair hung half-up, half-down from the upswept hairstyle, and he reached to pull out the remaining pins until the mass fell in a dark cascade. He smiled as the scent of lilacs surrounded him. "I couldn't come back to you until I was well."

Her eyes widened. "You were sick?"

He tucked a loose wave behind her ear. "Not sick. Malnourished and filthy. I didn't want to return to you an invalid in need of your care once again."

"But—"

"I know." He pressed a fingertip to her lips. "There's no one better qualified to restore me to good health. But I wanted to return to you whole and healthy—a *man*, not a patient." He dropped a kiss to her nose. "I'm still not as strong as I'd like and thinner than I should be. I promise to give myself over to your care from this point forward."

She studied his face, confusion evident in her bright green gaze. "You still could have contacted me—a letter, even a telegraph."

"I did write you. Every single day of my captivity." He shifted her on his lap to ease the pressure on his throbbing need. "But I didn't have pen or paper, so I wrote those letters all in my head. When the war ended and we were released, I tried putting the words to paper. But no matter how hard I tried, the words I wanted to say just wouldn't come."

"What…what did you want to say?"

Caleb smoothed the hair back from her face. "That I wouldn't be fully alive again until I was reunited with you. That I would die for just one more taste of your sweet, raspberry lips." He leaned in to kiss her, demonstrating that very fact. "That should I die in prison, my love would transcend death and find its way to your side and remain with you there until you joined me in the hereafter."

Tears slipped past her lashes. "You couldn't find the words to say that?"

"No...not until now. And the longer I waited, the harder it became." He shifted her again, settling her more comfortably. But the movement caused her to straddle him on the chair, hiking her dress to mid thigh. "I brought every half-finished letter with me; they're in my coat pocket."

"May I read them?"

He slid his palm over her thigh, cursing the pantalettes that stood between his hand and her flesh. Coherent thought was swiftly abandoning him. "*Now?*"

"Why not now?"

Pushing her hair aside, he leaned up to nibble at the curve of her neck. "I can think of a reason or two."

With a knowing smile, she cupped his head in her hands, and kissed him. Heat shot through him as her tongue darted between his lips. He reached behind her neck to unfasten the tiny row of buttons and didn't stop until he reached her waist. Alexa broke the kiss long enough to pull her arms from the dress.

Caleb couldn't help the moan that escaped him at the sight of her chemise. The dusky peaks of her breasts were visible beneath the thin cotton, nipples already swollen and eager for his touch. Without hesitation, he tugged the ribbon at her neckline and pushed the material aside. The feel of her firm, warm flesh in his hand was very nearly his undoing. She gasped, and moaned his name.

After so many nights of dreaming about touching her like this, longing for her until the aching need became his constant companion, he couldn't imagine how he would hold out long enough to make love to her properly.

She arched toward him, brining her breasts closer until he found one nipple with his mouth, licking, stroking, circling it with his tongue. She whimpered in pleasure, the sound skittering pleasantly along his spine.

Between them, his hand stole between her thighs where her pantaloons were split. She was hot and moist and moved against his hand as if she were every bit as impatient as he. He hadn't planned for their reunion to begin like this, but then, from the moment he'd discovered her on her front porch a lifetime ago, nothing had gone as he'd planned.

She hastily unbuttoned his trousers. Oh she was definitely as eager as he. The moment his cock sprang free, he lifted her hips and brought her down on top of him.

Her eyes, drowsy with passion, met his as he thrust deep. She arched again, and the sight of her creamy pale skin, breasts exposed, pushed him dangerously close to the edge. Yet even as he opened his mouth to tell her he couldn't hold out, he eased out and thrust deep again.

Alexa's body quivered around him, squeezing until his mind became a haze of white hot heat. Her fingers dug into his shoulders, and he buried his head between her breasts and let go the last hold on his own release.

She cried out and sagged against him. He wrapped his arms about her and held on, utterly spent and exhausted. He could hear nothing but their breathing, mingled, and nearly in perfect rhythm.

He became gradually aware of the sounds around them, the fading afternoon light filtering through the window at the other side of the room, the coolness of her exposed skin, the moisture at the curve of his neck where she had buried her face.

"Alexa?" He shifted, forcing her head from where she'd taken refuge.

At last she faced him, eyes shimmering with tears, cheeks wet.

She swiped at her cheeks and he smiled, reminded that she hated to cry. "I didn't believe you were coming back."

He brushed the tears from her face. "I promised I would."

"I know. I just didn't believe you."

"I'll spend the rest of my days making up for the years we were apart."

She sniffled, pulled the edges of the chemise together and re-tied the ribbon. "Caleb, if President Johnson doesn't pardon the men who served as officers for the Confederate army, what will you do?"

He helped her into her dress, reluctant to leave the little cocoon they'd created away from reality. "If I can't return to life as a soldier, then I'll try my hand at farming until I can."

"Farming? Here in Gettysburg?"

She moved from his lap and he rose to adjust his clothing and button his trousers. "Alexa, you know a wife goes where her husband goes."

"Yes, but—"

He pressed a fingertip to her lips. "I don't want to

have one of those marriages. You're far too independent to tolerate it anyway, and I relish the challenge of butting heads with you now and then." He quickly buttoned his shirt. "But I have a request."

She presented him her back, holding her hair out of the way for him to fasten her dress. "What is it?"

"The south is battered and beaten. It will take time to rebuild. I can't abandon Georgia when it needs me most." He sighed and began to work the tiny buttons. "How would you feel about leaving behind a town that has never fully appreciated you and starting your own medical practice where you are truly needed?"

She dropped her hair. "You think the people of the south would accept a female doctor?"

"They're in no position *not* to accept you. And once they meet you and see how dedicated you are to the care of others, how passionate you are about healing, I know they'll fall in love with you." Finishing with the dress, he turned her to face him. "Just as I did."

She chewed her lower lip thoughtfully. "Leave everything behind and move south?"

"No more pea hens. No more gossip. I can't promise my mother won't give you trouble at first, she's none too pleased that I went and married a Yankee." He winked and brought her hand to his lips. "But I have a feeling our beautiful daughter will win her over. Once the south is back on its feet, we'll go wherever you want. I've always had political ambitions, perhaps an opportunity will arise."

Her eyes welled with tears, and this time she didn't swipe them away. "I never could say no to you, Caleb McKenna. I'm not about to start now. My home is wherever you and our daughter are."

"Then come with me." He placed her arm in his and turned toward the door. "Speaking of my daughter, I have a good deal of lost time to make up for. Prepare to see her father spoil her rotten."

"I'd expect nothing less."

She laughed, and he couldn't help but realize how much he'd missed that sound.

Caleb unlocked the office door, but bent to drop a brief kiss to her lips, savoring the feel of the contact. "Once we open that door, we'll be facing our life together. Are you ready?"

Instead of answering, she bent to retrieve something from the floor. "Caleb, do you happen to recall the name of the foot soldier you chased off my porch that day? The one who was trying to force his way inside?"

He frowned. "Murphy, I believe."

"I'd very much like to find him one day and thank him."

"For what?"

She pressed something cool into his palm, and he looked down to find his wedding ring.

"Introducing me to my husband."

****

Felicity stood at the railroad station, waving a tearful goodbye. Alexa was safely off to Georgia with her husband and daughter, prepared to begin her new life, and new medical practice. Along with several bags of seeds from Grammy's garden of healing herbs, she'd taken a cutting from the willow tree in the yard, which seemed very important to her.

The past few weeks had gone by so fast. Meeting Caleb's relatives and packing Alexa for the move south had all happened so quickly. She could scarcely believe the time had come this morning when Uncle Edwin and Miss Adelaide had driven them all to the station for departure.

Tears blurred her vision as the train pulled out of sight. She would miss the cousin she had come to love like a sister, but she'd miss sweet Liberty most of all. Her little cousin would be fine, though, in three weeks Felicity had yet to see Caleb allow the child to use her own feet if he could carry her, and the feeling seemed to be mutual. She was head over heels in love with her papa.

Oh, there would be letters and visits, but it would never again be the same. And now she was faced with packing her belongings and returning home to Maryland; Uncle Edwin and his new wife didn't need her under foot as they began their new lives together.

She turned to look for them and caught sight of Will Carter, leaning against a hitching post, watching her. Her stomach flip-flopped as it always did at the sight of him, and she mentally cursed herself for her reaction. He'd never had eyes for anyone but Alexa, and now that she was gone, he'd likely be wed to one of the local girls within the year.

He pushed away from the post, ambling toward her with that confident, slightly bowlegged walk she'd come to love until he stood directly in front of her.

"It's nice of you to come and say goodbye, Will." She forced herself to sound cheerful, despite the lump of emotion still lodged in her throat.

"Miss Alexa's always held a tender spot for me." He slid his hands into his trouser pockets.

"Yes. I know." Heaven's, the whole town knew.

"Felicity?" called Uncle Edwin. "Are you ready?"

"I'll see she gets home, Doctor Winters." Will spoke up before Felicity could respond.

She stared at him, dumbfounded, but truth be known, her heart did a ridiculous little somersault at the thought of spending time in his company.

He walked with her toward his waiting buggy and helped her climb inside, then hopped up alongside her and urged the horses forward.

"I guess you'll be heading home to Maryland now."

She gazed down at the hands clasped in her lap. She didn't want to go back, but she really couldn't stay. "I suppose I will."

He glanced at her, then back at the road. "You don't have to. Seems to me this town has lost two of its best healers in the past year. You're the only other one knows how they did what they did."

She shrugged, ignoring a fresh wave of sorrow as it came over her. Gettysburg had become her home in all this time. "I don't want to be a burden to Uncle Edwin's new wife. I'm his relative, not hers."

He didn't take his eyes from the horses. "I meant you could stay if you got married."

Her jaw dropped. Was he suggesting she just go out and find a husband? Honestly, sometimes she just didn't know what to make of him. "Well then, by all means pull the wagon over so I can throw myself at the first man I come across."

A slow grin crossed his face, and he turned to look at her. "You sound just like your cousin when you get all riled like that."

She couldn't help the jealousy that nipped at her

insides. "You should know; you were the one in love with her."

Without a word he pulled the wagon off to the side of the road. When the horses came to a halt, he turned in his seat. "Where in thunder did you get *that* idea?"

"Where in—Will Carter, everyone in town knows how you felt about Alexa."

He rubbed a finger over his jaw. "Now wait a doggone minute. I'll admit, right after the battle, when I was here as a patient, I did have some feelings for Miss Alexa. But she told me I was just grateful to her for saving my life and nursing me back to health."

Felicity's jealousy was quickly turning to anger. Anger at Will for never noticing how she went out of her way to smile at him. How she spent extra time with her hair every Sunday before church just to look pretty for him. How she always managed to have his favorite cookies on hand when he stopped to visit. "But then she married Caleb, so it didn't matter how you felt."

"No." He climbed out of the wagon and strode around to her side, reaching up for her. "Come on down here, I can't talk looking at you sideways like that."

"I don't want to." Annoyance brought a chilly tone to her voice, but she didn't care.

He placed his hands to either side of her waist and hauled her none too gently to the ground in front of him.

"That can't be good for your bad shoulder."

"You let me worry about that." He pulled his hat from his head. "You're *listening*, Miss Felicity, but I don't think you're hearing what I'm trying to say."

Reluctantly, she faced him, plastering a bored expression on her face. She was behaving like a child but she didn't care.

"When I came back to Gettysburg, I saw what your cousin meant when she said my gratitude was getting confused with my true feelings. I cared for her—she's the whole reason I still have two arms—but I didn't feel what I thought I did the summer before."

Felicity folded her arms, staring up at the clouds in the brilliant fall sky. "You certainly made a good show of it, coming around all the time."

"Before Caleb took his vows, he asked me to look after Alexa and to take care of her if he didn't return. I agreed. A man doesn't take a promise like that lightly."

"So, you were just waiting to see if he'd return?" She chanced a sideways glance at him.

"Yes. If he hadn't a'come back, I might have even married her just to give that baby a father. But now that I've done my part, my promise is fulfilled. I can focus on the real reason I've been comin' by your uncle's place all this time."

A flutter of hope began to build inside her, but she didn't dare allow it wings, or let him see the hope in her eyes.

Will threw his hands in the air. "Naw—you know what? Forget it. I've been waitin' all this time for you to grow up, and you're still not there." He stalked off down the road.

"Will! Wait." She hurried after him. "What do you mean you were waiting for me to grow up?"

"For this." Without warning, he hauled her close and pressed his lips to hers. She'd never kissed a man, but in an instant, decided she liked the feel of his mouth on hers, the smell of him, outdoors and horses and a smell that was just Will.

He pulled back, and she blinked, disappointed to have it end so soon.

"I don't want to marry a little girl, Felicity. But I do want to marry *you*."

"You really do? This isn't just because Alexa is no longer here?"

"There you go again." He slapped his hat against his thigh and stepped away. "I've been in love with you since the night that fool Quentin Lord nearly shot his foot off. And then when I came back to town, you'd grown up so much and were so doggone pretty—I swear, every young man in town turns his head when you walk by. But I'm ten years older than you, Felicity. I had to wait for you to grow up before I could tell you how I felt."

"Yes." She could no longer contain the bubble of joy that threatened to burst inside her.

Brown eyes, as soft and gentle as ever, met hers. "Yes what?"

"Yes I'll marry you, silly." Laughing, she ran the short distance that separated them and all but leaped into his arms.

He caught her about the waist, lifting her feet from the ground as he swung her around.

She settled her hands on his broad shoulders and held on as he lifted her high in the air.

"Will Carter, I'm grown up enough to know what I want—and what I've always wanted is to marry *you*!"

Epilogue

Washington, DC
April, 1878

Seated at her writing desk, Alexa dipped her pen and pondered the blank parchment before her.

Beside the desk, seated in a wooden rocking chair that had once belonged to Grammy, Caleb gently rocked their youngest son. She smiled at the sight the two made, young Jackson's cheeks a bright pink, his maple sugar curls mussed as he snoozed on his father's chest. Caleb's large hands stroked the child's back and not for the first time, Alexa marveled at her husband's patient nature. The toddler had woke a short time ago, probably cutting teeth again, and Caleb had patiently rocked him back to sleep.

He rose from the chair, the sleeping child still pressed close against him. "I think he's out again. I'm going to try putting him down."

She nodded, warmth filling her as she watched him leave the room with the baby, then began to write.

Dearest Felicity,

I wanted to tell you again how much Caleb, the children and I enjoyed having you, Will and the girls for the holidays. The children love visiting with their Northern cousins, and I think Caleb enjoys rehashing those old war stories with Will.

Thank you for your congratulatory note on Caleb's election to the senate. The move to Washington has been an enormous change for all of us, but I think we're finally settling in. I look forward to beginning a new practice here as a physician, though the past thirteen years in the south has taught me much patience will be required before people readily accept a female as a doctor.

Of course we understand why you weren't able to travel here to see Caleb take the oath of office and we send our heartfelt congratulations on the birth of your eighth daughter. I cannot tell you how much it touches my heart to hear you've named her Alexandra Mabel. I do hope Will has kept his sharpshooting skills from getting rusty, with that many daughters he's going to need them.

We're looking forward to being able to visit with you more often now that we're in Washington and not so far away. Liberty, especially, enjoys the time spent with her female cousins. Having three younger brothers to boss around suits her, but I think she is secretly hoping this next one will be a girl. I confess I'm hoping much the same; with Lee, Stewart and Jackson already under my roof, I'm ready for a change from naming our children for Confederate generals. If it is a boy, I'll be suggesting we name him Lincoln or Grant.

She paused as Caleb came back into the room.

"Is he sleeping?"

"His thumb is in his mouth, I think he's out for a while."

She smiled, a tender image of her sleeping son coming to mind. Caleb stepped up behind her, his hands sliding over her shoulders. "Answering Felicity's letter?"

"Yes. It's been a week, and I never wait that long to answer her, we've just been so busy."

He bent to nuzzle the curve of her neck. "Don't take too long."

She reached up, sliding her hand behind his neck and pulled his head toward hers until his mouth met hers in a hot, openmouthed kiss that left no question about his intentions.

He unfastened the buttons down the front of her night dress, brushing the material aside until it fell from her shoulders. Sliding a hand purposefully down the length of her breast, he teased her swollen nipple until she moaned in sweet agony.

She tore her lips from his, scarcely able to think after his sensual play. "I'll just be another few minutes."

"I'll be waiting for you, Mrs. McKenna." She returned her pen to the paper, eager to be in her husband's arms

Please send Father our love. He is, as we noted over the holidays, beginning to slow down a bit, but I believe Miss Adelaide keeps him young. They seem so happy together.

Felicity, do you ever think back to that terrible summer when the battle came? I find myself thinking of it more and more lately. Especially when we were there visiting last summer. When the windows were open to catch the breeze, there were nights, I swore I could hear the cries and moans of the boys who fought and died so valiantly in Gettysburg that summer. Caleb says it's my overactive imagination, but I'm not so certain. I think for them, somehow, the battle goes on.

Well, my dear cousin, the hour has grown late and I must close and head to bed.

I think of you often and miss you terribly, but look forward to seeing you soon.

Yours with great affection,
Cousin Alexa

Author's Note

Most of us know that in July of 1863, the armies of North and South descended upon a small, sleepy Pennsylvania town and engaged in a horrific battle. What most of us don't realize is when those armies pulled out after the three-day battle, this town of 2,400 citizens was left with 22,000 wounded, more than 50,000 dead, and numerous horses, mules and livestock killed during the battle. It's their story, rather than the battle itself, that has intrigued me for many years.

Though the characters I created are purely figments of my imagination, the situations they encountered—a hungry Rebel soldier lured by the smell of oven-warm bread; a soldier with a femoral artery wound bravely dictating a final letter home; the soldiers coming down the stairs into the fruit cellar and telling the women they could come out; even Felicity telling Southern soldiers she'd have no eggs for "those poor Southern boys" if they stole her chickens—were all inspired by actual events the townspeople of Gettysburg endured during those three days in July of 1863.

Their courage during the battle and determination to rebuild their town afterward are truly a lesson in American resilience.

A word about the author...

If it's possible to be born a writer, then I certainly was. I'd probably have started sooner if there had been pen and paper available in the womb! But for as long as I can remember, I have heard voices in my head. Fortunately for me, they're all characters—begging me to tell their stories.

I've been married to Peter, my best friend, for fifteen years, and am a work-at-home mom with two busy boys, a teen and a tween. When I'm not working, writing, or buried nose-deep in a research book, chances are I'm baking, taking my dog for long walks along the beautiful shores of Lake Ontario, or just kicking back and hanging with my guys.

Visit Nicole at www.nicolemccaffrey.com

Thank you for purchasing
this publication of The Wild Rose Press, Inc.
For other wonderful stories of romance,
please visit our on-line bookstore at
www.thewildrosepress.com.

For questions or more information
contact us at
info@thewildrosepress.com.

The Wild Rose Press, Inc.
www.thewildrosepress.com

To visit with authors of
The Wild Rose Press, Inc.
join our yahoo loop at
http://groups.yahoo.com/group/thewildrosepress/